The Books of the Dead

Also available by Emilia Bernhard

Death in Paris

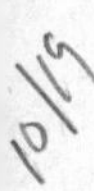

The Books of the Dead

A Death in Paris Mystery

EMILIA BERNHARD

NEW YORK

Published in the United States by Crooked Lane Books, an imprint of The Quick Brown Fox & Company LLC.

Crooked Lane Books and its logo are trademarks of The Quick Brown Fox & Company LLC.

Library of Congress Catalog-in-Publication data available upon request.

ISBN (hardcover): 978-1-64385-157-0
ISBN (ePub): 978-1-64385-158-7
ISBN (ePDF): 978-1-64385-159-4

Cover design by Mimi Bark
Map by Wikimedia Commons / public domain
Floor plan image and note image by Emily Bernhard Jackson
Book design by Jennifer Canzone

Printed in the United States.

www.crookedlanebooks.com

Crooked Lane Books
34 West 27th St., 10th Floor
New York, NY 10001

First Edition: October 2019

10 9 8 7 6 5 4 3 2 1

To Dr. Marren,
swan to my duck,
and to Jeremy Burns,
who does not need to get over himself.

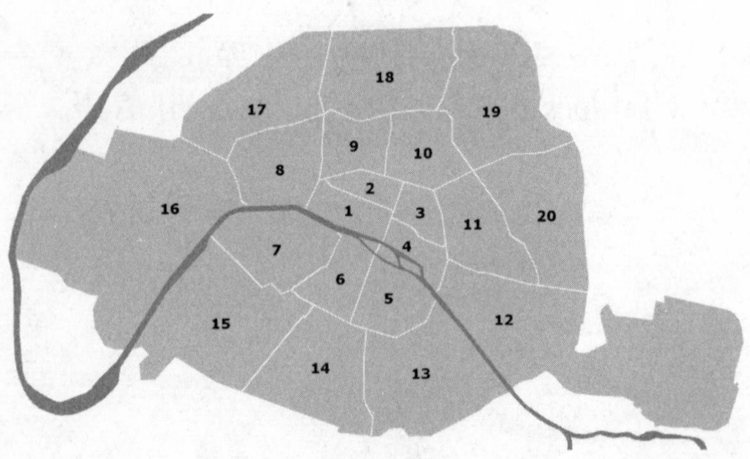

The *arrondissements* of Paris

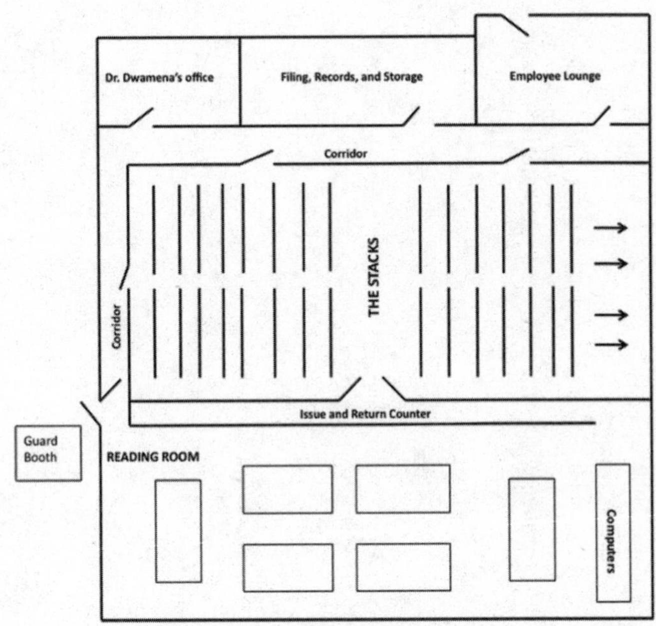

Floor plan of the Bibliothèque Nationale's
Rare Book Reading Room*

*Although the exterior and public spaces of the Bibliothèque Nationale described in this book are based on those of the real Bibliothèque, the reading rooms and private spaces are entirely the product of imagination.

Chapter One

If someone had told Rachel Levis that morning that by six o'clock in the evening she'd be face-to-face with a corpse, she wouldn't have believed them. Yet here she was at 5:55, bending over a dead man in a toilet stall.

The man was propped against the white tile wall. He wore an olive-green shirt and his black hair fell over his forehead, but after that normality ended. His face was purple and swollen, as if it had been beaten violently and then inflated. Open eyes, their whites turned pink, bulged out of their sockets; a swollen tongue poked out of his black-lipped mouth. His neck was bruised around a red groove that looked as if it had been incised into his flesh, the skin on either side of it swelling around the mark. A trickle of dried blood wound its way out of his left ear.

Rachel didn't scream. The rational part of her was surprised about that. She'd seen death before, certainly, but she hadn't stared it in the face. By rights she should have been horrified, terrified, or at least shocked. But after her first gasp she didn't open her mouth at all, maybe because she didn't want to alert the crowded room across the hall, or maybe because she hadn't fully processed what she'd seen—or maybe, she thought, because she had the instincts and sangfroid of a true detective. She backed silently out of the stall and closed its door. She didn't bother to try to avoid leaving fingerprints. She'd used a naked hand to open the door, so the damage was already done. She walked swiftly across the bathroom and out, then pulled the door closed, stood in front of the sign on it that said HOMMES, and reached into her bag for her phone.

The question was, whom should she call first? Her husband Alan, her best friend Magda, or Capitaine Boussicault, the policeman she knew from the last time she'd encountered a murder? The first would bring worry and common sense; the second would bring excitement and fellow feeling; the third would bring the law and an investigation. She thought carefully for a moment, then sighed and unlocked her screen.

* * *

"So you entered the *toilettes* and the body was there for you to see?" Capitaine Boussicault's pen hovered over his pad. He'd had his men clear the café immediately upon arrival, and now he and Rachel sat alone in the dining room as scene-of-the-crime technicians went over the men's room.

"No, when I came in, the door to the *cabinet* was closed. I saw the feet, and I swung the door open. Then I saw the body."

"And you touched it?"

"No. I only touched the door."

"I see. I'll tell the technicians. They will want your palm print to rule it out of what they find. But they will also want to know . . . and I myself would like to know . . ." He frowned. "Why were you in the men's room in the first place?"

"Well." Rachel had expected this question, and she began her answer at the very beginning. "It all started with the condom machine."

"The condom machine." Boussicault's tone was doubtful, and now that the words were out of her mouth, Rachel could see why. She plunged on. "Yes. I was actually going to the women's room. But the men's room is on the way, and when I passed by, the door was open. And I'm always curious about what's in the condom machines in men's rooms. Is it the same as in the women's room? So I decided to take advantage of the opportunity and go look. And as soon as I was two steps in the door, I saw the shoes inside the *cabinet*. But it was the *soles* of the shoes, and that seemed odd. So I went over and tapped on the door and asked if the person was all right. When there wasn't an answer, I gave it a little push to see if it was locked. It swung open. And"—she made an expansive gesture with one hand—"there he was."

Boussicault opened his mouth, but before he could say anything, Alan appeared in the restaurant doorway, his body momentarily blocking the early-evening sun. He crossed the room, wrapped her in a long hug, then peered into her face. "There was a delay on the Mètro. Are you all right? What's happening?"

"I was a little shaken, but I'm fine." She sat back down. "It's nothing to worry about, really."

He sat down next to her. "You're developing quite a tendency to stumble across murder in your middle age."

Rachel waved a hand dismissively. "Hardly a tendency. One eighteen months ago, and one now. Anyway"—she looked at Boussicault—"this might not even be a murder." *Although of course it is.*

"It is." Boussicault nodded. "Murder by ligature strangulation, to be precise."

"What were you doing over here, anyway?" By *over here*, Alan meant in Paris's second arrondissement. He and Rachel lived in the sixth arrondissement, across the Seine and a good half hour's walk away—a walk that, on this day of blasting July heat, would be more likely to keep Rachel inside than tempt her to go out.

"It was the hymns," she said. "The hymns Valerie's friend asked me to write."

Alan nodded. He was very familiar with these hymns, a commission from a church committee on the recommendation of a friend. They had been proving difficult to write for two months, and he'd heard all about Rachel's struggles.

"I tried all day," she said now, "and finally around four I thought I could go to the Bibliothèque Nationale for inspiration. I checked online, and they have a lot of medieval religious manuscripts at the site in the next street." She jerked a thumb to the right, indicating the location of the Bibliothèque Nationale's site on the Rue de Richelieu. "I took a Vélib', just to feel some sort of breeze, but by the time I got here it was only half an hour until the library closed. So I went to Bistrot Vivienne—"

Alan nodded again. Bistrot Vivienne, his wife's favorite restaurant, sat on a corner across from the Bibliothèque.

"But it was full," Rachel continued. "I couldn't even find a space to stand at the bar. So I started walking back to the Vélib' rack, and on the way I saw this place. I had a spritzer, and then I went to the bathroom, but the men's room door was open and—"

"You couldn't resist the condom machine."

"Right. Only, two steps over the threshold and—"

Rachel stopped. A technician had come into the room and crossed to speak to Boussicault. He kept his voice low. The *capitaine* nodded and the man sank back toward the hallway, his white paper suit slowly dyed gray by the gloom.

Rachel's natural detecting antennae tingled. "What was that about?" The *capitaine* shrugged. "Is there something about the body? Did they get a time of death? Did they find a weapon?"

The *capitaine* gave a little smile. He might have felt respect, and perhaps even some warmth, toward Rachel by the end of their earlier investigation, but his face said he was still a policeman first, and policemen did not answer questions from civilians. He shrugged one of the huge shrugs at which the French excelled and said, "It was nothing. Thank you for your time, Rachel. You've been very helpful."

Rachel didn't see that she'd been helpful at all, but he snapped his pad shut and rose. "If you will excuse me, I must go. Didier will help you out." His young blond *brigadier*, familiar to Rachel from eighteen months before, appeared as if conjured by his name. He waited, stone-faced, as she rooted under the table for her bag. Rachel hadn't liked this blankness a year and a half ago, and she found she still didn't like it now.

* * *

"Magda will be sorry she missed that," Alan said when they were out on the street. "Where is she, anyway? I was sure you would've called her."

Rachel shrugged.

In fact, she'd called Magda before she'd called Alan, but Magda's reaction had been anything but eager. "This is a terrible time!" Her tone had been sulky, as if the murderer had deliberately set out to inconvenience her. "You know I need to do all my ordering by the end of July if I want to be ready for the customers in September." Magda ran an online store that sold high-end French linens, and autumn was her peak season. "Look"—her voice became severe—"take copious notes. Copious. And I'll call you tomorrow to hear all about it. Now I have to clear the line, because I'm expecting a call back from a wholesaler in Alsace."

"Magda's busy," Rachel now said to Alan.

His raised eyebrow showed his surprise at the notion that she could ever be too busy for a murder, but all he said was, "Let's stop at Vivienne. If there's space now, I'll treat you to a restoring glass of wine." He put his arm out and drew her close as they walked.

Chapter Two

In the ten days that followed, Rachel got no further with her hymns. Part of the problem was simple lack of inspiration. The commissioning priest had asked her for compositions that, in his words, "found the marvelous in the modern world," but it was no easy task to produce these in the less-than-marvelous heat of a Parisian high summer, when the feel of sweat trickling slowly down her back made her skin crawl. Every day she would work until she could bear it no longer, then take herself out for a drink in an air-conditioned café—and every day when she returned from her drink she would see that what she had written wasn't much good. Natural heat apparently did not make for creative fire.

But there was another reason for her difficulty, she knew. She was distracted by the murder. She had begun to think of it as *hers*, an incident that belong to her. *Who was the man in the* toilettes? she kept asking herself. When she stood at the long window in her *séjour* hoping to catch a breath of air, the puffy purple face would float up in front of her and she would try to imagine it deflated, alive, full of expression and attached to a living being. She would feel a twinge of sympathy toward the unknown victim. No one deserved to die like that, disfigured and dumped in that humiliating position.

Then, hunched over her desk attempting to channel the wonders of a modern God she didn't believe in, she found herself trying to re-create the murder instead, trying to understand the murderer. She imagined the unknowing victim entering the men's room, pondered the sheer strength it would take for one person to strangle another—the *intention* that would be required, and required for all the long minutes it took to finish the job. And at the end of it all to saunter out of the café as if you'd done nothing more than have a drink after work! What kind of person could do that—what kind of person could want to do that—what kind of motive could push someone into doing it? No matter how she tried to focus on the hymns at hand, these thoughts kept elbowing their way in.

Perhaps that was why she wasn't surprised to pick up her landline when it rang ten days after the murder and hear Boussicault on the other end, asking her to come to the commissariat.

* * *

"Rachel." He was waiting for her in reception. He led her through corridors unchanged from her previous visit the year before, around the maze of desks that constituted his *dèpartement*, and into his office, its three glass walls giving it the feel of a giant aquarium. The last time Rachel had been here, Boussicault had dismissed her ideas and she had nearly wept. But, she reminded herself firmly, at the end of that experience she had solved a murder and they had formed a kind of friendship, so she had no reason to feel awkward or out of place. She tried to arrange herself in the chair in a way that suggested she was entirely at home.

The *capitaine* cleared his throat. "I asked you here because we've now finished our preliminary investigation of the murder at Chez Poule. I thought you might be interested in our findings and possible next steps."

Chez Poule: had that been the name of the place? Rachel realized she hadn't even noticed. But Boussicault was right, she was interested. After all, it was *her* murder. "Thank you." She leaned forward.

"*De rien.*" He opened a folder. "It turns out the victim was one Guy Laurent. He worked in the Rare Books and Manuscripts reading room at the Bibliothèque Nationale, and he was a regular client at Chez Poule." He flipped over a page. "Scene-of-crime examination suggests that Monsieur Laurent was killed one to two hours at the most before you found him, and the disarrangement of his clothing suggests that he was placed in the stall after he was killed." He turned another page. "His wallet was in his back pocket, and from his *carte d'identité* we learned that he was forty years old. We also know that he had just emptied his bladder." He glanced up. "His fly was still undone when he was found." Finally, he closed the folder and put it on the desktop, leaning back in his chair. "And, as I said, cause of death was ligature strangulation."

Once more the swollen face appeared in Rachel's mind. She swallowed hard. "How? I mean, what made the . . ." But she couldn't finish. She just gestured near her own throat.

"Well." Boussicault's voice was cool, and Rachel remembered that one of his best traits was his ability to meet horror with equanimity. "As you have seen, the ligature was narrow. Next to the body we found a length of string that appears to be a match in size. It was wet from lying on the floor, but we've sent it for analysis to see what it can tell us."

Grateful for his composure, Rachel tried to match it. "Did anyone see him come into the restaurant?" Her voice shook a little.

The *capitaine* gave her an approving look. "Exactly our first question. Unfortunately, Laurent was such a regular customer that no one can remember noticing him on that day specifically. In fact, they can't remember him or anyone else acting oddly that day. The place gets very busy in the afternoons."

"So there's no obvious suspect."

Again an approving look. "Exactly. And this may well be a random crime, or a crime of opportunity. It's hot; heat exacerbates instability. Random murders do increase in the summer. But the victim was an adult male, and there was no sign of sexual assault, both very unusual in stranger strangulation. Which makes it more likely that he was killed by someone who knew him and wanted him dead."

"Any plausible suspects in that category?" Rachel draped her arm over the back of her chair, trying to seem hard-bitten and worldly-wise. She still had no idea why she was here, but she had no objection to being a sounding board for the investigation.

"Nothing we could find. Monsieur Laurent lived out in Pont de Sèvres, so rather far for a neighbor to travel to kill him, and in any case his neighbors hardly seem to have known him. He kept to himself, apparently—his *portable* had only his mother and his job as contacts."

At this revelation of a limited life, Rachel felt another stab of pity for Guy Laurent. Nonetheless, "Maybe a resentful colleague?" she offered.

"Yes, our conclusion, too. So we questioned his colleagues. And it appears that among them Monsieur Laurent has not kept to himself. Their feelings toward him were quite strong. Very strong, in fact. His colleagues, well . . ." He said abruptly, "They all hated him."

Rachel frowned. "But surely that just makes your job easier. It's just a matter of finding out who hated him enough to kill him."

He sighed. "Under normal circumstances, perhaps it would be that way, yes. But Monsieur Laurent seems to have inspired equal loathing in all those he worked with."

"All of them?"

The *capitaine* opened the folder again and began to lay out a series of photographs, turning them so they faced Rachel. They were enlarged identity card photos, and as was the way with such pictures, each made its subject look not only as if they could commit a murder but as if they just had.

"Giles Morel." A man in his late twenties, with a thick blond beard and black-rimmed glasses. "He called Laurent"—Boussicault consulted a sheet of typed notes—"'a brainless pig whose remains he wouldn't wipe off his shoe.' He then refused to explain why he felt that way. Louise Fournier." A second photo, a pale young woman whose dark hair straggled into her eyes. "She first asked to be questioned by a female officer, but finally told us that in her opinion Laurent was"—another glance down—"'a better-dressed street mugger.' Then she wouldn't say any more." The next photo. "Docteure Alphonsine Dwamena." A dark-skinned woman in late middle age, silver hair cut close to her head. "Head of Laurent's department. She told me that Laurent was a troublemaker and that she found him"—again he consulted his notes—"'repellent as a person.' She also declined to elaborate." He looked up. "We can't determine which of these people hated him most, or whose hatred might push them into murder, for the very simple reason that they won't open up to us. They are like a little club—they won't say anything to outsiders—and without further evidence we can't make them."

He put down a final photo. "Laurent." Rachel bent over it. At last, the face she'd been trying to imagine for nearly two weeks. She couldn't find anything in it that would obviously inspire loathing. She knew people tended to find in photographs what they sought, so on being told that a man had saved a kitten from a tree, one group would see benevolence and decency, while on being told that the same man was a thief, another group would find thuggish shiftiness. But the person looking out at her was entirely unremarkable. She felt another twinge of pity. She reached out with her thumb as if to stroke the photo's hair, but pulled back. When she looked up, Boussicault was watching her. He said, "Rachel, I need your help."

He wanted her to help him identify the murderer. *That's* why he'd brought her in! Her heart leapt, then fell as she cast her mind back to the moments in the bathroom. "I'm sorry, but I really can't remember anything else. The door was open, and I went in. No one was coming out, and I didn't see anyone when I was inside except for him. I'm really sorry."

He shook his head. "Not that kind of help. You see, in summer crime goes up." He sighed. "It's the tourists."

Rachel nodded. All Parisians dreaded the arrival of the tourists in July and August. They blocked the sidewalks as they stood in groups trying to read their maps; they clogged the less defined sites like the Pont Neuf or Notre Dame by lingering in uncertain clumps. Somehow the temperature seemed to increase merely at the sight of them standing doggedly in line outside the Palais de Justice or the Eiffel Tower. And every year with their arrival came newspapers reports of a rise in pickpockets, in assaults, in public drunkenness and criminal damage. Most Parisians fled the city for vacations during this period, but of course the police had to stay to deal with the extra work as well as the usual Paris crime.

As if reading her mind, the *capitaine* said, "And in addition to the usual increase, we are dealing with a sudden influx of very good, very pure, heroin into the city. Many of my undercover people have been pulled into that investigation. And to add to that, two of my best women . . . maternity leave! It must have been a very cold winter, *hein*?" He tried for a grin but could only manage a weary smile. Then he collected himself. "And just when all I could think of to move forward on Laurent's murder was maybe to put someone on the inside . . . a new colleague in their department, one who needs things explained but who also might become part of their club—and maybe especially a woman, who is less threatening . . ."

Rachel caught her breath. *She* was a woman! She saw where he was heading: she was going to be part of a plan! She focused again on Boussicault's voice. ". . . only meant to listen and observe," he was saying. "I checked with my superiors, and as long as this remains a passive and time-limited undercover action, one in which I can guarantee there will be no danger, they will sign off. I remember that you were very good at blending into Monsieur Bowen's household, and your previous experience in libraries, and so I have brought you here to ask—"

A business card flashed before Rachel's eyes: RACHEL LEVIS, POLICE CONSULTANT. Or maybe RACHEL LEVIS, P.C.; initials were always better. She couldn't control herself any longer. "Yes! I will. Yes!"

Chapter Three

Later that afternoon Magda and Rachel sat on a bench in the Jardin du Luxembourg eating ice cream. Rachel had just arrived at the point in her story where Capitaine Boussicault completed his description of Guy Laurent's colleagues, and Magda took a luxurious lick of her pistachio gelato as she contemplated the situation. "So the most obvious suspects are also the least helpful. It seems pretty simple to me. Why doesn't he just put each of them in a room and sweat them?"

Rachel cocked her head. "From what he told me, they tried some version of that, he and his *brigadier*, and the people closed up. And also closed ranks, it seems."

"His *brigadier*? That blond boy we saw when we first went to see him? That guy couldn't sweat an onion!"

Rachel knew that Magda only started talking like a hard-boiled detective novel when she was excited at the prospect of investigation, but she still found it irritating. After all, she was the one who had been invited to help the police. If anyone had the right to talk like a Dashiell Hammett character, it was she. Then she remembered that Magda didn't know that. Then she remembered that she would have to tell her.

Magda took another lick from her cone. "So what does he want us to do?"

Rachel tried not to flinch at that *us*. Of course Magda assumed it would be *us*. It had been *us* all the way through their previous investigation, when they'd worked together against everyone else's disbelief. In fact, it had been *us* for pretty much all of their two decades of friendship. She bit her lip and delayed telling her friend the truth for just one more second. "Well . . . he needs some help."

"I got that. Otherwise he wouldn't want us to do anything."

Another inward wince. Rachel slowly licked around the outside of her cone. Finally she couldn't delay any longer. "Not us. Me. He wants me to go to work in the reading room where Laurent worked. He's fixed it with the Bibliothèque's head of security so that everyone in Laurent's department will think I've been brought in as a temporary replacement until they can hire someone qualified to replace him. He wants me to get to know them from the inside, to see what I can dig up that might point to one of them as Laurent's killer."

"Okay." Magda shrugged. "And what am I doing while you're doing that?"

Oh, dear. Rachel licked her gelato again, then again, then forced herself not to take a third lick but to speak. "No, it's just me. He just wants me to help."

Magda didn't say anything. Her gelato dripped down onto her fingers, and Rachel could tell she was working to keep her face blank. Rachel gabbled to fill the air. "He wants someone to go in, to blend in and see what they can find out. And he remembered that I did that on our last case. Remember how I did that? Then there's Edgar's library." A year and a half earlier, Rachel had worked to organize the library of her former lover, Edgar Bowen, after his death. In fact, that was how she and Magda had met Boussicault in the first place—and how they had solved their first murder. She went on. "He knew I worked there on that case, so I have experience."

"Well, I guess it depends on what you think of as 'experience.'" Magda's voice was tight. "Did you remind him which of us had her life threatened in the last case? Did you refresh his memory as to who was taken hostage by the killer and attacked with a deadly weapon?"

Rachel thought these seemed like reasons *not* to hire someone to spy on potential murderers rather than arguments in favor, but she didn't say anything.

Meanwhile, Magda fingered her neck, as if she could still feel the tines of the carving fork that had been pressed into her jugular. "You always do this. This is just like that time when—"

"Please don't bring that up." Rachel held out a hand. "That was more than fifteen years ago! And I have no control over Boussicault's reasoning. Plus, you said yourself that this is your busiest time, so I thought you'd be too swamped to do outside work. Anyway, I'm only supposed to be there for a month at the most, and I have to report to Boussicault every week. I'm not allowed to do anything but observe and report, and both the Bibliothèque's head of security and Boussicault's higher-ups were absolutely clear that if there's even the slightest hint of even the mildest danger, he has to pull me out right away." She made her voice slightly wheedling. "It's not like I'm going to be wearing a wire and infiltrating the Mafia. I'm just standing around watching."

Magda's face relaxed. "Well, you are good at blending in."

Ouch. But she was calming down, so Rachel let the comment go.

"And this *is* a busy time for me. And you *are* a better fit for an archive. You did organize Edgar's library." She thought for a moment. "Although I'm not sure that gives you the kind of knowledge someone needs to navigate a national library."

Ouch again. Rachel was surprised at this second jab. She could understand that Magda might be jealous, but weren't friends also supposed to celebrate your successes with you? Where was Magda's pleasure that her best friend had been invited to work with the police? Before she could control herself, she said, "Strictly speaking, *navigate* is only for bodies of water. And I'm supposed to be a volunteer, so I won't need to know much."

"Yet he thought of you because of Edgar's library," Magda said softly.

Neither of them spoke for a long time. Then Magda said, "Well, if anyone asks you a question you don't know the answer to, just sneeze. The other person will say *santé*, you say *merci*, and you can use the break to move the conversation onto another track."

Rachel recognized an apology when she heard one. She responded in kind. "That's a very clever idea. I'll bear it in mind."

Magda crunched another bite. "I learned it from that cute guy on that program with James Spader."

"What, the one with the glasses?"

"Uh-huh."

"Oh, yeah, he *is* cute."

Magda nodded. In the long light of the late summer afternoon, each woman crunched her cone contentedly.

Chapter Four

The first thing Rachel learned at the Bibliothèque Nationale was that it was full of corridors. When she arrived at the building on Monday morning, she was met in the marble foyer by a woman who introduced herself as Raida Dounôt, head of security. She handed Rachel an employee pass on a lanyard, led her up a spiral staircase discreetly placed in an out-of-the-way nook, then began to walk through a maze of hallways, all the while keeping up a brisk pace and addressing Rachel over her shoulder.

"I've explained to the head of the department, Docteure Alphonsine Dwamena, that you are a temporary replacement for Guy Laurent, drafted in while we go through the process of hiring someone permanent. Don't worry"—she looked back, and Rachel caught half of a reassuring smile—"she won't expect you to know how to do anything. I told her that you applied to be a volunteer and we asked you to help out in her department after . . . the tragedy."

Rachel would have thanked her for this reassurance, but she had neither the breath nor the focus. As she had entered the site that morning, she'd seen that the Bibliothèque was shaped like a rectangle around a central courtyard, but as she raced down unwindowed corridors, her impression was that she was working her way into huge maze. Just as panic began to overcome her, however, she and her leader arrived at a heavy metal door with a sensor on the wall next to it. Dounôt fished out her pass from her pocket and swiped it over the panel, then at last turned to face Rachel. Her expression was grave.

"This plan would not have been my choice. I agreed to it because I trust Denis from our time together on the force."

Who is Denis? Rachel thought. Then she realized the woman meant Capitaine Boussicault.

"But remember that all these people are suspects. If you see anything or hear anything that seems odd, do not engage with them. Come directly to me." There was a click, and Madame Dounôt gave a single sharp nod of her head. "*Bon. Alors.* We proceed." She pushed the door open.

* * *

The second thing Rachel learned at the Bibliothèque Nationale was not to touch Giles Morel's locker. Dounôt introduced her to Docteure Dwamena, who in turn introduced her to the other two employees, who were sipping coffee in the small room that served as a lounge. Having seen their faces only in the photographs, Rachel found it somehow disconcerting to see those faces attached to people. Louise Fournier turned out to be surprisingly tall and dressed from head to foot in rusty black. She offered Rachel a sinewy, long-fingered hand before retreating into a corner. Giles Morel, broad-chested and wearing a long-sleeved checked shirt that just revealed the end of a tattoo at his wrist, squeezed her fingers in a crushing grip. He smiled at her through his beard. But when Docteure Dwamena excused herself to answer a telephone that rang somewhere in the background, he dropped both the smile and her hand and said, "Don't touch my locker."

"Excuse me?"

"Don't touch my locker. You have a locker, so you don't need to touch mine. So stay away from my locker."

Rachel hadn't known that she had a locker, and she had no idea what it was supposed to hold or why she might want to touch anyone else's, but before she could say any of these things, Morel took a last gulp of his coffee and strode out. Should she record this exchange? Was it significant? She imagined writing VERY PROTECTIVE OF LOCKER in the notebook in her bag, but it didn't seem worth it. Then again, she reflected, past experience had shown her that you never knew what might be worth it. Maybe Morel had the rest of a ball of string stashed in his locker . . .

"He keeps his novel in there."

"I'm sorry?"

Louise Fournier took a step out of the corner. "He's writing a novel, and he keeps it in his locker. He doesn't want people to read it."

"Okay. Thanks, Louise."

Louise nodded, then gave a tight smile. "And call me Lou-Lou. No one calls me Louise." She turned and hurried out.

Rachel stood in the faded room, looking at its mini-fridge and its little coffee machine. As a poet she'd met plenty of eccentrics, but she hadn't expected to find an antagonistic hipster and an icy goth working at the Bibliothèque Nationale. She'd imagined the employees of a national institution would be more staid. Clearly she was in for a steep learning curve.

* * *

The third thing Rachel learned at the Bibliothèque Nationale was that she was going to need a cover story. On this first day she worked only two hours, but she was still asked enough questions to make her very jumpy. Trying to make small talk as she showed Rachel the stacks and explained how the book pick-up-and-drop-off system worked, Docteure Dwamena asked her why she'd decided to volunteer at the Bibliothèque, whether it was close to her home, and what kept her in Paris in late summer. Unsure of whether she should give true answers, Rachel sneezed after every question—and although the stacks were dusty, after the fourth time she felt the other woman looking at her strangely. Was she going to be removed from her post before she'd even started because of a fantasy dust allergy?

"You need a legend," Magda said as she, Rachel, and Alan ate dinner in Rachel's kitchen that night.

"A what?"

"A fictional back story," Alan chimed in. "Spies have them." Both women looked at him, and he shrugged at their surprise. "What? Didn't you notice me sitting next to you while you watched all those suspense shows?"

"Okay." Rachel bit her lip. "A legend." She shook her head with irritation. "Too bad it's too late to call myself Susan

Vandeventer. It's hard to be a different person with the same old name."

"Susan Vandeventer!" Alan said dismissively. He'd always disliked Rachel's in-case-of-emergency pseudonym, although she'd never known why. "Anyway, you don't want to be a totally different person. You just want to be a version of you."

"Oh, how *fun*!" Magda's eyes lit up. "You could be . . . a recently divorced socialite, volunteering as a way to give something back to the community. Or an unexpected widow, seeking to fill the gap left in her life by abrupt bereavement."

"Or a resting actress looking for something to do between jobs." Rachel pictured herself in a black turtleneck and leggings, reading Jean Genet on her lunch break and talking about the Theatre of Cruelty. That seemed like a good persona for a library. She could discourse knowledgeably about the Theatre of Cruelty, if she could just remember which one it was—did it come before or after Theatre of the Absurd? Or did they overlap? She foresaw a weekend spent on the Internet.

"No," Alan said again. "None of those are any good. A *version* of you. You need something like you, but not exactly you. The best lies are the ones that stick most closely to the truth. If you say you're a ballerina filling time between performances, then you'll have to remember everything that goes along with being a ballerina, and that makes the risk of forgetting very high. Plus, if they decide to look you up on the web, you're in trouble. What you need to do is design a life close to your own but with all the memorable details taken out. So you live in the sixth in an apartment, but don't mention that you're a poet.

And you have a husband, but he's not more like a god than a man . . ."

Rachel laughed, but she was impressed. She often found her husband's common sense irritating, but sometimes she saw how useful it was. He really could be quite an asset, she thought—the Bosley to her and Magda's Charlie's Angels.

Magda turned back to Rachel, "So . . . what would you do if you weren't a poet?"

"I don't know." Rachel thought of all the jobs she'd imagined having when the writing was going badly—shop girl, baker, costume restorer, hand model—and then of the only full-time employment she'd ever actually had. "I guess I'd work for a caterer?"

"I think we're a little too old to be cater waiters anymore." Magda tapped her dessert spoon on the table thoughtfully. "But something to do with catering . . ."

* * *

As they were undressing later, Rachel asked Alan, "What's your problem with Susan Vandeventer?"

He snorted. "You say that like she's a real person."

"Okay, what's your problem with *the name* Susan Vandeventer? I think it's the perfect alias; it's unlikely enough to be real, and classy enough to keep people from enquiring further. But you've never liked it."

He draped his shirt on the valet and turned to face her. "It's just . . . It's a ridiculous name. Who could forget 'Susan Vandeventer'? It's like calling yourself . . . I don't know . . .

Crystal Farnsworth, or . . . Ginevra Higginbotham. The goal of an alias is to make you go unnoticed. So if you want an effective one, it should be something easy to forget. Like Jane Smith, or Susan Davis. Or if it has to be French . . . uh . . ." He thought for a second. "Jeanne Martin."

"Jeanne Martin!" Rachel's tone made it clear what she thought of this simplistic effort. But as she got into bed, she thought, *Score another one for Bosley.*

Chapter Five

When Rachel arrived at the Bibliothèque the next day, she was a married woman living in the sixth arrondissement who was trying to build a catering business. Her husband, a lawyer at a successful firm, worked long hours, and she'd decided to do some volunteering while she waited for the catering to take off. At college in America she'd majored in drama ("There you go," said Magda comfortingly), but she'd worked in the university library to support herself. That was long ago, though (here, she imagined, she would give a little self-deprecating laugh; she spent her walk to the library practicing it in her head), so she had a lot to learn now.

Given the fully rounded back story she had ready, she was a little irritated when the first question anyone asked her was, "You're Jewish?"

"Yes." Turning from her newly assigned locker, she nodded at Giles Morel. "Yes, I am."

"I thought so." He looked pleased. "Rachel Levis sounded Jewish. And your accent sounds American." She nodded again, and he looked pleased again. "American Jews are cool." The word was English, but he pronounced it with the French intonation: *kuhl.* "American Jewish authors have really influenced me. Philip Roth, Paul Auster, Norman Mailer, Kurt Vonnegut . . . really questioning the imposed norms."

Who was she to tell him that Kurt Vonnegut wasn't Jewish? Rachel thought. He was in enough trouble if he thought Norman Mailer questioned norms. Instead she said, "You're a novelist?"

"*Mais bien sûr*!" As if it should have been obvious. "Although maybe not what *you* think of when you think of a novelist. I really distrust the givens of the form—well, of all form, really. I want to interrogate writing even as I write. Imagine a mixture of Georges Perec and Michel Houellebecq." He slid his eyes toward her quickly to see if she appreciated the names.

"Huh," Rachel said. She had difficulty imagining how anyone could combine French literature's most puckish writer and its most tedious satirist, but again, she wasn't going to say anything. She was there merely to observe and report.

"Yeah, not easy." Giles nodded. "But both of them leave so much undone, you know? I like to think my work pushes their approaches into new territory. I'm writing a *novel* novel."

He guffawed loudly and opened his mouth to continue, but Docteure Dwamena appeared in the doorway behind him. "Good morning! They just opened the doors, so we better get out there."

As she turned away, Giles rolled his eyes. "Okay, *Maman*." He looked back at Rachel. "She's always trying to control us. We'll have to talk later about my influences."

* * *

As it turned out, there was no later. Rachel was kept busy all day, except for a lunch break she spent sitting in the park across the road trying to gather her strength. The Rare Books and Manuscripts reading room was a light-filled square, its white walls and long windows set high in the walls providing illumination without the sun's heat, but the stacks behind it where Rachel worked stretched for what seemed like miles of dim shelves dotted with fluorescent lights. Whereas the reading room had a smooth carpet and air-conditioning set for maximal comfort, the stacks were dust filled, chilled and dehumidified to preserve the books, and whereas the reading room had glossy wood tables at which scholars sat while they leafed through what they'd ordered, Rachel had a metal trolley that she collected books on by reaching up to high shelves and down to low ones, then pushed to the swinging door behind the reading room's service counter to be picked up. The low light strained her eyes, the reaching and pushing strained muscles she didn't know she had, and trying to remember shelf numbers and locations strained her mind. By the end of the day she felt coated in book dust and was fantasizing about massages that would take in every inch of her back.

As they gathered their belongings from their lockers, Giles smiled at her. "We're always busy on Mondays. Let's have lunch tomorrow to talk about the novel."

As if there were only one, Rachel thought. But she nodded as he grabbed his messenger bag from his locker and left. She arched her back to ease a nagging ache at the base of her spine.

"Giles's novel is terrible," said a voice behind her. Startled, she turned around to find LouLou leaning against the doorframe.

"Oh?"

"Yes." LouLou gave a mocking half smile. "I thought you might want to know that if you're going to talk to him about his writing."

"Thank you."

LouLou shrugged and went to her locker.

"Have you read it? His novel, I mean."

She shook her head. "But I heard some of it once."

"He read it to you?"

"Not exactly." LouLou pulled her bag out of her locker. "About six months ago someone here figured out the combination of Giles's lock. He took the manuscript out. He made it look as if it had fallen out—the pages were all over the floor—but while we were helping to pick it up, he started reading it out loud."

Oh, dear, Rachel thought. "Was Giles angry?"

"Oh yeah. And embarrassed. He grabbed the page out of the other man's hand and ran around picking up the rest, and the next day he brought in a huge new lock." Rachel glanced across at Giles's locker, locked with a square steel block with a digital mechanism. It was the sort of thing you'd find on a warehouse, not a simple metal locker.

"Who was this man?" Although she bet she already knew.

"His name was Guy Laurent. He . . . used to work here."

"He doesn't sound very pleasant."

For a moment LouLou's expression was wounded. "Oh, no! He could be very pleasant!" Then her face closed again. "I mean, he could be charming to start off with. When he wanted."

Rachel waited, but LouLou didn't say anything more, and her face stayed the same. If that expression had been an opening, it had been a fleeting one—but still, it might have been one. Rachel had left a woman alone after spotting an opportunity once before, then kicked herself over the revelations she might have missed. She wasn't going to make the same mistake twice. "Listen, would you like to go for an aperitif?"

LouLou looked at her for a few seconds, as if weighing her up. "Sure, why not? But I can't stay long. I have an appointment."

Rachel's heart thumped. She was going to get to do some actual detecting. Too late, she remembered Boussicault's orders and Madame Duonôt's: only observe and report. But surely when Boussicault had said that, he hadn't believed she would have any actual chance to engage with a suspect? She was certain he wouldn't want her to pass up an opportunity to gather valuable evidence. In fact, he'd probably be upset if she *didn't* take this chance. He'd probably applaud her for taking initiative. "That's fine," she said to LouLou. Clutching her bag, she felt the outline of her notebook through the leather.

"I saw a place over on the Rue Chabanais. How about there?" She watched the other woman's face as she made the suggestion. Would she flinch at the mention of the street? Recoil at the thought of Chez Poule?

There was no particular change of expression. "Why don't we just go to Le Bijou across the road? It's closer."

They managed to snag a table in the crowded *tabac* that was Le Bijou. LouLou ordered a whiskey, which made Rachel feel that her own vodka tonic was unbearably feminine. But she noticed that LouLou's body language didn't match the strength of her drink; she crossed her legs and hunched her shoulders as if she were trying to avoid drawing notice—although as far as Rachel could see, no one was paying the least attention to them. Maybe she was embarrassed about her height.

"So . . ." Rachel leaned in a little, trying to create a sense that they were just two colleagues gossiping, the kind of intimacy that might lead to revelation. "You said Giles's novel is terrible. What's it about?"

LouLou took a swallow and frowned. Finally she said, "I don't know, really." She shrugged. "There was a man standing on a railway platform, but then he turned into a lobster, I remember. And there was a lot about how important it was to drive on back roads and see real peasant life."

Rachel longed to ask how a lobster could drive on any road, but she wasn't going to spoil her first opportunity for detection with logical questions.

"Well, it doesn't sound so awful to have some of that read aloud. Maybe Giles is a little oversensitive?"

LouLou snorted. "Giles is more than a *little* oversensitive. No defenses at all, that one. We used to be friends when I first started working here, and even now he still follows me around like a little puppy, trying to get me to like him again." She took a sip, but Rachel had no time to ask what had ended the friendship before she continued. "In any case, no, the reading aloud was the least of it. About a month later Giles received a letter from an agent saying they'd read his sample and didn't feel his novel was right for them. Then he started receiving emails and letters from other agents, all turning down his novel based on a sample he'd sent them. He finally figured out that the other man had sent what Giles had written to every agent in Paris, signing Giles's name to a cover letter. After that, Giles hated him."

Rachel couldn't blame him. Maybe you could recover from having your embarrassing work in progress displayed to your colleagues, but you had only one chance to impress agents with a manuscript. Laurent had essentially ensured that Giles's novel would go nowhere. Still—she thought of that puffy face—that didn't mean he deserved to die. Although she found it hard to square that story with LouLou's earlier assertion that Laurent could be pleasant.

"But you said the other man could be charming? That doesn't sound like it. What was so pleasant about him, this Guy Laurent?"

She used the name deliberately to see how LouLou would react. As she watched, LouLou's nostrils contracted for a moment; she pressed her lips between her teeth and glanced up to her left. The spasm passed in less than a second, but Rachel, veteran of many such twitches, recognized it with no trouble: LouLou had been refusing to cry.

When she spoke, though, it was in her usual vaguely caustic tone. "It doesn't matter. He could be pleasant, but only until he wasn't pleasant anymore. He was pleasant as a first step in breaking people down. That's what men like: breaking." Her upper lip curled back slightly. "Even the puppies. Giles thinks his book will be his 'big break'—he'll break the world of books. Laurent tried to break Giles; he tried to break everybody." She gave a little smile. "Then, of course, he got broken himself."

Three thoughts came to Rachel in quick succession. The first was that she sincerely hoped LouLou's verdict was not true. Level-headed Alan, Magda's delightful boyfriend Benoît, her own father: had she misread them all? Did they secretly long to be cruel?

The second thought was that LouLou was filled with rage.

The third thought was that Guy Laurent had something to do with that rage.

This was not the situation she'd imagined when she'd thought that going for a drink might lead to revelations about Laurent's death. She'd thought LouLou might tell her about Giles, explain why he'd stoop to murder, but while she *had* done that, she'd also made Rachel's sympathy for Laurent start to slip away. As a corpse on a bathroom floor he had seemed pitiful, but as a living human being he was sounding like a real bastard.

She knew, though, that a good detective would use LouLou's rage to learn more. *Anger*, she imagined Miss Marple saying in her tidy way, *is a very revealing emotion*. She leaned forward. "You say Laurent tried to break everybody. Did he try—"

"I'm sorry"—LouLou stood up—"but I must go. I can't be late for my appointment. This has been fun." She smiled the first real smile Rachel had seen from her. "Sisterhood is powerful."

* * *

"'This has been fun; sisterhood is powerful'?" Magda asked over the phone later that evening. "She actually said that? Did anything in the conversation suggest that pairing?"

"Not really. But she obviously doesn't like men, and she works—well, worked—with two of them. Maybe being with another woman and saying unkind things about men is her idea of fun sisterhood?"

"But why, is the question." Magda paused to consider it. "All that stuff about the evils of men, and she tried not to cry when you said Laurent's name. That sounds like love gone bad to me."

"Yes, Boussicault said something similar. I agree."

There was silence on the other end. Then Magda said, "You already talked to Boussicault about all this?"

"Yes." Rachel stretched out on the couch. "I'm supposed to check in, remember? It's part of the deal."

"You're supposed to check in once a week. It hasn't even been two days."

"What I found out seems important, so I called him sooner. After all, I'm working with him. I should call him with anything potentially important."

Another silence, but shorter. Then, "Yeah, okay. That's fine."

Rachel picked up the thread of the original conversation. "So the question becomes, was it unrequited love with Laurent, or requited love gone bad?"

"Was that Boussicault's question?"

"No, it's *my* question."

"Well, I don't see why it matters. Either way, she could be our murderer."

Rachel rooted down into the couch. Magda had a point: why *did* it matter?

"I know," Magda answered her own question. "It matters because one way Laurent still comes out looking okay. If it was unrequited love, then he's not to blame for how LouLou might feel, and he didn't deserve what he got. From what LouLou told you he did to Giles, though, he already sounds awful. So maybe he did deserve what he got."

"Nobody deserves to be murdered."

"Nobody? Really? What about Hitler? Was he worth trying to redeem?"

"I never said anything about trying to redeem people. Anyway, whenever someone brings up Hitler, they're just looking for a sure way to close down a discussion."

"Well, then, I guess this discussion is closed. I'll talk to you later." Magda hung up.

What was going on there? Rachel wondered. Magda hadn't hung up on her since an argument in the first year of their friendship—about Tonya Harding, as she recalled. And now she was hanging up because Rachel had called Boussicault first and didn't think their victim deserved to die? Well, she would get over it.

Rachel sank more firmly into the sofa, but she couldn't get comfortable. Shrug them off as she might, Magda's remarks stung. She knew that her friend thought she was naïve about people. And maybe she was right. But her feelings about Laurent's murder weren't really about him or his character. They were about justice. Not justice in the legal sense, but justice in the sense of how things ought to be. People shouldn't kill each other. They just shouldn't. And if that was true, it couldn't be a truth that was applied selectively. Valuing life didn't mean valuing particular people's lives, as far as she was concerned. It meant valuing life as a principle. She felt that now she was beginning to grasp her point. It was true that some people were terrible, cruel, some people were even Hitler, but that wasn't the fault of life; it was the fault of what they chose to do inside that life. Life didn't deserve to be extinguished for what people did with it. *That* was what she felt.

Or at least—since she sensed possible objections rising in her own mind—that was how she felt now, on this couch, with her legs stretched out and her head resting on a cushion. How delightful to lie still! How wonderful it was to rest somewhere soft and come to grips with her abstract thoughts . . .

When Alan came into the *séjour* ten minutes later, she was fast asleep.

Chapter Six

After the revelations during her drink with LouLou, Rachel could hardly wait to have lunch with Giles. It had been her general experience that the only thing people liked better than talking about themselves was talking about other people, and having learned all about Giles and Laurent from LouLou, Rachel had high hopes that she would learn all about LouLou and Laurent from Giles. The three days until their lunch hours aligned kept her on tenterhooks.

At last, on Friday, they met in front of the entrance to the Bibliothèque at one in the afternoon. "Where to?" She squinted against the sun and tried her ruse again. "I saw a place over on Rue Chabanais . . ."

"No." Giles jerked his head to the right. "We'll go to Le Louvois. They have a good red."

Rachel trotted behind his long steps, thinking how much she disliked people who told you what you were going to do rather than asking you what you wanted to do. At least LouLou had presented Le Bijou as an alternative rather than a foregone conclusion. She reflected for a moment on the silences and suppressions demanded by undercover detective work.

Fortunately, Le Louvois did have a good red. She forgave Giles a little.

"*Alors*," said Giles after the waiter brought their plates. "You asked about my novel." He knifed out some of his salmon *rillettes* and began to spread them on a piece of bread. "Well, what can I tell you? On paper, it's a work in progress, but in my mind it's complete. That is"—he popped the bread into his mouth—"its *purpose* is complete." Rachel waited. She knew he would tell her the purpose. "It's going to tell the real story of what it's like to be a man in France today. What it's like to be given just enough to know what you deserve, but not enough to be able to achieve what you deserve." He chewed another mouthful. "Of course, this would be too banal if expressed realistically. So I work through metaphor. The metaphor of the shell. My hero wears the shell of a lobster, an image of the crustacean extrusion that every man wears in one form or another to protect himself against life's disappointments."

Oy, Rachel thought. But she nodded and smiled.

"But enough about me and my work." He placed his hands flat on the tablecloth and leaned back. "We should talk about you! I want to hear everything about you."

Rachel took a deep breath. She was going to get to use her legend. "Well, I—"

"Just a second." Giles held up a hand. "I'm sorry, I don't want you to—that is, I want to—it's very important to me that you understand something right from the start. I might have given you the impression that I'm some amateur, pecking away at a computer as a hobby. I'm not. I'm a *novelist*. I'm simply employed as a librarian *at the moment*, to support my real work."

"Okay." Rachel nodded. "Well, I—"

"Not that I use a computer. I need to be more physical. I use a typewriter. An IBM Selectric, in fact."

"Hmm. So I—"

"The same kind as Hunter Thompson." He looked at her penetratingly, then added, "And Ernest Hemingway."

Rachel saw that she would not be using her legend. Nor would she be learning anything about LouLou's connection with Laurent. She was doomed to a lunch spent listening to this man offer a flood of clichéd allusions and information about himself. Well, she thought, if she could turn the flow in the right direction, she could still get something out of it. She put her elbows on the table and rested her chin in her hands, widening her eyes slightly.

"Is it difficult, being a novelist?"

It was almost too easy. Giles stopped, preened himself for a moment, stroked his beard thoughtfully, then said, "It isn't simple. Art is a cruel taskmaster."

"And being a novelist who's working as a librarian? Surrounded by so many books, is it hard to keep them from leaking into your own writing?"

"Oh, no." She could see him relaxing into the role of author explaining to acolyte. "In fact, the combination adds something. I sometimes come in early and write in the lounge, and I can feel the juxtaposition of old writing and fresh ideas giving the work a more piquant edge."

"Gosh!" Rachel gave a wide smile. "And what good luck

being surrounded by librarians! You have a ready-made readership there in front of you."

Giles snapped up straight. "I don't discuss my work with my colleagues." His mouth was a thin line between moustache and his beard. She had hit the right nerve. She was getting somewhere!

She filled her voice with surprise. "But I thought all writers loved an audience!"

"No. One wants the *correct* audience. There's no point in reading to those who wouldn't understand."

She shook her head as if amazed at his self-control. "I don't think I'd be able to resist sharing. I'd be tempted to leave a page or two out, just to see what they thought of it."

Giles was a better actor than LouLou; his face didn't change at all. But Rachel saw his hand shake a little as he raised his glass to drink, and when he put it back down, spots of red dotted the flesh above his beard. "I would never leave my work where it could be read by just anyone. Who wants the affirmation of the ignorant?" *Great line*, Rachel thought. Maybe he did have talent after all.

"Very sensible." She grinned conspiratorially. "So you have a secret life." She made her tone speculative, gently leading. "I wonder if any of the others do, too . . . Maybe LouLou is a showgirl on the weekends."

"No, she's a witch on the weekends."

"Excuse me?" Rachel hadn't expected to lead him there.

"She's a witch." Giles shrugged. "Well, she belongs to a coven. Out in Vincennes on Monday nights. But I think all they really do is sit around talking and then cast a few spells.

No child sacrifice, unfortunately." He laughed raucously at his own joke, but then, for the first time, his face softened. "I shouldn't laugh. I think it makes her feel strong, after—"

After what? After what? Rachel yelled inside, but she tried to speak calmly. "After what?"

For one terrible moment Giles looked at her closely, and she thought he was regretting his revelations. But he must have seen something in her (or wanted to be known as a source of inside knowledge, Rachel reflected later), because after that pause he just lowered his voice. "About a year ago—the novel was only in the outline stage—LouLou was assaulted while she was walking home. Near Les Halles." He looked at her, and Rachel understood. Until its recently begun renovation, Les Halles had been one of the most notorious areas of Paris. Her face must have revealed what she was thinking, because Giles said, "She wasn't . . . But it was by a man. It affected her very badly; she was very traumatized." *That explains LouLou's drink and her posture,* Rachel thought. One to seem tough, the other to avoid being noticed. "She started carrying a knife in her bag, and she took a different route home every day," Giles shook his head. "But she had a lot of therapy, and after a while it began to help." Rachel wondered how he knew all this, but then he said, "She and I, we used to talk. I was . . . we used to talk."

Rachel had no need to put fake emotion into her voice. "That's terrible. It's really awful."

"*Oui, mais* . . . It's not the worst of it." He stopped again, and again she feared he wouldn't continue. But he did. "A few months ago, a man who used to work here, the assistant head of the department, he began to be very kind to LouLou. She was much better by then, and he, well, he started *wooing* her. *Fils de putain*. Little gifts, listening carefully when she talked, always ready to help but keeping a respectful distance. And then after a while he swore he loved her; he told her he adored her. She was afraid, of course she was, so she denied him for a long time. But at last she gave in. And she . . . transformed. You could see the love shining off her." He paused, and Rachel held her breath. *What happened?* "As soon as he saw that glow, he dumped her. He did it in the lounge, in front of me. Told her he'd been wrong about her, didn't want to be with her now that he'd had some time to see what she was like. He said he found her plain and boring and too repressed." He closed his eyes. "*Enculé*." He opened them again. "After that, she—" He held up a hand and closed it into a fist. "With everyone, men and women. I try to speak to her now, and she acts like I've set out to injure her." Taking a drink, he looked at Rachel. "You see? My metaphor, the shell, is well chosen."

Rachel watched him. Although the last comment had returned him to his usual narcissism, she could see a change in his face, a small crack in the fatuousness. "What a terrible thing to do," she said softly. "I'm so sorry."

Giles shrugged. "*Eh, bien*, he ended up dead. In that *resto* you mentioned before, in fact. In a toilet stall. So one can't say there isn't any justice."

Chapter Seven

"Wow," said Magda. "You might have to change your opinion about his writing skills."

"Yeah, I might." But Rachel was willing to bet Giles's novel was nothing like the tale he'd told at Le Louvois. She knew his type from her creative writing workshops: their work was good only when they weren't paying attention. For a moment she felt a little melancholy for him. Then she remembered the many times he'd cut her off during their conversation, and her sympathy evaporated.

Magda took a sip of her smoothie. They had met in the Exki café near the Saint-Lazare train station, a short walk from Magda's apartment. The Exkis were a recent addition to Paris, and one Rachel entirely approved of. Their food arranged in tidy rows, their bright, well-scrubbed interiors, even their tables made of some gleaming varnished wood, soothed her. In an Exki, all was orderly and even. In an Exki, the world became a manageable place.

Magda broke her reverie. "So it was requited love in Lou-Lou's case. Or at least, allegedly, briefly requited love. Christ, what a shitty trick to pull."

"More than shitty." Rachel shook her head. "According to Giles, Laurent destroyed her emotionally. I believe it. She certainly seems to hate men now."

"Okay, so she's our prime suspect." Magda pulled a small hardcover pad from her bag and flipped it open. POSSIBLES, she wrote, underlining it heavily. Then she wrote LOULOU in block letters on the line beneath.

"Mmm." Rachel squirmed.

"No?"

"I just feel Giles is more plausible."

"Did Laurent break his heart, too?"

Although Magda was being sarcastic, Rachel took the question seriously. "In a way, yes. Being a writer is central to how writers understand themselves. Giles said it himself: he might work in a library, but as far as he's concerned he's an author, not a librarian. He thinks being a writer makes him special. So when Laurent showed that in fact he wasn't a writer, or at least not a very good one, it was a huge blow." She had a flash of insight. "And he kept the novel hidden. That suggests he already suspected it wasn't much good, or was scared it wasn't. And having your secret fear confirmed is even worse than simple humiliation."

Magda's pen hovered over the pad, but then she put it down. "I don't know. I don't think that reaches the level of what Laurent did to LouLou."

"Well, that connects here, too. I think Giles is in love with LouLou. At the very least, he's extremely fond of her. When he talked about her, he went all"—she wriggled again—"tender. And Laurent really did a number on LouLou. Wouldn't you want to kill someone if they did that to me? And we're just friends."

"Yes, I'd *want* to, but I wouldn't."

Rachel felt obscurely insulted.

Magda continued, "I just can't see a man in this day and age killing over a woman's honor, or over some wounded authorial pride. Whereas LouLou . . . she was severely psychologically damaged. It would hardly be surprising if she reacted violently."

"I just can't believe that. She's angry, but she also has some kind of residual feelings for Laurent. And we know women are less likely to be killers. Whereas a man, and an author's amour propre . . . Graham Greene said there's a splinter of ice in the heart of every writer."

"And someone else said hell hath no fury like a woman scorned."

They sat scowling at each other until at last Magda sighed heavily, picked up her pen, and wrote Giles's name next to LouLou's. Then, as if nothing had passed between them, she said, "What about Dr. Dwamena? Did you find out anything significant there?"

"She's mostly in her office. The only real interaction I've had with her was when she showed me the stacks."

Magda nodded. "Yeah, that makes sense. It's going to be harder to get info on the boss. Well"—her tone became brisk—"I've got to go home for a Skype appointment with another supplier, so I guess that's all for now. But things are winding down with my preparations, so next week I can start poking around for more useful information."

What could be more useful than on-the-ground reports about our two best and only suspects? The irritation that had popped up at Magda's refusal to kill for her grew stronger. This wasn't the first time Magda had suggested she was of more practical use than Rachel could be. But whereas Rachel would normally have snapped something back, this time she didn't say anything. She was feeling a little guilty about not telling Magda she was going straight from their meeting to report to Capitaine Boussicault.

* * *

The *capitaine* listened patiently until she finished her report and flipped her notebook shut. Then he said only, "They seem to have no problem talking when it's to a colleague."

"Well, not Dr. Dwamena."

"No, but the other two were very informative with you. Good work."

Rachel straightened in her chair. "Thank you." She felt an urge to add "sir," but held back.

"*De rien.*" His expression became parental. "But remember, please, that these were unusual opportunities. You are not supposed to be seeking suspects out. You're supposed to—"

"—observe and report," Rachel finished.

He smiled. "Exactly. And even if Dwamena is less forthcoming, a lot can be learned just from observing her. What you overhear can be even more important than what you elicit." Done with his sermon, he turned back to her report. "And you say neither Morel nor Fournier wanted to go to Chez Poule?" Rachel shook her head. "Of course, it's hard to know if that's significant or not, without knowing whether they used to go there when Laurent was alive. Is it bad food or bad memories that keeps them away?" He smiled at his own joke. Rachel joined him. "Well, I'm not sure it's very important, but it might help if we knew whether their reluctance to go there only began after the murder. I'll send Didier over on Monday to talk to the owner again. Good lead. Again." She looked modestly down at her lap. "Right, well, I must go to a briefing about heroin dealers in Porte de la Chapelle. Feel free to contact me before next Friday if you hear anything else that seems interesting."

At seven in the evening the Mètro was relatively empty, and Rachel had two seats to herself. She leaned against the window. Briefly, she replayed Boussicault's moments of approval in her head. It seemed she had a knack for police work. What's more, Boussicault didn't argue or dismiss her out of hand. He listened, and when he had a concern, he expressed it warmly and politely. There was something to be said for being part of a team rather than one end in an ongoing tug-of-war.

If only she could do something to be more useful! Okay, she told herself, he'd told her again that she was only supposed to observe and report, but he'd also been as impressed by her initiative as she'd thought he would be. So why not show some more? She remembered what he'd said about sending his *brigadier* over to the restaurant again on Monday. But he'd asked her to join the investigation because civilians wouldn't talk to the *brigadier* but they would talk to her. So why didn't she go over to Chez Poule and see what the people there would tell her? And she'd do it before Monday, which would move the investigation along faster. Besides, she pointed out to herself, she could do with getting a better sense of the scene of the crime herself. She had been too flustered to pay attention when she was there the previous time. And she knew Magda would want to see the place, too.

She was interested in this, she realized. After all those weeks of struggling with the hymns, she had almost forgotten how it felt to do something fulfilling.

Yet—she could never let a feeling go unanalyzed—this couldn't really be because she was bringing justice for Guy Laurent's lost life. She had to confess to herself that no matter what her abstract principles were, she was finding it difficult to be on fire for justice for Laurent specifically.

Unbidden, a vision of that afternoon's Exki café came to her. She saw its orderly counters, its bright light. She remembered her favorite supermarket, the Monoprix where the wine stood on the shelves in organized plenitude, where someone had arranged the fruit and vegetables into neat pyramids and piles. Solving a murder, she suddenly understood, was ordering the world. But it was also something more . . . She groped inside herself until at last she grasped what she felt. It was doing right. How often in the world did one have the chance to perform an action that was absolutely to the good, that absolutely righted a wrong? She thought of the hymns, precisely intended to offer and glorify hope in a debased world. Detection did the same, only more concretely. If successful, it was a demonstration that ugliness did *not* always win.

These thoughts absorbed her so much that as she came out of the Notre-Dame des Champs Mètro station, it was as if she woke up. The Boulevard Raspail stretched ahead, its thin trees the full green of summer and its grayish-cream buildings wavering in the heat. It had been a long time since Rachel had observed Paris rather than moving through it, and it was for a moment both completely new to her and completely familiar. *O so dear from far and near and white all / So deliciously you*, she found herself thinking, although she hadn't read Mallarmé for years. No murder should go unpunished in the middle of such beauty.

Chapter Eight

The Rachel who arrived at Chez Poule on Saturday with Alan and Magda was not the sweaty, thirsty, frustrated hymnist of three Wednesdays before but a focused, determined, attentive Police Consultant (in her mind the title was capitalized). In this guise she saw that despite its location, the café wasn't aimed at scholars or tourists. The menu in its plastic cover listed almost entirely dishes designed to see their eaters through an afternoon of heavy labor: *tarte flambée*, *choucroute* of sausages with sauerkraut and bacon, thick stews and soups. The dining area was a dim cave, its walls and ceiling stained by tobacco smoke so ingrained that it hadn't faded at all in the twelve years since the smoking ban. She knew that these days it was trendy to find such places charming, to relabel their insalubriousness as retro chic, but she didn't think that would be possible with this place. It was and always would be a dive.

A waiter appeared. "What can I get you?" He wasn't exactly smiling, but he wasn't completely antagonistic. Rachel felt hopeful about her information-gathering.

To increase her chances, she ordered something to eat.

After all, it was lunchtime. "I'd like the *choucroute* and a Coca Light, please." She smiled warmly.

"Stella Artois." This was Alan's standard weekend lunch drink.

"Café noir," said Magda.

The waiter took their menus and began to leave, but Rachel's voice stopped him. "This place is charming."

He seemed surprised at this description, but said, "I'll tell the owner you said so."

"Have you worked here long?"

He seemed even more surprised. "Two years."

"And you work this shift often, the lunch shift?"

"Why?" Now he was suspicious.

"No reason. Just—"

"You haven't come to talk about that *mec* in the toilet, have you? It was almost three weeks ago. Isn't it old news by now?"

Rachel felt the situation beginning to slip out of her hands. She tried to claw it back. "No, no, I haven't come to talk about that. As a matter of fact, I work near here. At the Bibliothèque." She couldn't see how to transition smoothly from explanation to question, so she just slogged on. "My colleagues recommended I try this place. Maybe you know them? A tall woman with long black hair and a man with a beard and a tattoo here?" As she touched her forearm to show the location of Giles's tattoo, Rachel realized how hopeless this was. They must have hundreds of customers a day. How would this man recognize Giles and LouLou from such vague descriptions? She should have borrowed the *capitaine*'s photos of them—except that then she would have had to tell him what she planned to do.

Unsurprisingly, the waiter said, "I don't remember anyone like that."

His tone suggested Rachel wouldn't be presenting Capitaine Boussicault with any new information from Chez Poule. Still, she tried once more. "Funnily enough, they did work with the man who died here. They all worked together. Maybe they all used to come in for lunch together, too?"

He gave her a long, level look, then said with precision, "No." He walked away.

Rachel flushed with embarrassment.

"Nice work, Jessica Fletcher," Alan said. She flashed him a look similar to the one the waiter had given her. "Sorry. But I still don't understand what you're trying to do here. And I don't see why you had to bring me."

He had a point. After all, she and Magda had been successful the previous year without his help. But when he'd found out then that she'd been investigating without telling him then, he'd been furious—and justifiably so, she saw now. As a result, she'd decided that this time he should know everything, right from the start.

Also, she needed his help.

"I was trying to find out if LouLou and Giles used to come here but don't anymore," she explained. "Obviously that didn't go the way I hoped. But I'm also trying to get a sense of the scene of the crime, because I"—she remembered Magda—"because we don't really have that. And I brought you because the scene of the crime is a men's room."

"But you've already been in it!"

"I wasn't really paying attention to my surroundings

then." The waiter reappeared and put their drinks down. She smiled feebly at him, but he just turned and walked away. "And now I can't go in without attracting notice."

"But *you* can," Magda chimed in, turning to Alan. She added helpfully, "Because you're a man."

"So I'm here as your proxy." Alan sighed. "Well, if that's the case, I better drink up so the whole investigation doesn't founder on my inability to play my vital role." He took a huge swallow of his Stella Artois.

Rachel put her hand on his raised arm. "Slow down. We don't want to be conspicuous."

No one pointed out that it was probably too late for that. In fact, no one said anything. Alan took a second swallow, then another, then another, then drained his glass. The waiter brought Rachel's *choucroute* and left again. At last Alan stood up. "*Aux armes, citoyens,*" he said, and walked toward the back corridor.

Rachel ate and Magda fiddled with her coffee cup. The silence between them felt natural, then strained, then endless. At last, Alan reappeared and sat down. The women waited, but he said nothing.

Finally, "What was it like?" Rachel asked.

He shrugged. "It was like a men's room. An ordinary, slightly run-down men's room."

"But we've never *seen* a men's room, so we don't know what that means. Describe it."

"Okay." Alan ran his hand through his hair, then took the last forkful of Rachel's *choucroute*. "As you come in—well, as I came in—the urinals are right there, against the back wall. There were four."

"I hate the word *urinal*," Magda said.

Rachel nodded. "Me, too."

"And *stall*. I mean, *stall* is okay if it's a barn stall, but as a bathroom word it's just horrible."

Alan cleared his throat. "Excuse me." The two women looked at him. He took a breath and picked up his thread. "So the ur—they're on the back wall. And next to them, to the right of them, are the, er—" He glanced at Magda and said with a slight upward intonation, "Cabins?" She nodded. "Directly opposite those are the sinks."

Rachel cut in. "Could you make us a floor plan?"

Alan knew she liked to see things in front of her. A few swift strokes and a rudimentary map drawn on a napkin lay on the table. She and Magda bent over it.

"Interesting," said Rachel.

"What?" Magda squinted.

"Boussicault said the evidence showed that Laurent was dragged into the stall *after* he was killed. And remember he was found with his fly unzipped? Put those two together, then add the fact that these"—she tapped the sketched urinals—"are next to the, uh, cabins, and we can assume that he died while or shortly after he was standing *here*." She put her finger on the space in front of the urinals. "That would mean there are two ways it might have gone down." She felt a thrill as she used the phrase. Who was being a Dashiell Hammett character *now*? "Someone could have walked up on him from behind, or they could have come up over the side of the first cabin."

"Oh my God, like in *Blow Out*. Remember John Lithgow—"

"I remember."

Too late, Magda recalled that the image of John Lithgow looming over a stall divider to garrote a prostitute quite literally haunted Rachel's dreams. "Sorry." She added, as if offering consolation, "Or the murderer could have killed Laurent while he was washing his hands."

"But you wouldn't wash your hands before you zipped your fly." Rachel looked at Alan. "Or would you?"

Alan shook his head. "I can't speak for every man, but I wouldn't, no."

"And what about other men you've been to the bathroom with? Would they?"

He gave a snort of laughter. "Now here I can speak for every man. We don't go to the men's room 'with'"—he made quotation marks with his fingers—"other men. While you're in there, the goal is not to look and not to listen. Even if you're talking to another man, you just stare at the wall."

Not for the first time, Rachel was struck by the complexity of men's relationships with each other. God knew they spent enough time worrying about the comparative size of their genitalia, but given an opportunity to compare, they actively avoided it! She recognized, however, that this was not the time to explore that piece of illogic. "Okay, then we'll just have to rely on your general feeling. Do you think he would have washed his hands before he zipped his fly?"

"No. But I also don't think anyone killed him over the side of a stall."

"Why not?"

"Think about it. The only plausible way to do that would

be to stand on the toilet seat and brace your feet. But if you did that, the pressure would push the seat off the toilet bowl, in which case you'd be thrown off balance and probably put at least one of your feet in the toilet, which would make you break your grip on your—what was it?—your piece of string. No"—he shook his head again—"you couldn't complete your murder standing on a toilet."

Rachel admired his reasoning skills. "An excellent point. Okay, so we can safely assume that he was killed either before or after he peed."

"But," Magda jumped in, "the *capitaine* told you he had recently emptied his bladder. So it had to be after." She turned to Alan. "Was the floor wet?"

He frowned. "No. Why?"

"Because the *capitaine* also told Rachel that the string the police found was wet, and they thought it was from being on the floor. But he didn't mention anything about scuff marks on the floor, which you'd expect to find if the killer had fought not to slip on a wet floor. If the floor was wet during the murder, then the killer would need to be heavier than if the floor was dry, because a lighter killer would slip, which would leave scuff marks. More body weight would help keep the killer planted. So if the floor was wet, but there were no scuff marks at the scene, then we can deduce that the killer is pretty heavy, and that narrows down our suspects." She shot Rachel a look. "Makes it more likely that it was a man, for example."

The women waited.

"The floor was dry." Alan grimaced. "Sorry. I really am. But it was."

"Okay. Okay. So we can't rule out anybody based on the floor." Rachel groped for an alternative scenario. "But . . ."

"Well, the floor is dry *today*," Magda interrupted. "We don't know what it was like on the day Laurent was killed. They could have had a leak that's been fixed since then."

She stood and walked to the bar. She smiled at the *patron*, pointed to their table, and wrote in the air with two pinched fingers. The *patron* nodded, then nodded again as Magda kept talking, then shook his head, then shook it more vehemently. Magda returned.

"What was that about?"

"I asked for the check." Magda resumed her seat. "Then I asked him if there'd been a leak in the men's room."

"You just asked? Without any excuse?"

Magda nodded. How did she do it? Rachel wondered. When Maga asked strangers bizarre questions, they just answered them. They didn't say "No" and walk way; they didn't even look irritated. But, she pointed out to herself, Capitaine Boussicault had asked her, not Magda, to help him. She felt comforted. "What did he say?"

"He said no. They had the plumbing overhauled last year, and the whole system is brand new." She lowered her voice. "I think he thinks I'm an inspector."

Rachel tried to arrange her thoughts so they worked as neatly as Alan's and Magda's. "Well, if the floor was dry and the string was wet, that means the killer must have wet the string beforehand deliberately."

"Maybe he peed on it." Magda looked pleased by this idea. "You know, to show contempt for the victim."

Alan was dubious. "He'd have to have good aim. Not to mention considerable dexterity, since he'd need to hold the string in one hand and his penis in the other, then pee in a straight line."

Unlike the previous moment, this was the sort when her husband's reasoning skills irritated Rachel. She liked the idea of a killer so filled with contempt that he urinated on his weapon—it sounded like something out of a Jim Thompson novel. Also, it would mean that the killer was a man, which might mean it was Giles. "Maybe he put the string on a counter," she said.

Alan laughed. "Okay, maybe. But I think if you're the sort of killer who goes in for symbolism, surely killing someone in a men's room is enough of a symbol of contempt. Or why not just pee directly on the body? Still scornful; much easier in terms of aim." When Rachel wrinkled her nose disgustedly, he said, "You *wanted* a man along on this visit."

"Okay." Magda spoke across them. "No peeing. Which makes sense if it's LouLou, anyway. So let's say the killer wet the string for practical purposes. What purposes?"

"Can string hold a fingerprint?" Rachel wondered. "He could have wet it to avoid that. if wetting would do that. Or to make it stronger? Is wet string stronger than dry string?"

Magda and Alan had no answers.

The waiter slapped the receipt down on the table and scurried away, casting one final angry glance behind him.

"I'll buy a ball of string on the way home." Magda reached in her bag to pay the check.

Chapter Nine

Rachel and Magda spent their Sunday afternoon wetting string and garroting Rachel's couch cushions. They found no difference in strength between dry string and wet string, and an evening spent searching the Internet didn't answer the question of whether string could hold fingerprints, or whether wetting it would make any difference to that. So it was a glum Rachel who made her way to the Bibliothèque on Monday. So much for ordering the world, she thought. She'd started with a body in a bathroom, and now she had a dislikable victim, a mysteriously wet piece of string, an angry waiter, and at least two potential murderers. If anything, she was disordering the world, especially since, she now had to admit, her belief that Giles was the murderer was largely based on the fact that the murder had happened in a men's room.

The day seemed determined to deepen her gloom. The reading room's patrons requested only the heaviest books, and all requested them at once; a wheel broke off one of her trolleys and she had to reattach it with tape; it turned out that the peach she'd included in her lunch was mealy. Rachel couldn't have been called a cheerful optimist at the best of times, and by six o'clock her back ached, her thumb had been jammed under a trolley wheel, and she had been denied dessert. She was beginning to regret deeply that she had ever agreed to help with the investigation.

So it gave her some pleasure to find Giles and LouLou arguing in the employee lounge. If she was going to be unhappy, she didn't see why she had to be unhappy alone. Also—her spirits lifted a little—who knew what the argument might reveal? It had been three days since she'd seen any sort of development in the case, but arguments, like anger, encouraged revelations. She pricked up her ears.

"It's rightfully mine," Giles was saying.

"I don't see why. You haven't been promoted." LouLou's voice was impatient.

"Not officially. But you were hired after me, so if either of us is going to get moved up, it's going to be me."

"There's no guarantee of that. It's not like a *tapis roulant*: one goes and the next in line takes his place. Anyway, even if you were moved up"—LouLou's tone suggested depthless scorn at this idea—"there's no reason why you would move into his locker. Yours is exactly the same."

They were fighting about a locker? Rachel moved farther into the room. Giles and LouLou stood in front of the double row of employee lockers, Giles with his hand on the handle of the central one in the upper row. It wouldn't take much of a detective to figure out that this must be the locker in question, and not much more of one to work out that the "he" in question was Guy Laurent. So they were fighting over Guy Laurent's locker. For a moment Rachel felt like laughing.

"The symbolism is obvious," Giles said patiently. He looked pained at having to argue with LouLou, but he also looked like he wanted to win. "Laurent was assistant head, and now that he's gone I will be made assistant head, and I should have the assistant head's central locker!"

LouLou snorted. She did not look pained. She looked derisive, determined, and very angry. "What is it about you men and your need to be superior?"

"I wish you wouldn't make everything about gender," Giles said plaintively. "Gender is just a construct."

LouLou snorted again. "Only the privileged gender would say that. Why don't we talk to Docteure Dwamena about your little masculine primacy issue? Why don't we see what another woman has to say about it?"

"*Bien sûr.*" Giles stuck his chin out. "Why not right now?" He picked up his messenger bag and slung it over his shoulder, gesturing for LouLou to precede him through the door. She did, but as she passed his outstretched hand, she gave an instinctive jerk.

They were gone so quickly that Rachel wasn't sure they even noticed her.

She sat down in one of the lounge chairs. *What a mess*, she thought. She had no idea if LouLou had ever been romantically interested in Giles, but he had at least some sort of affection for her. Yet here they were, Giles fighting for every crumb that could demonstrate his superiority and LouLou angry at every man on the planet, and all because of the nasty machinations of Guy Laurent. Just for a moment she wondered if it was all an act. Maybe Giles and LouLou had committed the murder together. Except that she couldn't see LouLou letting down her guard enough to work with Giles, or Giles giving her a moment in the planning process in which to speak.

She grinned at her own thoughts, then let the silence soothe her. After a few seconds it came home to her that she was alone in the lounge with Guy Laurent's locker. She glanced at it. Guy Laurent's lockless locker.

She bit her lip. Laurent wouldn't have touched his locker since the day he died, obviously. Who knew what he might have left behind? There could be an appointment book, or even a journal filled with—her imagination ran wild—entries detailing his cruelties and the victims of them. Perhaps there were further suspects she and the police knew nothing about. The uselessness of the trip to the restaurant and the disappointments of the day began to fade. Rachel Levis, Investigatrix and Police Consultant, was on the case.

She stood up. Like every person about to commit a furtive act, she suddenly became immensely fearful that someone with hyperacute hearing might be listening or someone with silent steps might sneak up on her in the middle of it. Gathering her courage, she walked to the central locker with a catlike tread. She lifted its handle, steadying the door with her free hand so it wouldn't rattle. After one more careful look around, she peeped inside.

The locker was empty except for a combination lock that lay on the bottom, its shackle cut open.

She resolved not to mention this moment to Magda. Why hadn't it occurred to her that, since the locker was missing its lock, someone might have gone through it already? How had she let her excitement get the better of her? With detective skills like this, she wouldn't even win a game of Clue. She opened the door further and picked up the severed lock. The bolt cutter had made a clean slice: the raw edges gleamed against the worn metal. She sighed and replaced it. Then she stopped. Had it been farther back? She pushed it slightly. Or had it been farther forward? She put her head inside the locker to see if the lock had left any trace she could use as a guide.

This, she reflected, would be the moment when someone walked into the employee lounge and found her.

Just as she was thinking that, she noticed a little flick of white on the locker's back wall. Reaching a hand all the way inside, she touched it with her index finger. It wasn't a place where the paint had peeled off or a nail head gleaming in the light. It was the corner of a piece of paper. She scraped at it with her thumbnail. It didn't move. She scraped it again. It still didn't move. She pulled herself out of the locker, checked once more to make sure the silent observer hadn't entered the room, then opened the matching locker on the row below. That one was empty. She stuck the top half of her body inside; she had to get on her knees, but it worked. There at the back, caught in the top of the locker, was all but one small corner of a piece of a paper. As she gently pulled it out, she saw it was a folded sheet from a school notebook. She unfolded it. The inner side was covered in scrawled numbers.

A clue, an actual clue! She was so excited that she spelled it the old-fashioned way in her head to give it added emphasis: a *clew*! The first real one of the investigation! Now she just had to get it out of the building without anyone's notice. She stood up, opened her own locker, and eased the sheet into the side pocket of her bag. Then she took the bag, shut her locker, and left the room. The back door, which led directly outside, was locked, so she used the one that opened onto the corridor next to the reading room. She could feel her heart pounding and breathed in and out deeply, trying to force a sense of calm. She made herself walk more slowly. *You're just leaving work after a normal day*, she told herself. *A normal day.*

Over these thoughts she gradually began to make out a conversation. The farther down the corridor she went, the louder it grew. It came from Docteure Dwamena's office. A second clew! Or was it? Could conversations be clues, or were they just leads? Could only material objects be clues? *Shut up, shut up*, she hissed to her whirling brain. *Calm down and listen. Observe and report.* She flattened herself against the wall next to the office and held her breath.

"—like this much longer," Docteure Dwamena was saying.

"But it's hard for me." The second voice was LouLou's. "It hasn't been that long since—"

"I know it's been difficult. I know you still have a lot to deal with. But you've been neglecting significant aspects of your job for quite a while now, and it's starting to cause problems."

"I'm sorry," LouLou said, but she added belligerently, "I come in early." After a breath, her tone became more conciliatory. "I know I'm very backed up."

"Of course I empathize," Docteure Dwamena said. "How could I not? As you know, he and I had—well, you know." *But* I *don't know*, Rachel thought. *Tell me.* Docteure Dwamena began again, her voice firm. "But now we all have a chance to wipe the slate clean and move on."

"He made some assertions about your behavior as head. That is not the same as what he did to me." LouLou's voice teetered on the edge of sullenness, but Rachel heard caution in it, too.

"Assertions," said Docteure Dwamena, her tone so flat that it could only be suppressing explosive emotion. "I wouldn't call them just assertions."

What would you call them, then? Please say what you would call them.

But the doctor moved on. "In any case, while as your friend I understand what you mean, as your *chef* I must tell you that you need to catch up on your outstanding work or I will have to submit a written warning." There was a long pause, and when she spoke again, her voice was softer. "Believe it or not, I do know what it is to feel that you will never recover from something. One must just work through it. Eventually one does heal." Another pause, the sound of hands meeting a hard surface, and then she said crisply, "*Alors*. There is nothing else to say, so now we go home, and tomorrow is a fresh start."

Taking the cue, Rachel hurried to the door that led out into the main hall. What had the doctor been going to say at the end of "he and I had—"? What did she mean by "I wouldn't call them just assertions"? What *could* she mean? Once out in the Bibliothèque's square courtyard, she had one thought: Magda. Her fingers itched for immediate consultation. She felt in her bag for her phone.

Then she stopped. She'd forgotten about the *capitaine.*

Should he be her first call? From a practical standpoint, of course. He was her boss. But Magda was her best friend. And she would recognize the drama of the discovery! She tightened her lips. Maybe she could scan the page, then take it to the *capitaine*, then share the scan with Magda? But what if the original had all sorts of clues that a scan couldn't capture? And was there even a place to scan in this area now that the Bibliothèque was closed? She stood in the courtyard, trapped on the horns of her dilemma. Her loyalties had never been so divided.

Chapter Ten

"A scan," Magda snorted half an hour later as she and Rachel sat side by side on a bench in the Jardin du Palais Royal. Rachel had slipped her feet out of her shoes and was resting them on a metal chair in front of her, feeling the curious combination of pain and bliss known only by those relaxing their overtaxed feet after a long day.

Now she leaned back on the bench and closed her eyes; her face was in shadow but she could feel the sun on her toes. Stretching them out the way she imagined a cat might stretch its paws, she looked down at Magda's long brown feet on the chair next to them. "But I didn't give you a scan, did I? I called you up and told you to meet me here before I took the page to the commissariat. I first read it at precisely the same time you did."

This was, in fact, exactly what she had done. After keeping her curiosity in check for twenty minutes while she waited for Magda to arrive, she had used the tweezers from her mini Swiss army knife to hold up the paper between them, her other hand behind it to keep the sun from shining through and making it illegible.

On the top line were written the letters BN. Beneath that, scrawled numbers and calculations covered nearly the whole page. Some of the numbers were large—tens of thousands or higher—but often they were then divided on lines beneath, or had amounts subtracted from them until they became

BN

17500 10000
145 000 14500 9000 2
90 000 9000 900 8500 5000
55 000 5500 224000 apd 4.7 950
4500 67272 750
11062 22000 7000 76000 700
17225-13000 4000? 60272 50000 625
18000 1800 420 26000 550
18075 1756 42075 2600 475
1215 1375 1300 150-
46000 37200 17050 15000
198000 186000 192000
123899 122500 122999 - 7999
8 115000 701
157512 1000 107999
1575 1500 150 1 100 19001 2000
525 10 900 2000 10 1900 280
20 1800 260 1500 120
11035 150 15
12000 300 M/F - 500 } (1500)
1200 600 SC - 1000 }

relatively small. The largest had APD 4.7 scratched next to it. Written neatly on a line underneath all the figures and calculations was M/F-500, and on the line beneath that, SC-1000. A bracket joined these two, and written next to its point was 1500, with a circle around it.

* * *

"We thought it might be a code," she explained to Capitaine Boussicault in his office half an hour later with Magda next to her. The sheet of paper now lay on his desk, encased in a plastic protector. "'BN' seemed to us pretty clearly to mean 'Bibliothèque Nationale,' so we thought it might be coded information about what he was doing there."

"Yes." He nodded, and she preened a little under his agreement. "Thank you very much. It has the potential to be significant." He put it on top of a pile to his left, then folded his hands on his desktop.

"That's it?" Magda said.

Boussicault smiled at her. "No. Tomorrow morning I'll take it down to the lab and see what they can do with it."

"But it could be a major clue. Your first break in the case!"

He fixed her eyes with his own. "Do you know what the numbers mean?"

"We thought that they might be some sort of calculations. And we thought the letters at the bottom might be the initials of people related to the numbers."

"Which means you don't know. It's plain that at least some of the numbers are calculations from the way they're arranged. And as for the initials"—Boussicault shrugged—"you could be right, but equally you could be wrong. They could stand for streets, or for restaurants, or they could be entirely personal mnemonic devices. As I say, it's a very promising item—but at the moment utterly inconclusive. We don't even know if Laurent wrote it or if it belonged to him."

Magda was outraged. "It was at the back of his locker!"

"The locker beneath his. Please, Madame Stevens. We can't move forward based on assumptions of what must be true or what could be true. There is a process. There are steps. The lab will compare the sheet to samples of Laurent's handwriting. They also have experts in codes who will be better equipped to decipher it."

Magda looked mutinous. She shrugged. It was not quite a French shrug, but it nonetheless managed to express both her belief that Boussicault was a hopeless slave to bureaucracy and her knowledge that she couldn't do anything about it. As if to drive the latter point home, she said, "Well, you've got the paper now, so it's not like we have any choice."

* * *

"You don't seem very troubled," Magda said as they walked down the steps of the commissariat.

"Oh, well, you know." Rachel was digging around in her bag.

"No, I don't know. I thought you'd be more upset."

"There's no point." She kept digging. "Like you said, he's got the page now. It's a done deal. Besides"—she pulled her hand out of her bag, holding a slightly crumpled sheet of paper—"I made a photocopy."

* * *

That night Rachel, Magda, and Alan had dinner together again. When they had finished their raspberries with cream and nearly consumed their bottle of wine, Rachel brought out the photocopy of Laurent's note and laid it on the table, smoothing it down so they could all see.

"And this is it," Alan said. "Just this one side."

She nodded.

Magda put an index finger on the top line of the sheet. "Since Laurent worked at the Bibliothèque Nationale, and since this was found there, we figured 'BN' must stand for 'Bibliothèque Nationale.'"

"Makes sense," Alan said. "And I'm guessing you also figured the letters at the bottom must somehow relate to that abbreviation, since they're the only other letters on the page."

"Yes," Rachel said, "but after that we're at a loss. They could be names"—she remembered Boussicault's comment and reddened—"or streets, or really anything. And what's happening with all those numbers in the middle?"

"Okay. Okay." Alan leaned closer to the sheet, idly tapping it with the side of his thumb as he focused. At last he said, "What if instead of trying to figure it out globally, we do it like for like? What if we work on the hypothesis that things that are similar stand for the same thing? Like you did with the letters."

"What?" Rachel said.

He put his forefinger on the letters at the bottom of the page. "Okay. So, because you assumed 'BN' was an abbreviation of 'Bibliothèque Nationale,' you also assumed that these letters were abbreviations for something."

Now Rachel understood. "So we would assume that the numbers are all the same kinds of numbers—that they're all doing the same thing."

"Right." He grinned at her, his hair flopping in his eyes. He loved numbers, Rachel knew. "Now, look at the numbers next to these letters on the bottom. They're smaller, yes, but this number"—he put his finger on the 1500—"is the sum of those two, and he's circled it. And it's been my experience that when people add two numbers and circle the result, they're only dealing with one thing."

"Money!" Magda slapped her hand on the table triumphantly. She also loved numbers.

Alan nodded. "Money. I don't know why, but they always circle the total if it's money."

"So," Magda continued, "using like for like, that would mean that all the numbers on this sheet were money. Okay. But that still leaves us with the question of what the money is doing. Or what Laurent was doing with it."

"Yes, that is a puzzle." Alan frowned.

"Or maybe . . ." Rachel bit her lip. "Not if we apply like-for-like again."

The other two looked confused, but she kept going. "First, let's think about what he was like."

"He was a shit," Magda said.

"Yes, but a particular kind of shit. A shit that liked to hurt people, and to hurt them by using their own experiences against them. Think about it. He hurt Giles with his own novel, and he hurt LouLou by playing on her attack. Now apply like-for-like. What kind of activity involving money would be like that kind of hurting?"

Alan still looked confused. "Say that again."

But the answer had come to Rachel in a flash. "Blackmail!" She slapped her hand on the tabletop. It did feel good. "Blackmail is like the other things he did. It's using someone's own experiences against them to get money out of them."

"Ooooh." Magda got it. "So this," she put her finger on the circled *1500*, "would be the amount he was asking for." Rachel nodded. "But what are all the other numbers?"

"I think they're calculations to figure out how much he could get. I think he's working that out somehow all over the page, and at the bottom he comes to a decision."

Magda looked at the page, then at her. "That's good. That's really, really good."

"Thank you." Rachel felt like patting herself on the back. Look how much she'd grown by working with the police! But her satisfaction faded quickly. "There's still the question of the letters, though. They could be the initials of the person—well, people—he's blackmailing . . ." She petered out uncertainly.

"Which means not either of your current suspects," Alan pointed out.

"Well," Magda said practically, "there are lots of other people at the Bibliothèque who could be suspects."

"Like who?"

"Whom," Magda corrected.

"Okay, like whom?" Rachel asked.

"Well, Docteure Dwamena, for one."

"Yes, I need to figure out how to find out more there." Aside from that afternoon's conversation, Rachel had hardly seen or heard the Head of Manuscripts in the two weeks she'd been at the library.

"Or maybe one of the people using the reading room."

"The patrons?"

"Sure, why not? They interacted with Laurent."

"But Capitaine Boussicault thinks—"

"Oh, Capitaine Boussicault thinks!" Magda was exasperated. "You didn't care so much what Capitaine Boussicault thought the last time you were investigating a murder."

Rachel was shocked. "What's that supposed to mean?"

Alan stood up and took his wine glass to the sink.

"It means"—Magda's voice was slow and clear—"that all your references to what Boussicault thinks and how Boussicault sees the crime are getting a little tiring."

Rachel was affronted. "He *is* a policeman. He does know best how to proceed with an investigation."

"He put this piece of paper on a pile! And he thought we were fantasizing about Edgar's murder!"

"He wanted to have professionals look at the evidence, not make guesses himself!" About the reference to their previous case she could say nothing; Magda was right.

"All I'm saying"—Magda's voice was weary now—"all I'm saying is that I think you're relying a little too much on the captain, when we're doing very well on our own." She gestured toward the sheet they'd just deciphered.

No one spoke. After a couple of minutes Magda stood. "I think I better go home. Thank you for dinner."

"Oh, come on, Da!" Rachel half-stood as she used the old nickname. "It's not a big deal. C'mon, Maggie May."

But Magda was immune to nicknames. She let herself out. Rachel sat in the cone of light shed by the fixture over the table and listened to Alan say nothing.

Chapter Eleven

On her walk to work the next morning, Rachel deliberately did not think about her argument with Magda. She observed the way the light glittered on the Seine as she walked over the Pont du Carrousel and noticed that people were already setting out towels on the riverside *plage*. She admired the shape of the Louvre against the sky as she approached it and again once she'd passed, and when she arrived at the Bibliothèque, she greeted the guard at the gate with such care and focus that an observer would have thought she'd recently done him a personal injury.

When she arrived in the employee lounge, LouLou told her that Docteure Dwamena wanted to see her. Rachel felt a sudden flip of the heart followed by a hot surge of questions. Had Docteure Dwamena somehow found out about her eavesdropping? Was she about to be fired? What would that mean for her investigation? She tried to calm herself by pointing out that, as a volunteer, she couldn't really be fired, but that just made her wonder if Docteure Dwamena was calling her in to tell her that she was such a terrible volunteer that they were firing her anyway.

She took a deep breath as she tapped on Docteure Dwamena's door, letting it out slowly as she entered the office.

"Ah, Rachel." Docteure Dwamena rose and gestured to the chair in front of her desk, waiting until Rachel settled before resuming her own seat. She smoothed her maroon leather skirt across her lap. "You've been with us for two weeks now, and I've been very impressed. Not just with your work in the stacks, but also with your outlook. Right from the start you've really connected with Giles and LouLou."

That was probably due to the minute attention she'd been paying them, Rachel thought. But people usually didn't praise you as a prelude to firing you, so she relaxed a little. "Thank you."

The doctor leaned forward and folded her hands on her desk. "Now I find myself in some difficulty, and I hope you can help. August is our busiest month, and we've been unable to find anyone to replace the colleague who . . . left us. This means we're going to be very short-staffed at our busiest period. Would you be willing to work in the reading room itself starting next week? We would ask for another volunteer to take your place here, and tomorrow LouLou could train you. It would only be very basic training, I'm afraid, but enough for you to help fill reader requests on Monday. Then you could continue to learn on the job. After another week you would know how to help patrons who have difficulty navigating the online catalog, and we could show you how to manage the record keeping and our other internal systems." She met Rachel's eyes and smiled. "Of course, you would become a paid employee from tomorrow—if you're willing to help us out?"

Rachel didn't know what to do. Would Capitaine Boussicault let her become a paid employee of the Bibliothèque? Would the increased access help their case, or would it leave her less time and attention to spare? Would the police higher-ups be okay with it? She opened her mouth to tell Docteure Dwamena she would like to talk with her husband before she made a decision, but just as her lips formed the first sound, the other woman's gaze shifted.

"Yes?" Turning, Rachel saw LouLou standing in the doorway, holding a book. She stepped into the office and held it out.

Docteure Dwamena seemed to know the significance of the gesture instantly. "No," she said. LouLou nodded. The doctor stood up and took the book, laying it carefully on her desktop before opening the center drawer and taking out a pair of thin cotton gloves. Drawing them on, she opened the vellum cover. She turned some pages, then drew in her breath through her teeth.

"What? What is it?" Rachel half rose and leaned over the desk.

"Here." One of the cotton-clad fingers pointed, and Rachel, leaning even farther forward, saw a vertical stub of paper close to the binding, a stub so narrow that a cursory examination might not reveal it at all. There were only a few pulled fibers to show where the rest of the sheet had been detached.

"A page is gone," Rachel said. The removal had been effected with great care; she couldn't see any damage to the facing pages. She straightened up.

"A woodcut." Docteure Dwamena brushed her hand over

the open book. "One of three woodcuts in here. This is one of the few remaining pristine copies of the *Supplementum Chronicarum*, written by Brother Giacomo Foresti and published in 1490. It has a complete set of some of the most complex and fully realized engravings of the late medieval period—well, I suppose it *had.*"

Rachel remembered something she'd learned in her previous case: without regular inspection it was difficult to trace changes to ancient books. "But the page could have been removed long ago! There's no way to know."

"No." Docteure Dwamena bent more closely over the desk. "One can see that this separation has no wear on it, no dirt. It's fresh, or at least relatively recent." She closed her eyes, then opened them slowly. "Again," she muttered.

"Again? What do you mean, again?" Then Rachel understood. "This has happened before?"

"Yes." The doctor rested her head in her hands. Then she pulled them back over her skull and stood with them gripping the back of her head for a moment before picking up the receiver of her desk phone. "Now if you'll both excuse me, I need to call the police."

There passed a half hour in which nothing changed. The readers in the manuscript room leafed quietly through the books they had ordered, and LouLou and Giles went about the business of handing Rachel request slips, then unloading the books she brought and giving her others to reshelve. Rachel felt a deep admiration for Docteure Dwamena. It took a rare steeliness to keep things running normally in the face of such a blow to her department.

Eventually LouLou came into the shelving area. "The *flic* is in Docteure Dwamena's office. He wants to see us."

The *flic* was Capitaine Boussicault. He was talking to the doctor when Rachel entered. She jumped slightly as she saw him, but when Docteure Dwamena said, "And this is Rachel, who was also here when the book was found," he raised his eyebrows inquiringly and shook her hand without a trace of recognition.

"If she was there when the discovery was made, she's a witness," he said, "so I would like her to stay."

The three women and the *capitaine* arranged themselves in the chairs that Docteure Dwamena had crowded into her office, and he began asking questions.

"Madame Fournier, you were the one who first discovered that the book was damaged?"

LouLou nodded.

"And how did you make that discovery?"

She cleared her throat. "Well, when a patron asks for a book, before we hand it to them we quickly look through the pages. We do it to make sure there's nothing inside that can get lost or misplaced. We just—" She made the gesture of riffling a book's pages. "When I did that with this book, one pair of pages fell open a little more heavily than felt normal, so I looked closer. When I saw a stub, I knew a page had been removed. I immediately brought the book to Docteure Dwamena."

"*D'acc.*" Boussicault nodded and turned back to the doctor. "And you . . . ?"

"I saw that there was a page missing. I judged that it had

been deliberately removed, and recently." She rested her hand on the book, as if it were an animal she could soothe by touch. "So I telephoned the police."

"How did you know the removal was recent?"

Docteure Dwamena gave the same explanation she had given Rachel, and the *capitaine* watched her closely as he listened. He used no notebook, Rachel noticed, just nodded and kept his eyes on the speaker. The effect was of a conversation rather than an interrogation, and she saw how this could relax people into remembering all sorts of half-forgotten details while at the same time allowing him to gather information they didn't consciously offer. She stored the method away for future use.

When Docteure Dwamena finished, Boussicault sat for a moment. At last he asked, "Is this your first such loss?"

Docteure Dwamena said nothing. Then she slowly shook her head. "We had a similar theft about a year ago."

"A year?"

"Yes. We found that a French translation of Machiavelli's *Speeches on the State of Peace and War* was missing its final leaf, an engraving of the author's portrait."

Boussicault cleared his throat. "I didn't see a report on that incident."

She looked down, then back up. "I didn't alert the police to that theft."

The *capitaine* raised his eyebrows. He didn't speak, but clearly he was waiting for an explanation. So was Rachel. What kind of department head didn't report a theft from her department?

Docteure Dwamena sighed. "Unfortunately, library theft is relatively common. I doubt there's a national archive or university collection open to the public that hasn't had something stolen. But this isn't generally known. It would do severe damage to libraries' standing. Not only would scholars devalue archives, since books might be missing or incomplete, but libraries would also get reputations for lax security. When we discovered the page missing from the Machiavelli, I had to balance many factors. The page had no particular value on its own: the book is old, but not so rare as to be particularly valuable or consulted particularly often. The stub was not freshly cut as it is here, so I had no idea when the theft might have occurred. I didn't want to risk what you might call collateral damage because of one illustration that I was certain would not be recovered in any case." She gave a thin smile. "Our books are rare, but library theft is even more rarely solved."

"I see." The *capitaine* shifted position in his chair. "You mention security. What was library security like at the time of the first theft?"

"Much the same as it is now. The library requires readers to fill out a registration form giving their name and local address, and after a short interview they are issued a library card with a photo. Visitors show their card to a guard when they enter the site, when they enter each reading room, and again when they pick up the books they ordered from the counter."

"And the readers in this room specifically, do they go through any kind of search on the way in or out?"

Docteure Dwamena nodded. "Both. We have a guard, like all the other reading rooms here. Readers may only carry their belongings inside in a clear plastic bag. They are not allowed to bring in computer sleeves or shells. As each patron leaves, they must give the guard any pads or notebooks they have brought in, and the guard—" She mimed shaking the pages. "Also, if they brought a computer, they must take it out and open it, then turn it over."

"And this room, specifically, added no further measures after the first theft? You didn't, for example, increase your oversight, your security?"

She shook her head. "Archival materials can't be electronically tagged, since it damages them, and we aren't allowed to have cameras in library areas used by patrons because of privacy issues. Given that, our security arrangements were and are the best we can do. And the truth is, no security setup stops thieves." She seemed to feel Boussicault might want to challenge her on this, because she continued, "Let me give you an example. Three years ago we switched over to our new ordering system. Now it's all done digitally. Patrons log on to the system with their identification numbers, tick a box to show which reading room they're using, and make requests by clicking on the items they want in our electronic catalog. *Bon*. A year ago the library received a phone call from a Dr. Charlotte Loftus from Widdowson University, Jerilderie, Australia." Seeing the captain's surprise at this total recall, she held up a finger. "You'll see why I remember. Dr. Loftus's university is very penny-pinching. If they fund a research trip, they demand a list of all the items consulted on that trip, to be sure the researcher did as they said they would. So Dr. Loftus accessed her Bibliothèque account to print out a list of her requests, and what did she discover but that, unbeknownst to her, she seems to have ordered a number of volumes of very hard-core gay pornography from our Jean Genet collection. Dr. Loftus's area of study, I should explain, is the connection between late Latin and French cognates in the eighth and ninth centuries. After some discussion with a system technician, she acknowledged that yes, she may have forgotten to log out of the computer terminal after she placed her request for materials. Someone used her identification number, then simply lifted the items off her trolley when they came and used them him- or herself. Nothing was stolen, but . . ." She raised her hands. "There is always forgetfulness, someone memorizing someone else's card number, human error . . . We can only do our best and then hope."

"And the Bibliothèque's administrators agreed with you? They suggested no changes after the first theft?"

"Well—"

For the first time, Rachel saw the doctor look flustered.

"I didn't tell them." She put her hands over her face again. When she removed them, she had aged ten years. "It seemed to me at the time that there really wasn't anything to be achieved by reporting it to those higher up. As I say, if we publicized the theft or drew any notice to it, there was every chance that the Bibliothèque's reputation would suffer. Our particular department would come under extra scrutiny that would almost certainly complicate our ability to do our job. So I decided to say nothing to anyone outside this department. We agreed among ourselves that we wouldn't say anything, but that we would increase our vigilance and watch the patrons more closely." She shook her head. "After a couple of weeks I realized I had made a bad decision, but by then . . . well, I would have had to explain not only that the page was missing but why I had decided not to say anything immediately. And, look at me." She gestured at her face. "I am the only person of my color who is a department head here. And I am the first. I have had to be the best in my cohort—twice the best—all through my training and career. What would be the result if I admitted that I had allowed something to be stolen from my reading room? That I had allowed something to be stolen and then kept quiet about it?" Her voice caught as she added, "Now, of course, it will all come out."

The *capitaine* waited a respectful moment, then turned to LouLou. "And you knew about this?"

She nodded. "We all knew." Then she clarified. "Except Rachel. She wasn't here then."

Boussicault appeared to consult the small notebook he now drew from his pocket. "So by *we* you mean you, Monsieur Giles Morel, and the unfortunate Monsieur Laurent?"

LouLou nodded again, although her lips moved slightly at this description of Laurent.

"And you all concurred with Docteure Dwamena's decision?"

"Yes. Well . . ."

The *capitaine* waited, then prompted, "Well, what?"

LouLou suddenly looked uncomfortable; Docteure Dwamena took over. “We did all agree at first. But then Guy Laurent . . . It was not in Monsieur Laurent’s nature to be loyal. I mentioned to your *brigadier* his unpleasantness in this area. He didn’t say anything about my decision for a few months, but then he began . . . poking.”

“*Excusez-moi?*”

“He started to make little comments. He said that it seemed to him that the theft showed I was growing lax. I couldn’t keep up with what was happening in the reading room. Apparently, I wasn’t able to take the appropriate security precautions for the current climate. Did I think it might be time to step down? When I didn’t give in, he began saying his conscience was bothering him.” She gave a little snort at that idea. “He said he had begun to feel it was wrong to keep the theft from the administration, that he was starting to believe it would ease his mind to tell them what had been stolen and what I had done about it. In other words”—she cocked her head to one side—“he never said it straight out, but he made it clear that he wanted to be head of the department, and if I wouldn’t move aside he would push me.”

“A very unpleasant man,” Boussicault remarked.

LouLou made a small noise, but Docteure Dwamena simply said, “Yes. Although he could be pleasant when it suited his ends.”

“I see.” A pause, then he became crisp. “Now, can you tell me who has been working in your archive over the past few days?”

Docteure Dwamena nodded. Obviously relieved, she

smiled and said to LouLou, "Could you bring me the slips?" As LouLou left the room, she explained, "Each time a patron requests a book, our computer prints a slip with the patron's name, number, and request on two identical halves. One half goes in the requested book, and we retain the *souche*. We order them and file them away as backup for our records."

So that was the work LouLou fell behind on, Rachel thought.

As if to prove her right, LouLou reappeared with a shallow box that held an untidy jumble of printed slips. Docteure Dwamena began sorting through them; Rachel thought she had never seen hands move so fast. After a few seconds she had a small pile. She tapped it sharply against her desktop and reached for her reading glasses.

"Right. So now I can tell you that today the reading room has been used by an Aurora Dale and a Dr. Robert Cavill, both of Cambridge, England, and a Homer Stibb from Tennessee in the United States."

Rachel felt an unexpected leap of pride: Americans used the Bibliothèque Nationale!

Docteure Dwamena looked at the *capitaine* over her glasses. "If you give me perhaps an hour, I can tell you if each reader has been here longer than just today, and if so, how long."

"No, thank you, that won't be necessary at the moment. But I would like to see—" He glanced at his watch and made a noise of irritation. "It's past closing time. In that case, please give my *brigadier* their contact information, so he can get in touch with them to arrange interviews. But I would like to speak to Monsieur Morel, assuming he is still here."

"Of course. He's probably closing up the reading room. LouLou can easily switch with him."

As if she took the announcement as an order, LouLou slipped out of the office. Rachel sat quiet; it seemed they had forgotten her, and she wasn't going to help them remember her.

A moment later, Giles came in, smoothing his beard nervously even as he tried to look nonchalant. He sat in the chair LouLou had vacated.

The *capitaine* smiled. "I assume Madame Fournier told you that I am here about a mutilated book."

Giles nodded sadly. "Yes." His voice was resigned. "I know. I already knew."

"*Pardonnez-moi*," Boussicault broke in. "I should have clarified. I'm not speaking of the mutilation last year. There has been a more recent theft."

"I—" Giles began, but the *capitaine* hadn't finished.

"Madame Fournier discovered a page removed from this book." He gestured at Docteure Dwamena's desk. "The, ah, *Supplementum Chronicarum*, I believe?" He cast a glance at the doctor, who nodded.

"The *Supplementum Chronicarum*?" Giles blanched beneath his beard. "There is a page missing from the *Supplementum*—" He stopped short. When he began again, his voice was more restrained. "But that's terrible. Who would do such a thing? What page is missing?"

"A woodcut," said the *capitaine*, just as Docteure Dwamena said, "'The Creation of Eve.'"

"'The Creation of Eve!' But that's the most—Why would someone do that?"

Looking at the expression on Giles's face, Rachel thought, *So he values books as well as Lou Lou.* Her heart warmed toward him a little more.

"You tell me," Boussicault answered him a trifle wearily. "You work with books."

"The *capitaine* thinks the thief may be one of our patrons," Docteure Dwamena explained.

"Yet they love books." Giles's expression changed from shocked to thoughtful.

"Never underestimate the power of love to prompt wrongdoing, Monsieur." Boussicault stood. "I will interview the patrons whose names you gave me as soon as I can arrange it," he said to Docteure Dwamena, "and then I'll get back in touch. But now I must go and write my initial report." He gave her a small smile. "I think I need not mention the earlier disappearance."

She smiled in return and pushed her chair back. "Thank you. Now please allow me to walk you out. It would be my pleasure. I could show you some of our treasures on the way."

"No, no." He shook his head. "You're a busy woman, and I don't want to take you away from your work. If your volunteer shows me out, we can discuss what she might have seen."

* * *

"What are you doing here?" Rachel listened to the soles of his shoes squeak against the marble floor as they walked toward the exit.

"I was at the commissariat when it was called in, and since I'm head of the murder investigation, I thought I was the natural choice to look into this."

"Do you think Laurent's murder is connected to this?"

He shrugged. "I have no way to judge at the moment. Docteure Dwamena's explanation tells me that thefts from libraries are common, and I have no reason to doubt her, although of course I'll check up on that. Laurent didn't find this book, obviously, and our only piece of evidence, your piece of paper, is so far inconclusive." He shook his head. "In fact, the only link I can see to Laurent's murder is that we seem to have picked up another suspect, given what the doctor told us about his behavior toward her."

And given that the piece of paper seemed to suggest blackmail and her story suggested she would be an excellent blackmail victim, Rachel added silently. But she wasn't going to present Boussicault with her ideas about the notebook page until she was more certain she was right. Instead she said, "But would a murderer really tell a story that revealed their own motive?"

"You'd be surprised what a murderer would do. She's a very intelligent woman; she could be trying a counterintuitive strategy."

They had reached the main entrance. He turned to face her. "Do you have anything to report, or shall I expect you on Friday as usual?"

Rachel remembered. "Docteure Dwamena asked me to work in the reading room over the next few weeks. August is their busy season. She asked me to take Laurent's place."

The *capitaine* frowned. "Not entirely a bad idea. Potentially more useful, in fact, since it brings you into closer contact. But I'll have to check with my superiors first, and Raida, of course. I'll let you know later tonight." He held out his right hand and smiled. "Now let us shake hands in case anyone is watching."

Chapter Twelve

Rachel hated the Châtelet–Les Halles Mètro station. She hated it viscerally and profoundly, with a passion she usually reserved for nylon clothing, basic punctuation errors, and people who said *passed* instead of *died*. The source of her loathing lay deep underground, in the long tunnel through which passengers needed to walk in order to change lines. Rachel felt that any Mètro stop that required its users to make their way further than three hundred yards in tunnels was in fact two Mètro stops, or possibly more, and she felt this most keenly when she stood at rush hour on one of the Châtelet–Les Halles tunnel's moving walkways, sweating in the oppressive air with a thousand other people trying to get home.

Today she tried to distract herself by thinking about what had just happened at the Bibliothèque. Was book theft so common that two thieves might operate in the same library? Or were book thieves so devoted to certain libraries that one might wait a year to strike again in the same place? And how on earth could Guy Laurent's murder connect to Machiavelli's speeches and the *Supplementum Chronicarum*?

"*Supplementum Chronicarum*," she suddenly said aloud. "SC!"

The yarmulke-wearing young man in front of her turned around, and she smiled apologetically, then folded her lips between her teeth to keep herself from crowing out loud. The SC on Laurent's sheet of paper could stand for *Supplementum Chronicarum*! And could M/F simply stand for *Machiavelli en Français*? What if Laurent had figured out the identity of the people who'd stolen the engravings and had been blackmailing them? And what if one of them killed him for it?

She burst out of the tunnel onto her Mètro platform. Normally she stayed on the train for as long as possible, basking in the air conditioning, but tonight she left two stops before it reached her stop at Notre-Dame des Champs. There was no wireless service in the Mètro, and she could wait no longer. This evening she had no desire to stand silent before Paris. Instead she walked with her head bowed and the side of a thumb stroking the screen, researching prices at an online bookseller and finding her way home by occasional glances and muscle memory.

As soon as she was in the apartment, she turned on her computer. She typed WWW.VITALIBRORUM.COM into the browser search bar; while the page loaded, she opened the narrow center drawer of her desk and took out the photocopy of Laurent's sheet. THE LARGEST ONLINE MARKET FOR RARE BOOKS, the screen now said. Underneath that sentence were thick blocks of text, sometimes flanked by tiny photos of books. She clicked on one of these, and a larger version of the text and the photo appeared.

"Yeah, baby," she said to the empty room. What she had in front of her was a precise description of a book, right down to the discoloration on page twenty-two, and a row of photos to match. At the bottom was a price in a blue box, another in a red box, and a third in a white box. Just what she'd managed to access on her phone, only large enough to read.

She heard the door open as Alan arrived home from work. "I know what the letters mean!" she called.

He appeared behind her left shoulder. "Huh?"

"The letters on Guy Laurent's sheet! I figured out what they mean."

"Oh, right." He bent over her and put his hand on the desk.

"Look." She pointed out the screen. "This is the website of an online clearinghouse for antiquarian books. So here"—she scrolled up for a second—"is a listing for a manuscript of the *Processional à l'usage des Dominicaines de Saint-Louis-de-Poissy.*" She made a face to show she had no idea what that was. "Published in the fifteenth century. And here's the price." She scrolled down a little and pointed again. "Thirty-three thousand euros direct from a single seller. But here"—she scrolled back up—"is Mozart's *Don Giovanni*, and there are three prices: two thousand euros, two thousand five hundred, and one thousand nine hundred and ninety-nine. That's because there are three different sellers; it's showing the prices of three possible places you can buy it. Now look here."

She pointed to one of the scrawled lines of numbers on the photocopy.

"Here's 123899, followed by 122500, followed by 122999.

If you read these as prices, they'd be one hundred twenty-three thousand eight hundred and ninety-nine euros; one hundred twenty-two thousand five hundred euros; and one hundred twenty-two thousand nine hundred and ninety-nine euros. Three different prices, but very close together, like with the Mozart. I think these are book prices. I think he was looking up books to see how much they were worth. And I think these"—this time she pointed to the letters on the bottom two lines—"are his abbreviations of two book titles. It turned out today that someone had stolen an illustration from a book called the *Supplementum Chronicarum*." She moved the pad of her index finger next to the SC. "And a year ago one had gone missing from a French translation of Machiavelli's speeches." Now she pressed it next to M/F.

"I think these numbers are his calculations of how much he could get from the person who stole those pages. He started with the price of the books, or books like them, tried to figure out how much the loss of an engraving might lower the value, and then tried to calculate how much he could ask for from the thieves for keeping quiet."

"Thief," Alan said.

"What?"

"I'd say it's one thief. You wouldn't add up the numbers and bracket them if you were dealing with two different people. Still"—he kissed the side of her neck and started to walk away—"good job. Now I have to go shower. Walk-home sweat is the worst kind of sweat."

Rachel sat alone in front of the computer. "Good job," and then a shower? What kind of reaction was that? There was supposed to be an exchange of proud glances, an acknowledgment of Rachel's craftiness, a silent agreement that they were a match for any police force. With Magda there would have been all of those. She knew Alan felt them, but—well, somehow it wasn't the same.

Chapter Thirteen

Wednesday morning was unexpectedly cool, the sky overcast. Rachel shoved her red umbrella into her bag as she left the apartment, but by the time she arrived at the Bibliothèque the sun had come out and she could feel the temperature beginning to climb once more. She had phoned Docteure Dwamena after she'd arrived home the previous evening to let her know that she wanted to accept her offer, and now they stood together in the empty reading room, waiting for LouLou to appear so Rachel's training could begin.

"Where is she?" Docteure Dwamena consulted her sliver of a watch. "She's been coming in early recently. I expected her to be here by now."

Rachel shrugged. "Maybe she's ill?"

"Maybe, although I would expect her to call to let me know." Docteure Dwamena frowned. "If she doesn't arrive in the next few minutes, I'll pair you with Giles. Of course he's late, too. As usual. No doubt lingering over a coffee at that little hole-in-the-wall he likes on the Rue Chabanais, talking to the barman about poetry. Although he said something about not going there anymore since Laurent—" She realized she was talking out loud and stopped.

So Giles *had* spent a lot of time at Chez Poule. And Capitaine Boussicault was right again: overhearing could be more useful than asking.

Docteure Dwamena flipped her wrist over to look at her watch a second time. "What on earth is going on with them?" She walked across the room and began flicking on the lights, then unlocked the reading room door.

A bell sounded: the Bibliothèque was open for the day. Rachel heard the sound of sensible soles squeaking on marble, and patrons began to trickle into the reading room. One of them, a man, immediately darted to the computers on the far wall.

"*Mon dieu!*" Docteure Dwamena moved to stand behind the counter, thinning her lips. "Was there some sort of librarians' party last night that I didn't know about? I see we will have to postpone the commencement of your training. I apologize on LouLou's behalf. I can deal with these people myself for a few minutes, if you'll collect their requests from the stacks."

The man began to bear down on the doctor, a sheaf of call slips in his hand. She smiled at him, tore the slips, and handed Rachel her halves.

The History and Wonderful Legend of Catherine of Siena
The Miracles of St. Otto of Bamberg

The Miraculous Visions of Brother William of Felpham
The Life and Miracles of Saint Opportuna

Boy, those medieval writers really loved their miracles. Rachel put out her hand to swing open the door to the stacks.

As her fingertips touched the dark oak a scream split the air, so loud it seemed to tilt the room. Without thinking, she pushed the door all the way open and began running into the stacks. The scream came again and again, each time loud enough to hurt Rachel's head. Fighting the desire to cover her ears and retreat, she ran through the maze of shelves, trying to find the source of the noise. At last, after what seemed like an eternity but could only have been about a minute, she tracked it to the far depths of the stacks, where one row was lit up, its fluorescent overheads flickering in the gloom. She rounded its corner.

On the floor in front of her sat LouLou, her mouth open, her screams now turning into one long keening yell. She held one hand out in front of her. Its fingers grasped the end of a serrated knife, the blade covered in blood but the handle clean. Lying facedown in front of her, at the center of a red pool that crept slowly toward the hem of her dress, was the body of Giles Morel.

Chapter Fourteen

Two hours later Rachel was in a low-slung white chair in the Bibliothèque's public lounge, which was now being used as an impromptu conference room and waiting area. In a far corner Capitaine Boussicault and Alan conferred, while here on the other side of the room she waited. In the background various police officers came and went, talking among themselves and making notes on little pads.

Libraries and bodies, Rachel thought. *Bodies and libraries.* Was this her fate now, to encounter dead bodies in or near libraries? First she had organized Edgar's library and discovered his son's corpse in a nearby room, and now there was Giles dead amid the medieval *Miracles*. Of the two events, she preferred the first—there had been blood everywhere then, too, but it hadn't been fresh. It hadn't been *moving*. She shuddered at the memory of Giles's blood oozing across the floor.

A shadow fell across her, and she looked up to find Capitaine Boussicault with a plastic cup in his hand.

She smiled. "I hear hot drinks aren't really a good idea for people in shock." She knew he'd recognize this reference to their previous case.

Indeed, he lifted the corners of his lips before he responded, "They find drinking difficult, or often they drink too quickly and burn their mouths." He handed her the cup. "You remember unexpected things."

"Well, you did say that to me in pretty memorable circumstances."

"*Vraiment.*" He bent his head. "But in this case, like the last, I think a cup of tea might be good for you. At the very least, its familiarity will soothe you." He crouched beside her, his trench coat brushing the floor. He had also dressed for rain, Rachel noticed. Or did he always wear that coat? He'd certainly been wearing it the last time he'd squatted next to her, which was also the last time she'd found a body. Substitute an expensive carpet for the marble floor, and it could have been a year and a half ago all over again.

"You are very brave, Rachel." Boussicault shook his head. "I know many policemen who wouldn't run toward a scream."

"Oh, well." She felt proud for a moment, then remembered the blood again. She took a gulp of the tea. It was only tepid, but it did soothe her. "Never mind me. How is LouLou?"

He dragged over a chair and sat down, facing her. "At the moment Madame Fournier is resting. She has been sedated."

"Was she able to tell you what happened?"

He cleared his throat. "According to Madame Fournier, she arrived late for work and was making her way toward the reading room when she encountered Monsieur Morel's body."

"That makes s—wait. *According* to Madame Fournier?"

He raised his eyebrows. "Madame Fournier was found

alone at the scene with Morel's body, holding a knife. She must therefore be treated as a suspect."

"Oh, no." Rachel shook her head vehemently. She kept shaking it. "No, no, no. Not LouLou."

"You yourself told me she was angry at and scared of men, and you told me she complained about Monsieur Morel's advances."

"I didn't say advances." But she remembered how LouLou had flinched when she'd passed by Giles on the way through the door the previous week. She'd been angry at even the hint of contact with him. Encountering him in the dimness of the stacks, with him perhaps saying or doing something unwelcome . . . *But still*, she thought. *Slap Giles, yes, maybe even punch him, maybe even scream as she had. But do something savage enough to produce all that blood?* She couldn't believe it. "There must be another explanation, surely. An accident, or . . ."

"Monsieur Morel was stabbed twice in the chest. That does not suggest an accident."

"Well, then, maybe . . . You said Laurent's death could have been an attack by a stranger, so why not this one, too?" She began to warm to this scenario that might clear LouLou. "Maybe there's some kind of serial killer on the loose. Someone with a grudge against librarians, or libraries, or rare book research!"

"*S'il vous plait.*" The *capitaine* leaned in and put up a hand. "Be calm. A good detective goes slowly." Go slowly? When a man had been killed and an angry woman was the prime suspect? Maybe Boussicault didn't know, but Rachel was well aware of how society reacted to female anger.

But the *capitaine* remained calm. "Don't try to guess the answer before you are sure you have all the available evidence. *Par exemple*, I would like to question all those who were at the scene when the murder was discovered."

"But that's just LouLou. And me. And you've—" Then she got it. "The people in the reading room?"

"And *la bonne* Docteure Dwamena. My scene-of-the-crime *médecin légiste* estimates that Morel was killed shortly before the Bibliothèque opened. Those using the reading room could easily have slipped in and out of the group of patrons waiting for the doors to open—or they may have seen someone else do so. These people are our best possible witnesses, and also possible suspects."

Rachel saw his point, but she was surprised by what he said next.

"And here I hope you will be willing to help again. You know the reading room and the area behind it, and you are the only person I can be sure didn't kill Monsieur Morel. I think it might be useful if you were to sit in on my interviews. You could spot any logistical inconsistencies in the stories I'm told. And at the same time you could assist with any translation difficulties I might have."

First a consultant and now a participant! She could hardly wait to tell Magda. Then she remembered they were in a fight. Well, Alan would be interested, too.

She opened her mouth to say yes to Boussicault's offer, but he again held up a hand. "*Tiens*. You need to be aware that this would mean abandoning your current role. Docteure Dwamena and all the patrons of the reading room would learn that you are working with the police, and this means you won't be able to act the part of a library volunteer anymore." He smiled. "Your cover will be blown." He said this in flawless and unaccented English. Rachel suspected that he didn't really want her translation skills. Perhaps he was just hesitant to admit he wanted a second mind on the case. He continued in French, "But in any case, I think we are beyond using subtle means to gather clues. We seem to have left the realm of subtlety."

Alan appeared behind the *capitaine*. "How are you feeling?" He sat down and put his arm around her.

"Better. Much better." Still, she rested her head on his shoulder.

"This is the second time in a month that the police have telephoned to call me away from the office. I think I'm starting to get quite a reputation."

She smiled feebly. If they had been at home, she would have asked to sit on his lap, then burrowed her face in his shirt to smell its clean, familiar scent, but here there was no place for such calming rituals. If she was going to persevere with Boussicault's interviews after this conversation, she suspected, she'd need all the adrenaline she could get. She firmed her smile and straightened up. "The *capitaine* was just asking if I'd be willing to sit in when he interviews the people who were using the reading room. He thinks I might be able to help spot if anyone's lying about aspects related to the library, and I could help with any translation problems."

"Surely n—" Then Alan stopped; he knew his wife. He sighed. "How long might this take?"

The *capitaine* gave one of his Gallic shrugs: *it's in the lap of the gods.* "A few hours, perhaps?"

Alan looked searchingly in her face. He was trying to decide if he was satisfied with her condition, she knew; he'd done it before when she'd been ill or hurt. At last he said, "I'll wait for you to finish. I couldn't get any more work done at the office anyway. So I'll be right here when you're done, and we can go straight home."

Rachel nodded. "It's a deal." She knew she should probably just go home right then, but she couldn't bring herself to miss the opportunity Boussicault was offering. She stood up and rolled her shoulders back. "Just let me get another tea, and then we can start."

Alan was still looking at her. Now his face was expectant.

"What?"

"Don't you want to—" He stopped and shook his head. "Nothing, never mind. Get your tea."

Rachel knew he meant, *Do you want to call Magda?* But again she steeled herself against it. Instead, she focused on gathering her mental strength. Shelving books and eavesdropping were one thing, but with the interviews she was getting to the meat of the matter. She was moving toward the center of the investigation, and she would need to pay attention.

Chapter Fifteen

Twenty minutes later, Rachel and Capitaine Boussicault sat in a small room that opened off one of the Bibliotheque's corridors. In front of them was a white Formica table, behind it was a single chair, and a window high up in the left-hand wall showed a rectangle of blue sky. Rachel was surprised to find a space so bare and utilitarian in a national library, but then she remembered that it was a bureaucratic entity as much as an ancient house of knowledge.

Boussicault cleared his throat. "Before we begin, let me explain what I have planned. The witness will come in, and I will explain that you are a translator, here to assist. You can greet them, but then just listen unless I ask you to help." He frowned, obviously realizing how hard this might be for a civilian with no training in remaining focused. "It might help you if you took notes." She dug her notebook and pen out from her bag and put them on the table in front of her. He nodded. "Okay. We start with the reading room patrons."

He rose and opened the door. In answer to his murmur, a tall woman, about sixty years old, entered. She crossed to sit behind the table, placing her navy shoulder bag in her lap. She was very slender, her hair was cut in a straight gray bob, and her rather hooked nose gave her the appearance of an intelligent flamingo. She craned her head to look around, lively, interested, and not at all scared.

"*Bonjour*, Madame." The *capitaine* gave her a small smile, gracious rather than warm. "May I ask your name?"

"I'm Professor Aurora Dale." Her voice was clear, although she spoke French with a noticeable English accent.

"Would you prefer to speak English? Madame Levis is here to act as a translator in case I have difficulties." *Confession of inadequacy*, Rachel thought. *Reassures the suspect.*

Aurora Dale nodded. "Yes, I would prefer that. *Merci*."

"What brings you here, Madame Dale?"

"Professor Dale. And I'm looking at accounts of early modern French midwifery for an article I'm working on."

"I see. And what is your home university?"

"I'm at Oxford. Shrewsbury College, Oxford. Here for three or four weeks, depending on what I find."

"When did you arrive?"

"Two weeks ago tomorrow."

"And this morning you were in the reading room as soon as it opened?"

She nodded, raking a hand through her gray hair. "Yes, but I'm not really sure I can be of any help. I barely made it in the door before . . ."

Boussicault gave his little smile once again. "Please, Professeure, let me be the judge of whether you can help. Now tell me, what time did you arrive at the library this morning?"

"Um, well . . ." Professor Dale looked upward, trying to remember. "I walked from home . . ."

The *capitaine* raised a finger. "Forgive an interruption, madame. Where is home for you in Paris?"

Dale recited in the voice of an obedient student, "Room five-twelve of the Auberge des Jeunesses, on the Boulevard Saint- Michel, across from the Jardin du Luxembourg."

It seemed to Rachel that writing down this address would make her look very much like one of the team. To her surprise, it also made her feel like one. She decided she would write down every witness's address.

Boussicault had moved on. "So, back to this morning. What time did you arrive, and which way did you come?"

"Well, there's really only one way to get into the library—unless I'm going to use the doors in front." She laughed a surprisingly—and delightfully, Rachel thought—hearty laugh at the thought of anyone coming through the blackened oak doors that faced the Rue des Petits Champs, the library's original entrance. "I left home at about quarter past eight, and it's around a half hour's walk, so that would make it . . . let's say eight fifty? Just before the library doors opened, anyway. And I stood in the courtyard with the others who were waiting—well, a bit off to one side. I was having a ciggy." She looked abashed. "My little vice, I'm afraid. I kicked them years ago, but I just can't fully *kick* them, if you know what I mean. One before work and one after, to round out the day on either end. That's the limit, though."

The *capitaine*'s smile said he empathized, although he did not go so far as to name his own vice. "And when you were off to one side," he responded, "did you see anything or anyone unusual?"

Professor Dale leaned forward. "I've been going over that. At first I didn't think I did. But then, working through everything carefully, I realized I had. Or at least I might have. Because I remember that just when I was finishing my cigarette, I saw someone go round the corner toward the back of the library. They were at a distance, and I only saw their back, but I do remember they were wearing something dark. Their clothing was dark, I mean. But then the doors opened and I switched my attention." She looked apologetic. "I'm sorry."

"Not at all." The *capitaine* steepled his hands in front of him for a moment, pressing the tips of his forefingers to his bottom lip. "You say you couldn't see their features, but did you perhaps get an impression of their gender? Perhaps something about their gait, or their body shape, made you think they were either male or female?"

She gazed into space, obviously casting her mind back. "Not really. As I say, they were quite far away. I am sorry."

Boussicault dipped his head. "It's fine. What you remembered is very helpful in its own right. Thank you for your time, Professeure Dale."

That was it? Professor Dale seemed to share Rachel's surprise at the brevity of the interview, because she stayed seated. After a second's pause she leaned forward and said, "Would I be right in thinking that someone has been murdered?"

"What makes you say that?"

Answering a question with a question: a police move Rachel recognized from *The Closer.*

"Well." Professor Dale's eyes were bright. "First, I saw an ambulance from the window of the room where they're keeping us. Second, there are a number of police officers here, many more than could be justified by the theft your sergeant mentioned when he rang me last night. Third, I doubt very much that you'd be questioning me about this morning if you were interested in something that you discovered yesterday. And finally, I also doubt you'd be asking me if I'd seen anything unusual if the dead person had died in some natural way. Although"—her voice grew reflective—"all deaths are natural, really, given that it's only natural to die when someone stabs you in the heart or pushes you downstairs so you break your neck."

Rachel decided she liked Aurora Dale. Capitaine Boussicault, however, only raised his eyebrows. "You're good at making connections, *madame la professeure*."

"Am I? Perhaps it's because literary criticism is quite a lot like detective work. At least I think so. You observe a text—more than once—look for the oddities and evidence, and try to see what they all might mean. Besides"—her tone now held a smile—"I'm an elderly English widow. We're obliged to be interested in mysteries. It's in the handbook."

Rachel couldn't suppress a smile, but Boussicault just stood. "You're free to go, but please don't leave Paris until you hear from us."

"Good heavens, I'm not going to leave! I still have research to do."

After the door shut behind her, Boussicault turned to Rachel. "An interesting woman. And her memory of seeing someone . . . Only employees can enter the Bibliothèque via the back." He thought for a moment. "Well, let's see if the others saw something similar. We will let them mention it themselves." He stood to open the door for the next witness.

Chapter Sixteen

The second interviewee was a young woman with pink hair gathered into shoulder-length pigtails. She seemed to have roses growing out of her upper arms, until Rachel realized these were remarkably realistic tattoos revealed by her sleeveless shirt. The flowers blossomed and rippled as she sat down in the chair and crossed her legs.

"*Bonjour.*" She was French.

Katja Bonsergent was a *maître des conferences* in the art history department at the Panthéon-Sorbonne, on the other side of the Seine in the sixth arrondissement. She was only at the Bibliothèque for the day. She was using the reading room to access two articles on Élisabeth Vigée-Lebrun, of whom she was writing a book-length feminist reassessment. No, she hadn't seen anyone or anything that seemed suspicious—not that, she said, she would know what was suspicious, given that this was the first time she'd used the Bibliothèque in at least a year. But in any case, she had walked from her apartment near the Panthéon and had only arrived just as the library was opening its doors.

The *capitaine* stopped her. "How long is the walk?"

"Perhaps half an hour."

"And can anyone confirm what time you left your apartment? Or arrived here?"

"Both." Bonsergent's firm nod made the pigtails bounce. "My girlfriend had breakfast with me before I left, and I showed my reader's card to the guard as I entered. He commented on my hair, so I know he'll remember me." She rolled her eyes at the small minds of the less cool.

"*Bien.*" The *capitaine* nodded his thanks. "We will be in touch if we need to. Don't go anywhere."

"Where would I go?" She shrugged. "I'm at the beginning of my academic career. I'm always working."

"I'll get Didier to contact her roommate to check her story," the *capitaine* said to Rachel once the door closed behind Docteure Bonsergent.

He scarcely had time to finish this sentence before there was a knock and a florid man put his head around the door. "All right to enter?" Not waiting for a response, he crossed and sat in the chair, brushing his hair off his face with a plump hand. He reminded Rachel slightly of Oscar Wilde—not in his coloring, which was an almost perfect example of Saxon blondness, but in his height and the fleshiness that lingered in his face and body.

"Robert Cavill. Saw the French girl leave and thought I'd just make myself known. Never can wait my turn, my wife would say." He gave almost a parody of a well-heeled English laugh—"haw-haw"—then took a handkerchief from his pocket and mopped his forehead. "Sorry. Always have been given to perspiration. And in this heat . . ."

"Yes, Paris in July can be miserable." The *capitaine* waited until Cavill put his handkerchief away, then gestured for him to sit. "So, Mr. Cavill, let me start by asking you what I asked my other two interviewees: what are you are studying here at the Bibliothèque?"

Cavill took a breath. "Hand-tinted engravings from books of the French Renaissance." Rachel was impressed by the brevity of this response, but it turned out he wasn't finished.

"I'm an art historian at Cambridge. Cambridge University. The Renaissance is my area of expertise. Well, I say expertise." He brayed again. "At the moment, I'm interested in the ways in which hand tinting on engravings from the French Renaissance encodes messages about rank and power. What the colors and styles telegraph to their viewers and readers."

"Mmm." Rachel realized that Boussicault didn't actually care what each person was working on. The question was just designed to check their plausibility and relax them a little before he moved on to what he considered the really important queries. Now he asked, "How long have you been working in the reading room?"

"A week tomorrow," Cavill replied. "I'm here for another week, and then my wife is bringing the children over and we're spending a fortnight in Provence."

"I see. And this morning? What time did you arrive?"

He thought for a moment. "I'd guess about ten minutes before the doors opened, maybe a little later. Professor Dale was just finishing her cigarette." He inhaled deeply, as if still smelling the smoke. "Made me wish I could join her. I wish it every morning, in fact. Quit ten years ago and never quite got over it."

Boussicault made no response to that, simply saying with mild interest, "And did you see anything unusual while you were waiting?"

"I don't know about unusual." Again Cavill used his handkerchief to wipe his brow. "I saw a couple of other faces one normally sees on mornings here, but aside from that . . . well, I remember seeing someone going round the back of the building, but I wouldn't call that *unusual*. People do it every morning. I assume they work here."

Boussicault gave no indication that the statement might be any more significant than any other. "And what did this person look like?"

"Gad! Now there you've got me." Like Professor Dale, Cavill thought for a few moments. Unlike her, he then said, "No, can't remember. I'm sorry."

"Could you say whether they were male or female?"

"No. They were quite far away. I'm sorry."

"Then perhaps what they were wearing? Or even just a color you remember?"

Cavill crinkled his brow for a long moment. Then, "No. I'm sorry."

The *capitaine* nodded. "As you say, it's understandable. Thank you. You've been very helpful. Now, where are you staying while you're in Paris?"

"The Hotel Etoiles." He recited from memory, "Room two-oh-nine, Hotel Etoiles, thirty-six Rue de Cléry."

"Good. We may well be in touch. Please don't leave the city until we tell you it's all right."

"But I've already given the deposit for Provence!"

"Well, it may comfort you to know that the police are also hoping this situation wraps up swiftly."

Going by Cavill's face, this did not comfort him at all.

Once the door closed, Boussicault stood up, gave a long backward stretch, and began pacing the little room.

"Why do you ask how long they've lived in Paris?" Rachel asked.

"*Pardon*?" He took a few more steps.

"You've asked every one of them except Docteure Bonsergent how long they've been in Paris. But the murder was committed this morning, so that seems irrelevant."

"I ask them, first, as a way of relaxing them. But I also ask because at this time I'm not completely sure that Monsieur Morel's death is unrelated to the theft we discovered yesterday. By asking them how long they've been here, I get an idea of who might have been here when the page was stolen." He gave a grin. "Which so far is everyone except Docteure Bonsergent."

Rachel's heart had begun to rise as his explanation proceeded, but now it fell again. So there was a chance that Lou-Lou might not be the culprit, but the alternate possibility was almost anyone else, too broad a group to help exclude Lou-Lou. There seemed to be no way to avoid the possibility that she was a murderess.

Chapter Seventeen

A knock on the door interrupted these thoughts. "Come!" Boussicault called.

A tall man came in. "Homer Stibb." He held out his hand to Boussicault. "University of Central Tennessee."

He wore aviator glasses and a short-sleeved checked shirt over chinos; his curly hair seemed slightly dusty, as if he had begun to resemble the books he worked with.

Boussicault ignored the hand and gestured to the chair across the table. "Please have a seat, Monsieur Stibb, and tell us what brings you to the library."

"Well." Stibb settled in the chair. He made a curious gesture, rolling his lips in and out, before he continued. "I'm a professor of medieval French literature. At the University of Central Tennessee, like I said. I'm here working on a project about medieval cipher manuscripts—you know, manuscripts written in code." Rachel must have shown her surprise that such things existed, because he angled himself to look directly at her. "Yeah. There are more of them than you'd think." He turned back so he was facing them both. "I'm comparing them to the nonciphered books and manuscripts they mention to see how the ciphers connect. And a number of those manuscripts are here."

"I see." The *capitaine* tapped his fingers on the table for a moment. "And how long have you been in Paris?"

Rachel paid closer attention now that she knew the purpose of the question. "Since last Saturday," said Stibb. "My plane arrived at seven forty-five in the morning."

"And you've been working in the reading room every day since then?"

"Well, since the Monday after that, yes. Last Monday."

"And what time did you arrive at the Bibliothèque this morning?"

"Mmm . . ." It was Stibb's turn to drum his fingers. "Eight forty-five? At least, I remember that Aurora arrived a few minutes later, and she usually gets here around ten to." He lowered his voice as if confiding a guilty secret. "She smokes. And she likes to have a cigarette before she starts work."

"Ah. And while you were waiting for the doors to open, did you see anything unusual?"

"Unusual? What do you mean, unusual?"

"Just anything you might have noticed that seemed out of the ordinary. Or that you might have noticed *because* it seemed out of the ordinary."

"Well . . ." Professor Stibb rolled his lips in and out again, sucking in his cheeks. He gazed into space just as Dale and Cavill had. "I'm not sure. I mean, I'm really not sure." He thought again, then said hesitantly, "Now that I'm focusing, I think I did see someone going around the back of the building. Maybe ten or so minutes before the doors opened? I remember it was right as Aurora was finishing her cigarette, because I was thinking how gross cigarette smoke smells and reminding myself not to sit next to her. And then in the distance behind her came this . . . person."

Boussicault asked his usual, "Can you give a more precise description?"

Again Professor Stibb gazed into space; again he rolled his lips and sucked in his cheeks. At last he said, "They were . . . tall? I remember that. And a jacket; I think they were wearing a jacket. Yes"—his tone became more animated—"or something dark, some dark sort of clothing." He looked at the *capitaine*. "Does that help?"

"Very much. And what about gender? Could you say whether it was a man or a woman?"

Stibb frowned. "Not really. I guess maybe a man, but I'm just saying that because of the height." He smiled. "Don't quote me on it."

Boussicault said only, "Thank you. Now, please, tell me where you're staying while you're in Paris."

"The Hotel Palais, just around the corner." Stibb shrugged. "It's only two stars, but it's near the books."

"We would ask that you not leave for a few days."

"Of course, of course." He nodded, then added as if to himself, "Yes, Aurora said it was a murder."

To this the *capitaine* also made no response, merely gave a curt nod and half rose from his chair. Stibb let himself out.

Boussicault exhaled. "So, three witnesses have seen this tall person. In a jacket or not in a jacket, at ten to nine or five to nine, but always tall and wearing something dark." After a pause he said, "And now we have one more interview. I need to talk to Docteure Dwamena."

"Really? She met me when I arrived at the library. She was next to me when LouLou started screaming!"

"Yes." Boussicault nodded grave agreement. "But where was she before that?"

Chapter Eighteen

Boussicault opened the door and nodded at someone outside. Docteure Dwamena entered. Then she stopped.

"Rachel?"

The *capitaine* gestured toward a chair, waiting for her to sit down. Then he explained, "Rachel is working with me. In fact, she has been working with me for the past few weeks. After Monsieur Laurent's death Raida Dounôt and I agreed it might be wise to have someone on the inside, since one possibility was that his murderer might have worked at the library." Rachel admired the vagueness of that "might have worked." Boussicault continued, "I asked Rachel to work here to see what she could find out about Laurent's colleagues. In case there was something significant." His voice weakened on the last sentence, as if he had only just realized how distressing this revelation might be. Rachel, too, suddenly felt guilty for what she now understood was an ongoing trick she'd played on her colleagues.

Docteure Dwamena's expression didn't change. The skin around her eyes tightened for a moment, but she said, "I understand."

"I'm sorry." Boussicault sounded as if he really was.

Unexpectedly, Docteure Dwamena waved a dismissive hand. "I think we have more pressing concerns now. And perhaps it wasn't such a bad idea. After all, look at what's been happening. First Laurent, then the book, and now this!" She folded her hands in her lap, but Rachel could see the tips of her fingers digging into the flesh beneath them.

"Yes." The *capitaine* shared her sorrow for a moment. When he began speaking again, to Rachel's surprise he didn't ask about Giles Morel. "How long have you worked here, Docteure?" His tone was conversational.

"Fifteen years. I started in 2000."

"As head of this department?"

"No, no." She smiled. "I began in cataloging. At that point we were just beginning to switch to the Internet as our primary interface, and it was my job to think about how to position the Rare Books and Manuscripts catalog so the public could know easily what we had and how to find it."

"And how long have you been head of Rare Books and Manuscripts?"

"Almost ten years. Since the autumn of 2005."

"Do you enjoy it?"

"Yes, very much."

"All the time?"

"Well"—she smiled—"no job is enjoyable all the time. But I've enjoyed it for the most part, with some occasional dissatisfactions." Rachel saw that her fingers had unhooked; her hands were now clasped softly in her lap.

Boussicault leaned forward. "I was interested by what you

just said, grouping Monsieur Morel's death with the theft from the book and the death of Monsieur Laurent. If you don't mind, I'd like to begin by asking you some questions about Monsieur Laurent, since his murder is still unsolved." Docteure Dwamena nodded. "Was he one of the job's dissatisfactions?"

"He was certainly a grain of sand in my shell."

"Did it irritate you that you couldn't turn him into a pearl?"

The doctor crossed her ankles and sat up straight. "*Capitaine*, it may surprise you to hear me say this, but until recently Laurent didn't need smoothing in any area that concerned me. He was an excellent librarian."

What makes an excellent librarian? Rachel wondered. *Did he always check the date on his book stamp? Did he have an especially fierce shush?*

As if reading her mind, Docteure Dwamena offered a more serious answer. "He knew how to build a collection. He could spot gaps in our holdings that, when we made acquisitions to fill them, became new connections for scholars and made us unique among national libraries. He had a superb sense for the possibilities of holdings. In that way, he was a great asset."

"But not in other ways? After all, he was quite deliberately antagonizing your employees."

"Yes, I knew about his personality." She sighed. "He was a true sadist. Not a sexual sadist, but someone who loved to cause people emotional pain, ideally lasting emotional pain. When he first began working here, I was made aware of some behaviors, but after a couple of warnings it stopped being a problem in the workplace. Until recently. I knew what he did to Giles and to LouLou, of course"—she sighed again—"but as you must know, there is a great deal of difference between knowing things and being able to prove them. And proof is what matters to an employment tribunal." She spread her hands. "You can't fire a man for breaking his coworker's heart, and with Giles—well, there was a chance, however small, that Giles could have left his locker unlocked, or that someone unknown tampered with his manuscript."

"But if you can't fire someone," Boussicault said, echoing Rachel's thoughts, "removing them another way comes to look very attractive."

"But murder is a rather extreme form of removal. And what if they have saving graces? As I say, he was a gift to the profession." She gave a tiny smile. "As it happens, I had begun the process of having him transferred to the Mitterand site, so that they might benefit from his talents. With a nice raise, so he wouldn't be inclined to angle for my job here."

Checkmate, Rachel thought. Even Boussicault looked impressed. He continued, "Now, tell me, Docteure, what did you do this morning before the library opened?"

She gave him a level look. "From seven-thirty to eight AM, I was in the Café Korcarz having a croissant and coffee, as I am every morning before work. I then walked here, arriving at eight thirty, as I usually do. From eight thirty to nine I was on the telephone with our conservation team. They are about to take annual holiday, and we were covering some final issues before they did so. At nine I went to the side door to let Rachel in."

"I hope you don't mind my saying that we will check all

this." She nodded, and Boussicault scarcely took a breath before he moved on. "Now we come to Morel. Was he a gift to the profession?"

The smile vanished. "No. He was a man with hopes beyond his talent." She looked sad. "And without any self-awareness."

"And Madame Fournier, what is she like?"

Docteure Dwamena pressed her lips together before she spoke. "Yes. Yes, that is the question, isn't it? You know all about her assault, I assume?" When Boussicault nodded, she went on. "Before that, she was very shy. Quiet, sweet-tempered . . . But she changed. Immediately after the attack she became very fearful, very fearful. She showed me a knife that she kept in her bag; she told me she held on to it as she walked home every day, just in case. But then she got survivor's counseling, and things were much better. She and Giles were friends, you know. He was very supportive—he was a little in love with her, I think. But then Laurent—" She looked at Boussicault. "I don't have to tell that story, do I?" He shook his head. "Thank God. He ruined her. He really did. *Salaud*. He confirmed what she feared about men. In fact, he did worse. After the attack she was afraid of dangerous men. He convinced her that all men are dangerous."

Just at that moment, as if on cue, the door opened and the young blond *brigadier* came in. He leaned over Boussicault and whispered in his ear. The *capitaine* stood. "*Pardon, mesdames*. I will return in a moment."

LouLou and Docteure Dwamena sat silent. At last Rachel said, "I'm sorry."

"*De rien*."

"I really enjoyed working here."

"I'm glad."

The door reopened, admitting Boussicault. In his hands was a large plastic bag, doubled over and stained rusty at the bottom. Sitting down, he put it on the table. "Docteure, would you be willing to tell us if you recognize this item?"

At some point, Rachel was sure, Docteure Dwamena's composure would crack, but this was not to be that moment. The doctor nodded, her only sign of tension being that she pressed her lips together once again. The *capitaine* unfolded the bag.

Rachel leaned forward, too. She saw a serrated knife, its blade around five inches long. It was the knife that LouLou had been holding. Dried blood coated its tip and sharp edge, but its riveted handle was completely clean, and the tip was smudged where LouLou had held it.

"Do you recognize this?"

The skin around the doctor's eyes pinched again. "It's a steak knife."

"Yes, but is it one you've seen before? Is it at all familiar?"

Docteure Dwamena leaned back and flicked up her eyes to meet Boussicault's. "I know what you're asking, but I couldn't say."

"Couldn't say, or can't say? One is definitive, but the other implies a personal choice." Abruptly, Boussicault's tone became hectoring. "Which is it: you don't recognize, or you prefer not to admit that you do?"

"All right." Docteure Dwamena looked down at the knife, then back up at the *capitaine* again. "I want to say first that this is an ordinary steak knife. I have seen thousands like it at restaurants or in people's homes. But . . . yes. It does look like the knife Louise Fournier had in her bag last year."

She looked at Boussicault. Boussicault looked at the knife. Rachel looked at Boussicault. His face said the interviews were over.

Chapter Nineteen

The next day at breakfast Rachel told Alan all about the interviews. When she finished, he shook his head. "It doesn't look good for LouLou."

Rachel really did not want LouLou to have murdered Giles. Hadn't the poor woman suffered enough? "But what's her motive? And what about this tall person?"

"I thought you said she was tall." Alan took a bite of his croissant, and a few crumbs drifted onto the tablecloth. "As for motive, I'd think a police interview with her would help uncover that. They have one scheduled, right?"

"Yes. She was still sedated when we finished yesterday, but I assume they'll let me know when she's ready."

"Okay, so then you'll know more about her possible motives." He bent his head over his tablet.

How could he be so unengaged? How could he not want to run over scenarios with her? "But what about other possible suspects?"

He scrolled down the screen. "I thought Boussicault didn't think there were any other possible suspects."

"That was for *Laurent*'s murder. Now everything's changed.

LouLou would want to kill Laurent, but why would she want to kill Giles? They used to be friends."

He looked up reluctantly. "And she used to date Laurent. People kill former friends all the time." Seeing her face, he sighed and put down the tablet. "Okay. You told me she'd been assaulted, right? And that she'd started carrying a knife afterward? Well, maybe he startled her in the stacks, or they got into some kind of argument, and she's got the knife. So she stabs him." He took his dishes into the kitchen.

Rachel bit her thumbnail as she considered his scenario. "LouLou locks her bag in her locker, so she wouldn't have had the knife with her—assuming she's even still carrying it."

He shrugged. "Well, then, I got it wrong." He put his jacket over his arm. "Look, I'm sorry, but I need to go to work. You were at all the interviews, so you're more likely to come up with a good idea than I am. I have faith in you." They kissed, and Rachel listened to the door thump shut behind him.

She had indeed been at the interviews. So what did she know? Well, she knew all the addresses. She tried to smile at this feeble joke, then frowned. No, seriously, who else looked good for it? She thought for a long time. Well, all of them. Except for Katja Bonsergent all of the current patrons of the Rare Books and Manuscripts reading room had been working in the library long enough to have interacted with Giles. And they'd all said they'd arrived early yesterday, but none of them had spoken to the others when they got there. Which meant no one could back them up, which in turn meant any of them could be lying and could in fact have been killing Giles.

And yet—she rose and took her own dishes to the sink—at

the same time none of them was obviously good for it. They'd all said separately that they'd seen a someone tall going around the back of the Bibliothèque, which meant they independently corroborated each other's alibis. Besides, if she couldn't see a motive for LouLou, what motive could one of the patrons possibly have?

God, how did detectives do this alone? No wonder they always had some sidekick to run their ideas past. Her fingers itched to pick up her *portable*, but she held back. Magda had insulted her, had . . . had impugned her character. She wasn't going to climb down first.

As if understanding, the *portable* rang. She snatched it up. "'Allo?"

"Rachel. Boussicault." His tone was calm, but she heard barely suppressed excitement beneath. "I wanted to let you know of a development. The scene-of-the-crime agents found something while they were making their final sweep." He took a breath. "*Pardon*. Let me explain. A final sweep extends out further than the other searches. It's designed to make certain that the agents have missed nothing, to avoid nasty surprises in court."

Get on with it, Rachel thought. She'd watched *Forensic Files*; she knew how it worked. But all she said was, "Uh-huh."

"The sweep extended to the adjacent aisle. And, as I say, it uncovered something." He paused. "On the floor one aisle over." He paused again.

Damn the French and their love of drama. "What was it?"

"It was an illustrated book of medieval psalms."

"A psalter." Rachel couldn't help herself; irritation brought out her inner pedant. "It's called an illuminated psalter. And he did die in the medieval religion section. It probably fell off a shelf."

"I don't think this fell off a shelf. For one thing, it was under a shelving unit. And for another, it's missing a page."

It was Rachel's turn to be silent. She almost dropped the phone, then gripped it more tightly. "No way."

"Indeed." He paused again, but this time more like a man standing back to watch his effect. "Obviously this is a significant development."

"Obviously. Should I come to the commissariat?"

"No need. I just thought you'd like to know. *Au 'voir.*"

Rachel put the phone down on the counter and stood processing the news. A book, a missing page, the body. She tried to see a connection.

All of a sudden one burst into her brain. *What if Giles was the book thief?* She remembered his response when Boussicault told him a book had been mutilated. *I know*, he'd said. *I already know.* And he'd looked anxious even when he first came into Docteure Dwamena's office, before Boussicault had said anything. What if he'd already known because he was the one who'd stolen the engraving from the *Supplementum Chronicarum*? What if his voice had been heavy because he'd thought he was about to be found out?

"What if it's the books?" she said aloud to her silent apartment. "What if the murder isn't about rage but about the books?"

All the details fell into place at once. Giles had been

stealing book illustrations! Laurent had caught him at it and was blackmailing him! Giles had killed him for it! Then he had been killed himself by a disgruntled customer—a disgruntled tall customer he'd let in the back door!

She heard Magda's voice in her head. First it asked, *Why did he kill him with a piece of string?* Then it asked, *Why aren't Giles's initials on the notebook page if the blackmail is all about him?*

"Oh, shut up," she said aloud. But fine. Those were fair objections. So maybe Giles wasn't the thief. Maybe he'd found out who the thief was, like Laurent, and he was also trying to blackmail them. After all, both Laurent and Giles were librarians. If one discovered theft, so could the other.

Rachel listened, but she heard nothing inside her head or out. She smiled. Maybe this wasn't going to be so hard on her own, after all.

The next question, she thought, was obviously, who was the thief? Well, someone who knew a lot about books, who knew their value—and who needed money. And who would know how to turn book illustrations into money. She had another epiphany: who needed money more than academics? Probably all the reading room visitors she and Boussicault had interviewed needed money. And who would know how to turn antiquarian illustrations into money better than academics who studied antiquarian books? Probably all the reading room patrons they'd interviewed could do that easily, too.

If only the interviews had been more informative! If only she'd known in advance that she'd want to ask about finances.

Now she had no way of finding out; Alan had made it very clear on her last case that to help her would put his job in jeopardy, and there was no one else.

But there was. There was someone who had used computer skills to access private information on their last case, and the results had been very useful. Someone free, someone accessible, someone only a phone call away.

No. She crossed her arms and whirled around to look at the refrigerator, the cabinets, anywhere but at the solution in front of her. *No, no, no, no.* But she couldn't avoid it. The only other way to get help was to hire someone. Did she want to reveal her purpose to someone else? Someone she didn't know and didn't know if she could trust? Did she have the time to waste locating someone and explaining herself? The answer to those questions was also *no, no, no, no.* Since that was the case, she really had no other choice.

It wouldn't be a climbdown, she said to herself, lifting her chin a little. It would be a sacrifice in the name of the higher calling that was detection.

* * *

"That's ridiculous," Magda said.

"You're free to say no to my request." Rachel's voice was stiff.

"No, not that, the other. Your goal was to find an alternative theory, and you devised a line of thinking that led directly to that goal. You're avoiding considering LouLou at all costs, even at the cost of clear reasoning. What evidence do you have that Giles was blackmailing anyone?"

"As I said, you're welcome to decline."

"I'm not going to decline." Magda sounded impatient. "I will help. But I want it understood that I'm still upset. I'm only helping you out of duty to the higher calling of detection." She paused. "And because I've finished my ordering and organizing for next season, so space has opened up."

"Fine." Rachel lifted her chin again.

"Fine. The next time your phone rings, it will be me with the information you requested. Because Magda Stevens does not let the personal interfere with the professional." She hung up in Rachel's ear.

Rachel stood staring at her *portable.* She had wanted to hang up first. Just for good measure, she stabbed her finger at the red receiver that lingered on the screen.

Chapter Twenty

But when Rachel's cell phone rang at nine o'clock the next morning, the person on the other end was not Magda but Docteure Dwamena.

"I wanted to call you right away." Her voice was as calm as always, but somehow it sounded more urgent. "Personnel gave me your number, and I wanted to reach you before you were too busy. I have found something that might be important to your investigation."

Rachel sat up in bed, pulling the sheet around her. "Really?" Then good sense prevailed. "But if it's important, you should get in touch with the police."

There was a pause. "I thought you were the police."

Rachel understood: Boussicault had said, "Rachel is working with me," and Docteure Dwamena had drawn the perfectly sensible conclusion that Rachel was part of his team. A natural mistake, and easily fixed.

Yet if she fixed it, she would miss hearing what the doctor had found. And she was almost a member of the police. *Almost*, said a voice in her head, *but not fully*. Yes, but she was fully a member of the investigating team, which meant she was working to gather information on the case, and this was a moment when information was being offered.

She considered these truths, trying to reconcile them. At last she said, "Yes, of course I am. Tell me what you found, and I'll let you know if it's worth alerting my superiors."

"Well, as you know, the reading room has been closed for the past two days. I thought it might take my mind off our losses if I used the time to catch up on work. I decided to go through and file the backlog of reader request slips. And while I was doing that, I found a slip from two weeks ago requesting the *Supplementum Chronicarum*."

Rachel gasped. "Have you saved it?"

"Yes. But that's not the reason I decided to telephone. After I put it to one side, I kept working, and I came across some slips from Tuesday and Wednesday. There weren't very many, but there were a few. And one of them had the same name on it as the *Supplementum* slip."

It took Rachel a few seconds to figure out what this meant. When she did, she didn't quite believe it. "You mean you have a slip with the name of the last person known to have requested a damaged book, and another slip from yesterday morning with the same name?"

"Yes."

Miss Marple, Rachel reminded herself, did not scream with amazement; Sam Spade did not let out bellows of joy. She inhaled and said calmly, "And what is the name?"

"Jean Bernard."

"Jean Bernard?"

"Yes, Jean Bernard."

A good French name. But not the name of any of Rachel's French friends, or of any French lawyer, banker, or even handyman she had ever dealt with. Why, then, did it sound so familiar? Where had she heard it before? *Had* she heard it before? She tried to remember. *Never mind that. Focus on the detection at hand.* She shook herself.

"Whom else have you told about this?"

"No one. I thought I should call the police first."

"Good thinking." Then Rachel remembered the second half of her compromise. She sighed. "Now, I'm going to give you the number for Capitaine Boussicault. He's the man who was with me on Wednesday. Just tell him exactly the same thing you told me."

When she hung up, she hit speed dial without thinking.

"No, it's not too early." Magda was too excited to remember to be haughty. "Because I've found something. Listen to this."

Chapter Twenty-One

"Robert Cavill," Magda said to Capitaine Boussicault as she and Rachel sat across the desk from him, "does not work at Churchill College. In fact, he doesn't work at Cambridge University at all." She tossed a printout on his desk triumphantly. "He works at *Anglia Ruskin* University."

Boussicault looked puzzled. "But we already know this." He picked up the piece of paper and moved it to one side.

Magda was surprised. "You already know that Robert Cavill lied about working at Cambridge?"

"*Mais oui*."

"And did you know that his salary at Anglia Ruskin is much lower than at Cambridge?" Again her tone was triumphant.

"Well, we know that Cambridge offers many benefits that Anglia Ruskin University does not—mortgage assistance, free lunches, that kind of thing. So although the salaries are almost the same, the Cambridge salary covers more, as it were." If Boussicault noticed Magda's crestfallen face, he gave no indication of it. He continued, "And we know that even though he is not at Cambridge, he is very well regarded in his field, and his field is specifically medieval religious iconography. His most recent publication, in fact, was a book called *From the Dragon to the Law: Uses and Meanings of Scales in Medieval Religious Illustration*."

"I knew that," Magda said.

"I see. And you knew that in addition to the twin sons he mentioned in his interview, he also has a daughter?"

"Yes, I knew that."

"Then no doubt you also knew that all three attend the Perse School, in Cambridge, where the fees for each are roughly fifteen thousand pounds a year."

It was stiflingly hot in the office, Rachel realized. The air conditioning was broken. She listened to the second hand of the wall clock moving for a long, muggy ten seconds before Magda said, "I didn't know that."

"And did you know that Professeure Dale, so interested in determining if we thought Monsieur Morel's death was murder, has for the last five years run a very large overdraft with her bank, an overdraft partially paid off in the past year by a number of payments she received from"—he checked a sheet of paper in front of him—"Peter Harrington Rare Books, London?"

"No." Magda's lips thinned. "I didn't know that either."

"Or that Professeur Stibb is up to his ears in debt? Student loans, credit card debt, a mortgage . . ."

Why is he being so unpleasant? Rachel wondered. There was no need for him to be belligerent when all they wanted to do was help.

"Forgive me," Boussicault said, as if he had heard her. "It's this heat; it's made me short-tempered. They were supposed to come and fix the air conditioning this morning, but no one arrived." He sighed, "But, *mesdames*, information gathering is what the police do. You might say it is our *métier*. We have databases; we have computer networks—one of which I used yesterday to examine Madame Fournier's bank account to see if she might have been connected with the books thefts and somehow killed Monsieur Morel because of that." Rachel waited for him to tell them the outcome of that examination, but he just continued on. "And we can call upon Europol, as I did to learn what I just told you. Pan-European agencies are very helpful when national treasures like irreplaceable books are at stake." Rachel looked at her lap. She hadn't known that. "And we are able to move quickly," Boussicault continued. "At this moment my team is using all these connections and resources to find the Jean Bernard Rachel instructed Docteure Dwamena to tell me about."

Magda cast her a look.

"Our job is made harder by the fact that the Bibliothèque is having difficulty finding an address that matches his reader ID number," Boussicault went on, "but I have sent someone there to collect the slips to take them to our lab, where the technicians can try to find fingerprints. If he's the thief, matching fingerprints may already be in our system. These same technicians will soon be handing in detailed reports that will tell us about Laurent's murder, Morel's murder, and their scenes. We are also waiting for full coroner's reports on Laurent and Morel. In short, the investigation now proceeds along lines we know very well and in which we are trained experts."

"How soon is soon?" Magda asked.

"I'm sorry?"

"You said"—Rachel recognized Magda's quoting voice—"'these same technicians will soon be handing in detailed reports.' How soon is soon?"

Boussicault considered. "For the coroner's report, perhaps next Wednesday; the forensics, perhaps the week after next."

"The week after next!"

The *capitaine* sighed once more. "Madame Stevens. Real police work is not like television police work. On television everything goes quickly, but here. . . . For example, it is very hot. In hot weather there are many more suicides. Each suicide must be signed off by a coroner. More bodies to sign off means more autopsies, which means a backlog of bodies. As for the forensic reports, even normally these take time, but again, hot weather increases the rate of violent crime. More violent crime equals more evidence; more evidence equals more lab work. More lab work equals more delay. In fact, the end of next week is refreshingly soon, given the circumstances."

Magda crossed her arms, her face a thundercloud. She made one more attempt. "What about the tall person?"

"The tall person." For a moment Boussicault looked confused, but then his face cleared. "Ah, the tall person possibly wearing black! As it happens, employees of the Bibliothèque must fill out a medical form when they start, listing, among other things, their height and weight. Of course, Madame

Fournier is tall and wears almost entirely black, but I nonetheless have a man currently working his way through these forms to see if any other employees are notably tall. But Madame Stevens"—here he leaned toward her—"can you imagine circulating a notice in Paris that says, 'Be on the lookout for a tall person wearing a black jacket'? Three-quarters of the men in Paris would be arrested!"

Magda had to concede that point. She uncrossed her arms.

Rachel tried to steer the conversation in a more hopeful direction. "Well, what about LouLou? When will that interview happen?" The rest of them might not have been much use, but surely her interview would be revealing.

Boussicault checked his watch. "In fact, Madame Fournier is being interviewed right now. I sent a female officer in my place, since I thought it might help produce more information."

"You sent another—" Rachel clutched at her composure. "You should have sent me." She felt her nails digging into her palms. "I could have used our friendship to get better results."

"Y—" The *capitaine* stopped, puzzled. Then his face cleared. "I think I may have given you a wrong impression, Rachel." His voice became gently polite. "I asked for your assistance at the Bibliothèque because I admired your talent for observation in connection with Monsieur Bowen's murder. I asked you to sit in on the preliminary interviews because I knew you would be interested, and it seemed a good way to thank you for your work. And also"—he looked abashed—"I liked the idea of fostering a budding interest in investigation.

But I didn't mean to give you the impression that you were a part of this one. I see now that I seem to have done so. My apologies."

They all sat still for a moment. *Budding talent for investigation?* Rachel thought. *Talent for observation "in connection with" Edgar's murder?* She and Magda had solved that murder! Hell, she and Magda had recognized that there was a murder to solve in the first place!

Unaware of her blossoming anger, Boussicault drew a breath. "Now, *ecoutez-moi*." His tone was weary. "We are moving forward at a good pace, and I anticipate developments very soon. Madame Fournier, the other readers as witnesses or suspects, Jean Bernard: we are exploring all possibilities. I will keep you informed. And Rachel, to apologize for the earlier confusion, I invite you to sit in on the next round of interviews." Rachel noticed his stress on *sit in*—in case she hadn't grasped his point about her outsider status, she supposed. "But the police are doing our job to the best of our ability, which is very high indeed. You must trust us."

* * *

Outside, it was Paris at two thirty in the afternoon in late July. They sought shelter. Even here, next to the brutalist concrete of the commissariat, they could see two bistros a few steps away. It was pointless to try to make a considered choice, so they simply turned into the one that said CLIMATISÉ in the window. A cold blast hit them as Rachel opened the door.

They chose a table far back in the room's and settled in.

Rachel felt the backs of her thighs slip moistly against the padded vinyl seat.

"Well," Magda said.

"Yes." Rachel wiped her forehead.

"He dismissed us."

"Yes." Rachel was grateful to Magda for not saying *dismissed you*. She would have been within her rights.

"Politely, but dismissed us."

"Yes." She was too distracted by her own thoughts to say anything else. She had imagined that Boussicault thought of her as an equal, or at least an apprentice he was mentoring into equality: a capable professional who might bring a more maverick eye to his investigation. Now she had to accept that she had never been a Police Consultant. She hadn't even been consulted by the police. Instead, she had been drafted in to do a job for which her qualification was precisely that she wasn't police. She had been an ordinary member of the public when they needed someone to look like an ordinary member of the public. She hadn't been necessary; she had been used. And she had misunderstood, which was in a way even worse.

If there was one thing Rachel hated more than being used, it was having to rethink her opinions, and she found the combination of the two almost too much to bear. When the waiter approached, she ordered a hot chocolate. Cold drinks were for relief and celebration. In moments of deflation, only a hot drink would do.

"I don't like being given the brush-off," she said to Magda.

"Well . . ." Magda smiled slyly.

"What?"

"I don't know if he realized it, but while he was brushing you off, he also brushed a lot of information your way."

"Like what?" All Rachel could remember was a detailing of police superiority.

"Well, now you know that each of the reading room patrons we interviewed has a motive."

That was true, Rachel realized. She tried to put her personal feelings aside and reexamine what the *capitaine* had said. "They don't have any forensics available yet beyond what they gathered at the scene."

"They haven't found the tall person," Magda added.

"Or Jean Bernard, who was there Wednesday morning, but nowhere to be found after that." Rachel remembered something else. "And because of the murder and the interviews, I completely forgot to tell Boussicault what we figured out about Laurent's sheet of paper."

The two women looked at each other.

"So"—Magda's voice was precise—"the police don't know five things, and of those five we do know one."

"Yes."

"I'd say that puts us ahead."

"Yes." Again Rachel luxuriated in that *us*. She felt her own blood rise. She realized that she hadn't wanted more vocal support from Alan, and she hadn't wanted to work on equal footing with Boussicault. She'd wanted to be working with Magda. She put her left hand on Magda's where it lay on the table. "I'm sorry."

Magda met her gaze. "You should be." She shook free of

Rachel's hand and waved her hand for the waiter. "Two spritzers." When she turned back to Rachel, her eyes were glowing. "Now who is Jean Bernard?"

We can do this, her eyes said. *We're more than a match for any police force.*

Rachel explained about the phone call, and the way the name echoed in her head.

"It's not one I know," Magda said. "But that doesn't necessarily mean *you* haven't heard it before. Maybe a poet? Or a publisher?"

"No." Rachel shook her head. "It's not someone I know through work. That's the problem: I know who it *isn't*. I just don't know who it *is*."

"Oh, wow." Magda was distracted by the ghoulish possibilities. "You could have met the murderer without even being aware of it." She sounded pleased at this notion. "Some Jean Bernard you ran into at an event could have killed two people you knew."

"I only knew one of them. And I just said it wasn't someone I met through writing. It was closer to home. Anyway, I don't believe murderers can be good writers."

"What? That's ridiculous."

Rachel shook her head. "All that time planning crimes would take away from the focus you need to produce good work."

"What about that serial killer in Germany? He was a writer. Remember, they said that in the documentary."

"He was a journalist. The only real book he wrote was his autobiography." Rachel made this sound like the basest sort of labor.

Magda raised her eyebrows at such foolishness. "Back to the original topic. Just let it go and focus somewhere else. The memory will come to you." As if she were eager to help with that, she reached into her bag and pulled out her pad and pen. "Let's think about where our investigation should start."

Chapter Twenty-Two

Magda had to admit that Boussicault was right about trying to find a specific tall person with a black jacket in the middle of Paris—"Not that I'm going to stop looking." But there also didn't seem to be any point in interviewing the suspects they knew were in Paris. In fact, Magda pointed out, there were good reasons not to do that: "The *capitaine* promised you could come to the second interviews, and if they're moving as quickly as he says, then that should be soon. It would be a waste of energy." LouLou was the logical place to start—"Just a friend, dropping in to check up on her and have a little chat," Magda cooed—but Rachel not only foresaw great difficulties in extracting LouLou's phone number from the Bibliothèque now that she no longer worked there but also pointed out to Magda that she didn't have the skills necessary to deal with a grieving, possibly sedated, potential murderess.

So they started with Jean Bernard. Finding him involved only collecting addresses and then visiting them. It was easy to access addresses via Whitepages.fr, Magda explained. and although visiting each of them would be tedious, they could do it. And how many Jean Bernards could there be in Paris? They could work through the ones they found in a couple of days, and if they didn't locate their man, they could move further afield. They arranged that Magda would take the weekend to gather the information. Then they'd start their investigation on Monday—and although neither one said it, both thought of the pleasure they'd get by bringing their results to the police a couple of days later.

Rachel spent her weekend wrestling with her hymns and her calling. She couldn't really remember ever wanting to be anything other than a poet. Even when she hadn't believed she could be a poet—when she hadn't known she had talent and when she'd had no notion of what being a poet might actually involve—she'd loved the idea of putting words together to tell the truth through emotion. And even though the world of poetry writing had turned out to be pretty thankless—self-printed pamphlets outnumbering published collections a hundred to one, readings supposedly made worthwhile by small but devoted audiences and access to free wine, the rare event of publication battling the sinking feeling that you were claiming a title you had no right to—her interest in and love for the art had waned only twice: first when investigating the death of Edgar Bowen eighteenth months previously, and again now. She thought of all the saints gathered in the stacks at the Bibliothèque Nationale. Had they ever doubted their vocations? As she worked, she tried to access the grace they must have felt in the presence of God, but at the end of the weekend all she had of the hymns were some vague lines about sheep. She went to bed on Sunday night longing for the quick arrival of Monday morning.

She and Magda had arranged to meet at the Anticafé on the Rue de Richelieu. Rachel was intrigued by the Anticafé, which she had discovered walking home from the Bibliothèque the previous week. A sign in its window told her it charged by time spent rather than by food consumed, and this arrangement struck her as so eminently sensible that she longed to try it. Pushing the door open now, she found herself imagining a cheap quick meeting amid a paradise of free snacks.

Magda sat at one of the rickety wooden tables with four sets of stapled pages in front of her. As Rachel sat down, she pushed one of the taller stacks toward her. It turned out that the Jean Bernards of Paris filled ten double-sided pages. But whereas to Rachel this would have indicated that they should abandon the search, to Magda it meant only that they would need to move at a brisker pace. She took a map out of her bag and unfolded it on the table between them.

"I've made a series of concentric circles, with the Bibliothèque as the central point. Since we're right here, I thought we'd start with the smallest circle and work outward." Rachel glumly recognized her tone as hearty. "Each circle has a radius of a kilometer. In our first circle—that's on the first page of your document—there are fifteen Jean Bernards. The second circle has twenty-five. There are twenty circles in total. I reckon we can do one circle a day."

Twenty doors average per day! Rachel felt her heart sink.

Maybe Magda sensed this dismay, because she added, "Although I doubt we'll even have to cover all of them before we find our man." She snapped the map closed with an air of satisfied finality. "Now, I've put together a questionnaire for us to use as a guide. I thought we could say we were doing outreach to determine how well the Bibliothèque is known to Parisians." She shoved one of the smaller sets of pages across the table.

The questionnaire was two pages long. Rachel glanced down the first page. HAVE YOU EVER BEEN TO THE BIBLIOTHÈQUE NATIONALE? HAVE YOU USED THE BIBLIOTHÈQUE NATIONALE IN THE PAST SIX MONTHS? WHICH READING ROOM DID YOU USE THERE? "'Try to determine if subject wears dark outerwear,'" she read aloud. "How? Are we going to ask to use the toilet at every stop, so we can get inside and check out their coat stand?"

"No, one of us can just—" Magda craned her neck and mimed moving her head to get a better look.

Rachel envisioned a long line of doors being slammed in the faces of two twitchy emissaries from the Bibliothèque Nationale. But Magda seemed to have no such qualms (*of course she didn't*, Rachel thought). Instead, she placed her two stapled sheets on top of her thick stack and considered the pile. Then she placed her thick stack on top of her two stapled sheets and considered that. She nodded approval, then straightened the edges of the resulting pile with a look of enormous satisfaction on her face. She looked up. "Ready?"

Rachel, who hadn't had the chance to consume even one cookie, nonetheless saw no way to stall. A Magda with her hands full of printed pages and her heart full of determination was a force to be reckoned with. She took a deep breath. "Ready."

* * *

No one answered the door at the second-floor apartment of the first Jean Bernard.

The second Jean Bernard lived on the fifth floor of a tall, slender building where, once Rachel and Magda climbed the stairs, they discovered no one was home, either.

The third Jean Bernard lived three flights up, around the corner from the second. His door was answered by a young woman with an anxious face holding a King Charles Spaniel with an equally anxious face. Yes, she said, Monsieur Bernard did live there, but he and his companion were in Nice until the end of August. She was taking care of their dog while they were gone. She'd be happy to give Monsieur Bernard a message, if they wished. Rachel and Magda shook their heads, patted the dog, and apologized for wasting the girl's time. Then they caught their breath and walked down the thirty-six steps they had just climbed up.

For the next three days they trekked all over Paris. There were Jean Bernards living near Les Halles; there were Jean Bernards living in the tourist-thronged streets of Montmartre; there were Jean Bernards who could pop out for a stroll in the nearby Jardin des Plantes—and once, to Rachel's mingled excitement and relief, there was a Jean Bernard in the building next to hers, which meant they could stop home for a rest before gearing up to go visit the Jean Bernard who lived across the Jardin du Luxembourg near the Sorbonne's

Faculté de Médecine. These various Jean Bernards were tall, short, elderly, young, frail, hale, at home, at work, and often away on vacation having left behind locked doors and knocks that echoed in their empty apartments. Those who were at home had dropped by the Bibliothèque Nationale to see the famous Labrouste reading room with its ballooning glass ceiling, or had casually noticed the blackened original doors on their way to somewhere else. In one exciting case the Jean Bernard had actually used the library, but only the previous January and not the Rare Books reading room; in one depressing case the Jean Bernard did not know there was a Bibliothèque Nationale, nor what its purpose might be, and couldn't be made to see why that purpose might have value. But not one of these Jean Bernards had filled out book request slips at the Bibliothèque Nationale anytime in the previous six months.

Rachel reflected that perhaps before starting they should have considered the wisdom of trying to track someone down in the month when most Parisians fled their city. She felt so silly trudging from door to door all over Paris with no luck that she didn't say a word to Alan about what she was doing, instead telling him that her feet hurt from long walks seeking inspiration.

But their lack of success didn't seem to bother Magda; she walked each area with her list in hand, checking off names and making notations. If it hadn't been unbearably hot, and if the search hadn't long since become utterly boring, Rachel might have admitted to being impressed—Magda could get excited too quickly and too completely, but once she had the bit between her teeth, she would follow an idea to the end. In a heat wave, though, three days of temporary failure felt like an eternity, and as they turned from the most recent Jean Bernard's home street, the Rue Dubois, into the Rue de l'Ecole-de-Médecine on Wednesday afternoon, Rachel was too tired to admire anything.

She stopped. "I need a rest."

"But we have . . ." Magda looked at her pad. "Three more people to see in this circle."

"No." Rachel shook her head. "No." She knew she was being childish, but she couldn't help it. They were on a fool's errand, she thought, and she had gone along with it and gone along with it until she could go along no more.

She turned sharply to the right and marched up the street, Magda trailing behind. After about a minute she made an equally sharp left through a pair of double doors. Two more sets of doors and one marble entrance hall farther and she and Magda stood in a long wooden room: the Musee d'Histoire de la Medecine, an oasis of quiet in the crowded Odeon area. Glass cases, crowded with antiquarian medical instruments and anatomical models, were set into the walls on either side and around the long gallery above. The silence was absolute.

"We've been here before," Magda muttered.

"I know." Rachel's whisper was flat.

Magda waited a moment, as if to show respect, then hissed, "Why are we here?"

Rachel sighed. She longed to sit on one of the steps that led up to the balcony, but she was sure it was forbidden. Instead she put a hand on the iron balustrade and closed her eyes, letting her lids rest for a moment before she opened them. "It's just too much. We've chased Jean Bernard for three days with no luck." She saw her friend's face fall. "And that's fine. But we're getting nowhere, and I need some time to regroup."

"But we could find him at the next address!"

"Or we could not. We haven't so far."

Magda waved a hand as if such failure were long behind them. "But that just means we're getting closer to the time when we will."

Or to the final time we won't, Rachel thought but did not say. "Wouldn't this be easier if we used phone numbers rather than addresses?"

"You have to pay to access the phone numbers."

Rachel thought of *Law & Order, Law & Order: SVU, Law & Order: Criminal Intent*—all the Laws & Orders—where the detectives sat at their desks and called potential witnesses, not moving until they'd separated pointless leads from useful ones. She thought of the Rue de Vaugirard commissariat with all its rows of similar desks, each no doubt fitted with a phone on which Boussicault's officers could make countless calls, their backs untouched by sweat and their feet nestled comfortably in cushioning shoes. She wondered longingly if they'd fixed the air conditioning there. She decided she would pay for the access to the phone numbers.

She was opening her mouth to say this to Magda when her *portable* rang, unbearably loud in the silent room. She groped it out from her bag and looked at the screen. It was Boussicault.

She stared at the phone, divided, as it rang again. She knew for a fact that she had two more rings before it went to voice mail. Boussicault could be calling about the interviews or to tell her that the police had tracked down Jean Bernard themselves. But he had dismissed them and their possible contributions, and she was with Magda now. They were sisters doing it for themselves!

A third ring broke the peace.

"Answer the fucking phone!" Magda snapped.

Rachel answered the phone. She slipped back out through the door into the foyer, Magda following.

"'Allo, *capitaine*?"

"'Allo." Boussicault's voice was businesslike. "I hope I don't disturb you?"

"No, no, not at all."

"Put it on speaker," Magda hissed.

Rachel put her hand over the *portable*'s microphone. "No."

"Why not?"

She thinned her lips and swept her hand around the marbled hall. Echo would make it impossible to understand Boussicault on speaker. Magda rolled her eyes, but she squashed her head up next to Rachel's ear. Rachel tilted the phone outward. Now they could both hear, but neither could hear very well.

"We've had the coroner's report on Morel."

"Oh?"

Magda poked her in the ribs with excitement. Rachel pulled away, taking the phone with her.

"There's not much I didn't expect. He was stabbed twice in the chest; death was from a tension pneumothorax."

"A tension pneumothorax?" As Rachel spoke, Magda began to dig in her bag.

"The knife punctured the lung, and the escaping air blocked possible breathing space. It's a very quick death. The knife found next to him was definitely the murder weapon. But there are two unexpected details, and interestingly both link his death to Laurent's."

"Oh?" Rachel struggled to keep her voice casual.

Magda came up with her policeman's pad.

"There was saliva on both men's necks."

"*Saliva?*" Rachel's voice echoed off the walls.

Magda began to write furiously.

"Yes, a good deal on Laurent, a small patch on Morel. I'm not sure what to make of it. It was too degraded to get any DNA, but it does connect the two murders and suggest some form of contempt was involved in both. Spitting on the bodies, perhaps? A partnership gone wrong, or a confrontation ending in violence, with the murderer showing what he thinks of the victims by spitting on them?"

Rachel's mind went back to Magda's hypothesis about the murderer peeing on the string used to murder Laurent. Suddenly it didn't seem quite as implausible. But, just as in that scenario, what could inspire such scorn that you would mark a corpse by spitting on it? She was making a mental note to ask Boussicault this when Magda held up the pad. LET ME TALK TO HIM, it said. Rachel shook her head.

Boussicault was still speaking. "The arrival of the coroner's reports makes me hopeful that the full forensic reports will arrive shortly. I'm also aware that two of our suspects' teaching periods begin again soon, so the longer we keep them in Paris, the more tense and less cooperative they may become. In light of that, I'd like to begin our next round of interviews quickly. The day after tomorrow."

"The day after tomorrow for the interviews." Rachel looked at Magda, who held up the pad again.

LET ME TALK TO HIM.

Rachel shook her head again.

"Yes," the *capitaine* said in Rachel's ear. "I plan to begin at ten AM."

Magda had flipped over her page and was scribbling again.

"You are available?"

Magda held up the pad once more. LET ME TALK TO HIM!!! Rachel noted the three exclamation points—Magda was usually restrained when it came to punctuation—but she still shook her head. What in Magda's previous interactions with the *capitaine* made her think they could have a useful conversation? Rachel moved the pad-holding hand out of her sight line.

"Yes," she said, "I'm available. So, ten AM on Friday?"

"Let's say nine forty-five. That will give us some time to get organized before we begin."

She knew she should be angry at him for dismissing the two of them from the investigation. She *was* angry at him for that. But she really did want to be at those interviews. She wanted to find someone besides LouLou who could be the murderer; she wanted to know if any of the witnesses could be possible suspects. And she wanted to know if the superior abilities of the Commissariat Rue de Vaugirard had managed to locate Jean Bernard. At the very least, if she sat in on the interviews, she would learn everything that Boussicault discovered, then bring that to Magda for their own use. And she knew that if a true detective had to choose between her personal feelings and aiding the investigation of a crime, there was no question which was the choice to make. "I'll be there at nine forty-five."

Magda's pad appeared in front of Rachel's nose. ASK HIM IF I CAN COME. Rachel pushed it aside again, but it appeared again, and when Rachel tried to push it away, Magda pushed back. When she drew her head back, Magda made the pad follow.

She sighed. "Magda would like to speak to you."

Chapter Twenty-Three

"I can't believe he said no!" Magda sat on Rachel's sofa with her arms crossed.

"You said that all the way home, but you didn't tell me why he said it." Rachel spoke from the kitchen area, where she was making them both gin and tonics. After Boussicault's call she had been too excited, and Magda too irritated, to be able to focus anymore on looking for Jean Bernard. Instead they had come straight to Rachel apartment. So she did have something to thank the *capitaine* for after all, she reflected as she whacked an ice cube tray against the countertop.

"Oh, he said the interview room was too small to fit four people comfortably." Magda's tone said she considered this an obvious lie. "You're going to have to tell me every single thing." She took the glass from Rachel. "In fact, you can start by telling me exactly what he said to you on the phone. What was this about saliva?"

Rachel sat in the chair across from her. "The coroner found saliva on Giles's neck, and on Laurent's."

"Saliva? The murderer licked him?"

"Or drooled on him, I guess. From the exertion, maybe?"

"Who drooled on whom from exertion?" Alan had appeared behind Rachel, still wearing his suit. He put his keys down on the counter.

"Oh, hey. We don't know; that's the point. I was just telling Magda that Boussicault told me the coroner found saliva on Giles Morel and Guy Laurent's necks."

"You're talking to Boussicault again?" Alan had heard all about the second meeting in the *capitaine*'s office.

"Well, he called me."

"To tell you someone drooled on a corpse's neck?" He sat down in an available chair.

"I was thinking they spat on it. On them."

"Maybe the murderer has a thing for bodily fluids," Magda said. "That could explain why they killed in a bathroom."

"But not why they killed in the library stacks," Rachel pointed out. "Although . . . I remember reading somewhere that dust is sixty percent dead skin. So if they had a thing for bodily waste—"

"They'd also have to have a thing for librarians." Alan broke in. "Bodily waste, necks, and librarians. That's one picky killer."

Despite herself, Rachel laughed. Magda, however, kept a straight face. "How would you explain the saliva?"

"I wouldn't. And neither would you, I thought. I thought Boussicault told you you weren't needed anymore."

"He did." Rachel nodded. "But he also told me I could sit in on the second round of witness interviews, remember? He just called to tell me when they are."

"Which is?"

"Day after tomorrow. Which means we get a day off from trying to track down Jean Bernard."

"Who's Jean Bernard?"

Too late, Rachel remembered that she hadn't told Alan about their search. She took a breath to prepare herself, but Magda got there first.

"Jean Bernard is the name of a man who was in the reading room on Tuesday and on Wednesday morning," Magda said. She didn't look at Rachel. "The Bibliothèque found his request slips, but he'd left by the time the police arrived, and Boussicault said they haven't been able to find him yet, so Rachel and I thought we'd fill up some time by giving it a try ourselves."

Rachel let her breath out like a balloon expelling air. An explanation that both was true and made the truth sound innocuous. She gave Magda a grateful glance.

Alan looked confused. "Why don't the police just use his address?" He turned to Rachel. "You told me everyone had to register their address when they first use the Bibliothèque, right?"

"They don't have it. In fact, the Bibliothèque can't find his registration at all." She shrugged. "It happens, apparently."

"Jean Bernard?" Alan said the name again, slowly this time. "Some man named Jean Bernard has filled out request slips at the Bibliothèque, but there isn't any record of his registration and the police can't find him?" He frowned, then pulled his cell phone out of his breast pocket and typed into it. After a moment he stopped. He started to laugh.

"What?" Now it was Rachel's turn to be confused.

"Jean Bernard," he said, as if this were an explanation.

"Yes, Jean Bernard. I don't see what's funny. It's a perfectly ordinary French name."

"That's what's so funny." He sobered and explained. "Because my division is International Major Finance, the bank has to be careful that all our transactions are on the up-and-up. One thing they do to ensure that's so is give us a list of the most common French names, the ones people are likely to use if they want an alias that won't be noticed. You know, like Pierre Durand or Jean-Luc Richard. Those totally ordinary names."

He turned his screen to face her, and she squinted enough to read COMMON FRENCH NAMES as a website headline.

"Jean Bernard is the second most common name in France. Someone who didn't want to be found filled out those slips to throw the police off. It's a fake name! I can't believe the police didn't make the connection." He nodded at Rachel. "Now, *Jeanne* Bernard would be a much better alias for you than Susan Vande-whatever."

That's why it sounded so familiar, Rachel realized. It had the same rhythm and half the same sound as Jeanne Martin, that silly fake name Alan had suggested to her. She kicked herself for being so slow on the uptake, then took refuge in the fact that the police hadn't figured it out, either.

"It isn't necessarily a fake name," Magda pointed out. "It could just be that the murderer has a very common name."

"That is true." Alan nodded. "But how likely is it that someone named Jean Bernard would show up at the Bibliothèque only on the day before he killed someone and the day that he killed someone, and that he would pass the time before the murder by filling out some request slips in his own name when he could've just sat in the room and left no indication of being there?"

Well, Rachel thought, *put like that* . . .

But Magda said, "It's not impossible."

This was Magda's go-to answer when she was backed into a corner, Rachel knew. Next she would start quoting Sherlock Holmes about how if it wasn't impossible it was likely, or whatever it was. Now it was her turn to play rescuer.

"But it's more likely that the actual murderer filled out some slips with a very common French name in an effort to distract the police and hopefully keep himself safe." She made her voice soft. "Occam's razor."

For a few long seconds, the *séjour* was silent.

"Okay, maybe we should concentrate our efforts elsewhere." Magda held up a clarifying finger. "Not give up on Jean Bernard, but just delay the search. Until we see what your interviews turn up."

"Very good idea." Rachel slapped her hands on her thighs and stood up swiftly. "Now who wants a drink?"

Chapter Twenty-Four

The interview room at the Vaugirard commissariat did not have one-piece aluminum chairs and tables specifically designed so that enraged suspects couldn't break them and use the pieces as weapons. Nor was it an anonymous carpeted square with a frosted window or poorly disguised two-way mirror set into one wall and a camera on the ceiling to capture all the action. Instead, it looked remarkably like the room in the Bibliothèque Nationale in which Boussicault had conducted the first round of interviews: the walls were white and the furniture consisted of a table with two chairs on one side and one on the other. The only addition to the commissariat's decor was an inoffensive painting of two tall poppies in a glass on the wall behind the two chairs. This was hardly what television had led Rachel to expect, and she felt vaguely disappointed. What was the point of being involved with something in real life if it didn't live up to the expectations raised by make-believe?

Capitaine Boussicault came in, shutting the door behind him. Some of Rachel's disappointment must have shown on her face, because he said, "This room is designed to be both comfortable and neutral. No clocks, no windows, nothing to show the interviewee how much time has passed or what time of day it is. At the same time, a reasonable amount of comfort and even some inoffensive decoration. The idea is that this relaxes them, so they might let their guard down." He smiled. "Let's hope it works."

He sat down next to her and put a *bloc-notes* on the table, flipping it open and flicking through the first few pages until he reached a list. "*Bien*, okay. First I will talk to Professeure Dale, then Professeur Stibb, and finally Docteur Cavill. The mysterious Jean Bernard we are still trying to track down."

Rachel's said nothing. She would tell him the truth about Jean Bernard, she knew, but she wasn't quite ready to do it yet. After the interviews. She just wanted a little more time to feel they were ahead of the police in one small area.

For a moment there was a slightly awkward silence. Then Boussicault stood up and turned to look at the painting. "Inoffensive, isn't it?" He reached behind the lower portion of the frame; suddenly there was a brief, high-pitched whine. He grinned at Rachel's surprise. "In here"—he flicked one of the poppies and the canvas rippled—"are a camera and a microphone, recording everything. That's why we want people to be relaxed. "High-tech, *hein*? We are not the police of Arsène Lupin these days." He grinned again and sat down.

"Now"—he looked at his watch—"are you ready?" Rachel nodded, and he said to the empty room, "Send in Professeure Dale."

* * *

When Boussicault's *brigadier* led her in, Aurora Dale looked much the same as she had in the first interview, only a little more worried. This time she didn't smile at them. She just sat down and settled her bag on the floor next to her. The *capitaine* nodded at the silent Didier, who settled into a chair by the door; Rachel took this as a signal that these interviews were no longer preliminary.

Boussicault tried to set Dale at her ease. How had she been finding Paris since their last interview?

"Hot," Professor Dale said tightly. "But fortunately the reading room is air-conditioned. And where I'm staying is near several cinemas, so I take refuge there in the evenings. Last night I saw a revival of *Rififi*." She looked across the table. "Would you like to see my ticket stub? I saved it because I know the police like that sort of thing."

"That won't be necessary, thank you," Boussicault said. "But I would like to ask you a few questions about events further in the past, if I may."

Dale nodded. She settled more comfortably into her seat.

"Thank you. Could you begin by reminding me how long you've been working in the reading room?"

"I was there for two weeks before that young man's death."

"And had you visited the Bibliothèque before?"

"No." Which put her out of the running for the earlier theft, Rachel thought—before remembering that she could be lying.

"And in the two weeks before Monsieur Morel's death," the *capitaine* continued, "which books did you consult?"

"What, all of them?" Professor Dale looked incredulous. "There were about a hundred. I don't know if I can remember them all."

"Well, just the ones you can remember, then."

At first with some speed and then with an increasing number of pauses, she listed an array of titles. The *capitaine* scribbled on his pad as if he wanted nothing more than to acquire a reading list on early modern French midwifery.

"I see. And during your time there, did you notice Guy Laurent?"

"I'm sorry, who?"

"Guy Laurent. He was working in the reading room during the early portion of your time there."

"Oh, is he the other librarian? The one who died?"

Rachel noted the form of this description, which suggested Dale imagined a natural death—then remembered that that, too, could be a ruse.

Professor Dale, meanwhile, said, "I didn't care for him."

"Why not?"

"There wasn't a particular reason. I just—I found him disquieting. He delivered some of my books, and whenever I saw him coming—" She acted out a shiver. "And he had greasy hair. There's no need for that sort of thing."

Boussicault hid a smile as he noted down this lapse in hygiene, then looked up. "But you never had a conversation? Never ran into each other outside the Bibliothèque?"

"Absolutely not. First, I would have gone out of my way to avoid him. And second, staying in the sixth I never run into anyone from the Bibliothèque."

"You don't remain in the second arrondissement when you finish your day's work?"

"No."

"You and Professeur Stibb and Docteur Cavill never have a drink together after the library closes?"

"No. Just a chat before we go sometimes. One sees the same faces over and over; it would be churlish not to say hello and good-bye."

Boussicault nodded, made another note. "And Monsieur Morel? Did you notice him in your time at the reading room?"

"Only as someone to hand slips to and receive books from. Why?" Professor Dale straightened. "Are the two deaths connected?"

The *capitaine* ignored these questions and sailed smoothly onward. "You never talked about books with Morel?"

"Not beyond saying, 'Thank you for this psalter.'"

Rachel's ears pricked up at the final word; she also noticed that Professor Dale sounded irritated.

Perhaps Boussicault noticed the same, because he changed the subject. "Now I wonder if you could answer a few questions for me about your life in England?"

Dale looked puzzled but said, "Certainly. I'll try."

"When you are in Cambridge, you bank with National Westminster Bank?"

"Yes. They've been my bank for thirty years."

"You have a current account with them, and until five years ago you had a savings account as well?"

"Yes."

"May I ask, what became of the savings account, Professeure?"

"May I ask why you've been prying into my finances?" Dale shot back.

The *capitaine* raised his eyebrows. "I checked into the finances of all the witnesses, madame. I like to be thorough in my investigations."

For the first time, she looked worried. "Then you know I closed it."

"Well, yes." He gave a little laugh, as if she had made a mildly funny joke. "I'd like to know why you closed it."

"I had transferred its balance into my current account, and there didn't seem much point in keeping an empty account open."

"And why did you transfer the balance? It was a sizable amount."

The *capitaine*'s tone remained calm as he asked this question, but Professor Dale had become increasingly tense. Now she snapped, "You can see that I did it over time, in increments. I did it first to pay the death duties on my husband's estate, and then to help with my grandchildren's school fees. It was all aboveboard, I assure you."

"Death duties?" Boussicault looked puzzled. *Droits de succession*, Rachel said silently, reflecting that if he'd kept up the pretense of wanting her help with translation, she could have helped him with the term. But since she was present just as a courtesy to her, she said nothing.

Fortunately, Dale responded. "Yes, taxes. Our house was

in my husband's name—the legacy of nonsensical prefeminist British laws—and that pushed the value of his estate up. I had to use some of my savings to pay tax on the estate, and of course also the expenses of the funeral. And we had promised to help with the school fees, and I wanted to keep that promise. So my savings went."

"And your current account, too," Boussicault observed genially. "I saw that until relatively recently you were running a very large overdraft—one that grew larger every year, in fact."

"Well, if you have very little money and you take not-very-little sums away from it repeatedly, you'll find that it grows into a very large overdraft."

Rachel felt great respect. Obviously taken off guard, plainly angry, clearly discomfited, Professor Dale nonetheless managed to retain both her wits and her power over words. Rachel didn't think she could've managed as well.

Boussicault, however, seemed untroubled by admiration. Unrelentingly affable and unrelentingly calm, he was nonetheless unrelenting. "And then, about a year ago your financial situation began to improve?" He made it a question, but it required no answer. "You started to receive generous payments into the account." He stared at his *bloc-notes* as he threw his last card on the table. "From a London antiquarian bookstore. Peter Harrington."

Professor Dale stayed silent for a very long time. She thinned her lips, then sucked the left side of her lower one between her teeth. At last she said, "Yes."

"Yes, you acknowledge that you received these payments?"

"Yes."

"Would you tell me, please, what they were for?"

Again she thought. Then, "No." The word came out of her thinned mouth like a flat package through a mail slot.

"No?" Boussicault repeated. "No, you won't tell me why you are receiving money from this antiquarian bookseller?"

"No."

"Did you sell him books? Engravings? Illustrations?"

Still Professor Dale said nothing. Rachel wasn't quite sure what was going through her mind. Perhaps fear had made her careful—or perhaps, a voice in Rachel's head murmured, knowledge of her guilt had done it. But certainly she had changed. Now she opened her lips a little wider and said with controlled calm, "I have no desire to discuss my private money matters with you, nor with anyone else. And I have no intention of doing so, either. If you want this conversation to go any further, I demand to be allowed to call the British embassy for assistance."

The room was silent. Then Boussicault raised his eyebrows. "Innocent people don't usually need consular assistance."

"Nonsense!" For a moment Rachel saw how Professor Dale dealt with flawed reasoning, and she was glad she wasn't one of her students. "That's the oldest line in the police book: innocent people don't need lawyers. I should think innocent people need lawyers more than anybody else. I'd have to be mad to sit here blithely answering questions in a foreign country, whose legal system I don't understand, without legal assistance." As if to underline this observation, she picked up her bag from the floor and planted it firmly in her lap.

Boussicault smiled. "I'm not going to steal your *portefeuille*,

Professeure. In fact, now that you have asked for embassy help, I'm not going to do anything except provide you with a telephone number and request that you wait in the commissariat until that help arrives." He rose and opened the door. "If you step outside, my *brigadier* will show you to a telephone."

With dignity worthy of a wronged Edith Sitwell, Professor Dale did just that.

As Didier shut the door behind them, Boussicault exhaled a long rush of exasperated air. Rachel marveled at the range of meaning the French could achieve with breath alone. "Probably her consulate representative will advise her to say nothing, and so that will be that for us. But in the meantime"—he raised his voice—"Professeur Stibb, *s'il vous plait*."

* * *

Like Professor Dale, Homer Stibb looked slightly worried at being called in for a second interview. Unlike her, as soon as he sat at the table he began to complain. "When is all this going to be over? It isn't cheap living in Paris, and my research money will only go so far. I'm already carrying significant debt, and I'd like to get home before I incur more. How soon can I leave?"

If Boussicault was taken aback by this deluge, he didn't show it. He did, however, skip the opening questions he'd used to put Professor Dale at ease, instead moving right to the point. "We already know that you have significant debt, Professeur Stibb. It's exactly this I wish to ask you about."

Stibb crossed his arms and slouched lower in his chair.

"Sure, go ahead." But his jaw made its nervous back-and-forth motion.

Boussicault removed some printed sheets he had tucked into his *bloc-notes.* "You have thirty thousand dollars in education loans."

Professor Stibb nodded.

"You have an outstanding mortgage of ninety-two thousand dollars."

He nodded again, and Rachel saw his arms tense across his chest.

"You have three credit cards, with a total balance of ten thousand dollars."

Homer Stibb's lips rolled and his cheeks moved in and out, as if he were sucking a gobstopper, but his voice was calm. "Did you bring me in here to tell me about a bunch of debts I already know I have? Yes, I owe a lot of money. That's not news to me. Thanks to the American government's decision to keep its future and current academics financially strapped, I had to take out student loans, and it took me years to save up for a down payment on a house. So now I have a high mortgage, and if I want to make any big purchases I have to put them on a credit card."

"And I see these credit cards are also how you pay the fees on your mother's retirement home."

"Community," Stibb corrected. "They're called communities now. Yes, I use the cards to pay the fees."

"Used."

"Excuse me?"

"You said *use*, but I notice that you haven't paid any fee on a card for the last . . . three months. So it should be *used*, really. And in any case, none of them has enough credit left to pay any large fees." He appeared to consult the pages and do some quick mental arithmetic. "Even if you split it between them."

Stibb reddened. "What business of yours are my credit cards? Where did you get that information?"

Exercising his policeman's prerogative once again, Boussicault ignored the second question. "Your credit cards are very much my business, Monsieur Stibb, when I'm dealing with a murder that seems to be linked to theft and blackmail."

"What? What do you mean?" Stibb's face now paled, and his lips tightened. "What theft? My God, I've never blackmailed anyone in my life!"

"Your financial records back you up," Boussicault observed drily.

Stibb winced. "It's been a hard couple of months. I've had to use the credit cards for other things. But I'm managing."

"Ah, you are." Boussicault put down the sheets of paper. "I'm relieved to hear that, because I see from your credit card records that you haven't been managing to pay these retirement community fees." Stibb gave a little jerk, and the *capitaine* gave a little sigh, as if it pained him to admit what he knew.

"Okay." Despite his reaction, Stibb's voice was level, even reasonable. "Look, you know how it is. You have rough patches. I had a rough patch. And my university doesn't pay for travel up front. They reimburse us. So I nearly maxed out my credit cards to pay for this trip, but by the end of the summer I'll get it all back. So I told my mother's place I'd give them a large payment in September. I thought it might get them off my back, and it worked. They agreed to wait, provided I'd make payment in full then, and I promised I would. Then when I pay down the cards I'll hold some back, and I'll pay the community that. It won't be what I promised, but it'll be enough for them to be willing to wait for a little more the next month, and a little more the month after that. I say big, but I pay little; that's how I do it." He leaned forward. "Look, this isn't *The Name of the Rose.* I don't steal medieval manuscripts, and I don't murder people. I'm an overextended academic who teaches French to bored twenty-year-olds and has to connive a little to make ends meet. Who doesn't?"

Where she'd felt respect for Dale's steely reserve, Rachel now admired Homer Stibb's frankness. In might be humiliating to own up to your terrible financial habits, but his willingness to do so looked like it might save him from being a viable suspect in a murder.

But again Boussicault obviously didn't share her admiration. Rachel saw a muscle on the left side of his mouth give a small jump, then another, before he spoke. "What makes you think I suspect you of those things?"

"Oh, come on!" Stibb ran his hand through his curls. "I was contacted Tuesday night and told the police wanted to interview me about a library theft, and when I arrived on Wednesday morning, someone who worked in the reading room was dead. It isn't too hard to put those together. Especially given that literary analysis uses some of the same skills as detection."

"Yes, Professeure Dale made a similar observation at her first interview."

"Did she now." Stibb looked mildly surprised. "Well, I may have made the point to her while we were waiting to talk to you."

Rachel saw the muscle in Boussicault's cheek twitch once again. Finally he stood up. "You may go, Professeur Stibb. But don't leave Paris until we tell you it's all right to do so." He waited a moment, then added, "The prefecture of police can cover your expenditures, if that becomes necessary."

As the door closed behind Stibb and the *brigadier*, the *capitaine* sat back down. For a moment he rested his fingers lightly on the spot where his muscle had jumped. Then he said, "These people have seen too many films. Or watched too much television. This was all easier when the police were more mysterious."

Rachel wasn't sure if by *this* he meant investigating, interviewing suspects, or simply having the upper hand in any scenario, but she thought she understood how he felt. They had been in this room for—she checked her watch—over an hour, and all they had to show for it was the obduracy of one academic and the rudeness of another.

"This man," Boussicault went on. "One step further and he would be *un escroc*. He tells us how he has managed in the past as if that's an indication of how he is managing now, but that is a false equivalency. And *la bonne professeure*, she saves her ticket stub as if going to the cinema proves she isn't a murderer, while she refuses to explain the behavior that makes her look good for the crime!"

"But doesn't that suggest that they're innocent? I mean, wouldn't a murderer try harder *not* to suggest any reason for suspicion?"

The *capitaine* frowned and stared at the floor for a minute. Then he shook his head hard and looked up.

"Well, there is still Monsieur Cavill. Let us see what he has to say for himself." Once again he spoke to the air: "Please send in Docteur Cavill."

Chapter Twenty-Five

There were some words and phrases, Rachel knew, that were impossible to understand until you saw them in action: *wuss out*, *chillax*, the true meaning of *that sucks*. When Robert Cavill entered the interview room, she realized that until that moment she'd never really grasped the meaning of *flop sweat*. Cavill's face gleamed with a clammy perspiration, and Rachel could smell the fear coming off him. As he sat down, he tried for a smile, but it was a poor half-born thing.

"*Bonjour*, Docteur." The *capitaine* waited until Cavill settled himself in the chair. "How have you been enjoying Paris since we last saw you?"

"How do you think?" Cavill spoke sulkily. Like many men, he made his fear take refuge in belligerence. "A man was killed meters away from where I work, I saw the murderer entering the murder site, and I've been told not to leave town. It hardly makes for an enjoyable stay."

"But you've still been using the reading room."

"Yes, well, work is the best distraction, my father always said."

"An interesting expression." The *capitaine* made a note. "What do you need distraction from in this case?"

Cavill's face flooded with red. "Oh, I don't know. A violent death that I might be accused of causing? In a country where I don't speak the language fluently and where I don't know anyone? Which of those do you think might preoccupy me?"

"If you have done nothing wrong, you have nothing to fear," Boussicault said.

Cavill snorted—apparently Professor Dale wasn't the only one too smart to fall for that, Rachel thought—but the *capitaine* continued as if he hadn't heard.

"Now, I wonder if you could once more lead me through your memories of the morning of Monsieur Morel's death."

For the next five minutes, Cavill repeated the story he had told them the week before. Rachel could see him begin to breathe evenly, and when he wiped his face with his handkerchief in the middle of his recitation, no more sweat appeared.

"Thank you." Boussicault turned a leaf of his *bloc-notes* and gave Cavill a small smile. "Now, if you don't mind, I'd like to ask you some questions about yourself."

Cavill looked surprised but said, "All right."

"You have three children, is that correct?"

"Yes."

"And they go to the . . ." Boussicault pretended to look at his notes. "The Perse School, yes?"

Cavill nodded.

"And this is a fee-paying school."

He nodded again.

"And you also have a mortgage."

"Yes."

Having let Cavill calm himself by retelling his story and regain his confidence by answering some factual questions, Boussicault now made his move. "Churchill College must help you with these expenses, yes? Even here in France we hear how rich Cambridge University is, how it pays its lecturers' mortgages . . ."

Cavill stared at the tabletop. He took several huffing breaths, clenched his jaw, then loosened it. He looked up. "I want to confess."

Rachel couldn't believe it. Just like that? She ground her teeth, cursing Magda's absence: she was missing the best bit!

"Ah," said Boussicault. "Well."

"Yes." Robert Cavill nodded his head a few times. "Yes. I lied to you. I'm not who you think I am. I don't work at Cambridge. I work at a university called Anglia Ruskin—it is *in* Cambridge."

What? All that lead-up and his "confession" was just to something they already knew? Rachel was outraged.

"Yes." Boussicault sounded reflective. "We knew that. We already discovered that Anglia Ruskin University is your actual employer."

Rachel looked at his smooth face. He had known Cavill wasn't confessing to the murder; he'd just let him go on because relief would lower his defenses.

Now Boussicault said, "But if you don't work at Cambridge, all your expenses must leave you in a great deal of debt."

"Presumably you know they do." Cavill was sullen.

"I do." Boussicault was almost apologetic. "And I also know that you are a world expert on medieval illustration and iconography."

"Yes." They were back to monosyllables.

"Which would mean that you know the values of many medieval woodcuts."

"Ye—" Cavill caught himself. "I mean no. I mean yes, I would know the value, but I would never take one. Never. Illustrations are an integral textual element. And aside from anything else, it's very difficult to separate medieval paper. It has a very high rag content. You'd need a very sharp blade."

"You've given it some thought." Rachel couldn't help feeling that, robbed of Professor Dale and Professor Stibb, Capitaine Boussicault was lingering over Dr. Cavill.

"I haven't—or rather, yes, I have, but only now, here."

"I called the Cambridge University Library," Boussicault said suddenly.

Rachel started.

"They told me that a number of items have gone missing over the last two years or so. When I gave them your name and asked if you had used their special collections in that time, they very kindly checked for me. And it turns out you had."

He steepled his fingers, resting his lips against them as he watched Cavill's face. Rachel marveled. Was Boussicault telling the truth? Docteure Dwamena had said libraries didn't like to admit to theft. Would Cambridge really give such information to an unknown foreign policeman?

Apparently Robert Cavill believed they would, because,

after being shocked into silence for a moment, he became almost hysterical. “No! I am not a thief! I would never harm a book! I admit it, I live beyond my means.” His voice was high and thin. “I want to have the life I deserve, and I want my children to have the right sort of education. I confess all that, and that I'm swimming in debt to get it. But I don't confess . . . I don't confess . . .” He took a gasping breath, and as he let it out, he suddenly burst into tears. “I didn't steal from any library, and I didn't *kill that man*! I'm not a murderer, and I'm not a thief!” He buried his face in his hands.

Boussicault waited. If there was one thing Rachel had learned from this afternoon, it was that a good detective cultivated an almost zenlike calm. She'd have to start yoga again.

After a few moments, Cavill stopped crying, wiped his face, and smoothed his hair, breathing deeply. At last he said, “I know my rights. I'm leaving, and I'm going to contact my embassy. You can deal with *them*.” He stood and took his sport coat from the back of the chair. It was tweed, Rachel saw, a ridiculous English weave much too heavy for the current weather. It sagged open as he shrugged it on, revealing its lining, and she noticed a small shape pressing against the brown satin. As she watched, the shape fell forward a little.

“What's that?” She hadn't meant to say it aloud, but she spoke without thinking.

“What's what?” Cavill was settling the jacket on his shoulders; Boussicault was looking at her.

“What's that in the lining of your jacket?”

“There's nothing in the lining of my jacket. This jacket is

from Ede and Ravenscroft. I assure you it has nothing wrong with its lining."

Rachel didn't know who Ede and Ravenscroft were, but they didn't sound like the sort of place where a man swimming in debt should be buying his clothing, and they also pretty clearly didn't make their clothing as well as Robert Cavill thought, because she knew she had seen something in the lining. She met Boussicault's eyes.

"Monsieur Cavill, may I see your jacket, please?" The *capitaine* held out a hand.

"Certainly not! I've spent hours in here being interrogated by you, ending in a very unpleasant scene, and you've been able to prove nothing. And now you want me to hand over a piece of my clothing? Absolutely not."

"I'm afraid I must insist. If you don't feel able to hand it over to me yourself, I can call some officers to help you."

It was a standoff, and Cavill lost. He stood still for a moment and then, with a sigh clearly meant to indicate his contempt for the whole scene, shrugged off his sport coat. As he did so, Rachel saw that his shirt cuffs were monogrammed. She suddenly felt enormously sad.

Taking the jacket, Boussicault slowly turned it inside out and ran his hands over the front lining. One of his fingers snagged on something: a horizontal slash near the breast pocket, about three inches long. He looked at Cavill.

"I've no idea what that is." Cavill's face was growing red again. "Or where it came from. I must have ripped the lining somehow."

The slash was very clean, Rachel could see. It certainly wasn't an accidental rip. It looked more as if it had been made with a sharp blade. Boussicault inserted his thumb and forefinger into the gap it left, his other hand lifting the remainder of the jacket so that the bottom eventually met his grasp. Rachel could see his fingers grope, then grope again. They pinched something. He let the bottom of the jacket fall and drew out his fingers. Between them was a piece of paper. It had been folded so it was perhaps one inch square, but the folds weren't tight. They had bulged and separated, and it was this that had made the shape noticeable against the lining.

Boussicault put the jacket down, placed the paper on the table, reached into his own breast pocket for a pair of tweezers, and began to unfold it. After what felt like an age but could only have been about thirty seconds, it lay open before them.

It was very old, and all four of its margins were filled with elaborate patterns of curling stems and fleurs-de-lis, with what looked to Rachel like a disembodied angelic head at the center bottom. In the middle of the page was a woodcut of a man bending over another man, who appeared to be fast asleep. Out of the side of the sleeping man the bending man was lifting a tiny woman. After a moment, Rachel recognized it as a picture of the creation of Eve. After another moment, she realized it was the missing page from the *Supplementum Chronicarum*.

She didn't say anything.

Boussicault didn't say anything.

Robert Cavill said, "No. No. No, no, no. I have no idea how that got there. I had nothing to do with it. I would never steal. I would never deface a book. Someone planted it. Someone must have planted it . . ."

The room became silent. Then Boussicault looked up from where the page lay on the table.

"Robert Cavill," he said, "I am detaining you on suspicion of the *délit* of theft, and on suspicion of the crime of murder against Giles Morel on thirtieth July, as well as suspicion of the crime of murder against Guy Laurent on sixth July. You have the right to answer questions, make statements, or remain silent. You have the right to an interpreter, if you need one. You have the right to an attorney and the right to notify your embassy, or to have us notify them for you . . ."

Chapter Twenty-Six

Rachel sat alone in the timeless, airless interview room. Once he had charged him, Boussicault had left with Cavill, taking the young *brigadier* with him and saying to Rachel only, "Wait here." So she waited. She had been required to leave her bag at reception ("to ensure no interviews are recorded," the young *gardien* at the desk had explained apologetically), so there was no way to message Magda about developments, to look up French arrest procedures, or even to play a game.

After fifteen minutes the *capitaine* had not returned. Nor had he returned after twenty minutes. After half an hour Rachel opened the door and poked her head out. The only person in the hallway was a harassed-looking woman frowning at a clipboard as she walked swiftly past Rachel.

"*Excusez-moi*?" The woman stopped. "I was helping Capitaine Denis Boussicault to interview suspects, and he told me to wait here. Do you know when he'll come back?"

The woman transferred her frown from the clipboard to Rachel. "Boussicault is in booking."

"Do you know how long he'll be?"

She shrugged. "Booking is like purgatory: no one knows how long anyone will be there."

Rachel admired her turn of phrase, but she still wanted to know how long she was supposed to wait. "Well, I've been waiting here for half an hour, and this is a lot like purgatory, too. Could someone go ask Boussicault what I should do?"

"No one goes to talk to the arresting officer when he's in booking." But she thought for a second. "*D'acc.* Come with me."

She led Rachel through the corridors, then the familiar maze of desks, and at last deposited her in Boussicault's aquarium office. "I'm sure he won't be long." She gestured to one of the chairs in front of the desk. "Have a seat."

Rachel sat. The minutes passed. Gradually her bored gaze focused on the piles on Boussicault's desk, then on the specific pile where he'd placed their sheet of notebook paper in its plastic protector almost two weeks before. Was it still there? She could see a little corner of plastic sticking out midway down the pile. *Seriously? Hasn't he even made use of our discovery?* She slid her eyes left, to the desks outside; no one seemed to be watching her. Half standing, she leaned forward to ease the plastic further out of the pile. In this awkward position her gaze fell on the folder on top of the pile. Its label said Fournier.

There was no question of making a choice. She slid the folder toward her with her index finger and then, angling her body away from the window, opened it in her lap. The top sheet inside was a form headed Interview Transcript Summary. She kept reading.

Difficult interview, began the typed paragraphs beneath.

LF both belligerent and in some degree of shock. Stated that she had intended to arrive early on 29 July to "catch up on work," but due to commuting issue arrived at BN only fifteen minutes before opening. Left travel card @home: used cash for bus. Entered via employee lounge, placed personal items in assigned locker, proceeded to record room. Only five minutes remaining before BN opened, so proceeded to reading room via stacks. [LF crying.] Found Morel facedown. Blood clearly present. "Lost control."

Further questioning: Stated she does not carry a knife, or any weapon. Did carry one, but stopped due to therapy. "Why don't you ask my therapist if you don't believe me?" Found Morel "like a puppy. More irritating than threatening." Voluntarily added that she is "More than able to defend myself against any man, inside a library or out."

Refused to answer further questions. Demanded a lawyer.

A few lines below, where the form offered the options Accusé / Non accusé, the interviewer had circled Non accusé. But beneath that someone—Boussicault, she assumed—had written in script that somehow seemed to telegraph irritation, Aussi non exclue.

Not charged, but also not ruled out. Rachel had to agree that that was about the size of it. She didn't blame the second writer for being peeved. There was just as much in the summary to raise doubts as to allay them. A suspect alleges she no longer carries a knife but is antagonistic about it; a suspect says she didn't consider the victim an antagonist, then asserts that in any case she's more than a match for any antagonist, then demands a lawyer. You didn't have to be a criminal mastermind or an ace detective to see how all this sowed confusion—nor to see how this confusion might let a murderer slip free.

Was the interview transcript itself any more helpful? Still mindful of the rows of police behind her and aware that Boussicault could return at any second, she flipped through it.

> *LF: I forgot my Navigo. I used cash. LF: We had been friends. We were not anymore. LF: It did affect me, yes. But it doesn't anymore. LF: I know how to take care of myself if I need to.*

At this last remark Rachel groaned softly and closed the folder.

She looked at her watch. It had been over an hour since Boussicault had abandoned her in the interview room. By anyone's reckoning that was a long time to wait. No one would be suspicious if she left. As she walked through the halls to reception, she repeated the contradictory substance of what she'd read over and over in her mind until it became matched to the rhythm of her footsteps: *no knife, lost control, puppy dog, clammed up.*

"Could I have my bag?" There was a different *gardien* at the desk. "I was with Boussicault," she explained, "and I had to leave my bag at reception. Rachel Levis." He unlocked the bottom drawer of the desk, checked for ID to confirm her identity, then handed her the bag. "Thank you." She took the notebook and a pen out and wrote on a page, I WAITED AN HOUR. YOU CAN REACH ME AT HOME. Not, she suspected, that he would try to reach her. She ripped the sheet out, folded it in half, wrote CAPITAINE BOUSSICAULT on it, and handed it to the *gardien*. "Please give this to him when he becomes available." And with that she left the commissariat and headed home, her feet still drumming out what she'd discovered. She needed to talk to Magda as soon as she could.

Chapter Twenty-Seven

"What about the saliva?"

"What about the saliva in relation to what?"

Magda thought. "In relation to anything, I guess. Was it mentioned at all?"

Rachel shook her head. "Once Boussicault found the woodcut, he didn't say anything to Cavill besides the charge. And Cavill didn't say anything else before they took him away. As for LouLou, that interview was before they knew about the saliva, remember?"

"Oh, yeah. Goddammit. Well, what do you think?"

"About what?"

Magda thought again. "About Cavill, to start with. Do you think he's the murderer?"

"Well, they caught him. Red-coated, as it were."

"Yes, they found a piece of evidence on him, and they arrested him. But do you think he *did* it?"

Rachel bit her lip. She'd been thinking about this on the Mètro over. She didn't like Cavill's pretensions, and she'd seen evidence found on him with her own eyes. But without that piece of evidence, Dale and Stibb had just as much motive. And LouLou . . .

"I just think other people have motives, too. Maybe better ones."

"Such as LouLou."

"Yes, such as LouLou. But I—"

Magda held up a hand. "Do you remember Dr. Gilbert?"

"Yes." Dr. Gilbert had been Rachel's freshman writing instructor.

"Remember the time you went to see her about your gun control paper? And she said to you, 'Rachel, every time you don't like something—' "

Rachel chimed in from bitter memory, " 'You say it's stupid.' Yeah, yeah."

"Well, I think you're doing that now. Yes, LouLou's had a shit time. Yes, you really don't want it to be her. Yes, sisterhood is powerful. But still . . . Just because you don't like it, that doesn't mean it's a dumb idea. You have to acknowledge that it *could be* her."

Rachel looked into her friend's kind but firm face. Magda was right. Dr. Gilbert had been right, and Magda was right. The last time they'd solved a crime, she'd refused to entertain certain suspects until very late, and because of that she'd missed an important clue. Okay.

"Okay. All right." She took a huge breath, focusing. "Well, we already said LouLou could be the book thief. She could have killed Laurent and Morel because they were interfering with business." She stopped, frowning. "But why one with string and one with a knife? And why one in a men's room and the other in the stacks?"

"Those are fair questions." Magda thought for a second. "Maybe just because that's what was available. Think about it. Laurent takes her to Chez Poule to discuss the blackmail—he certainly wouldn't want to have that talk in the library—and she's enraged. Plus, she's already angry at him for destroying her, as Doctor Dwamena put it. He goes to the men's room; she finds a bit of old string she's left in her bag, follows him in, and does him. Then she starts carrying the knife again because she's paranoid she'll be found out. Or maybe she never stopped. We only have her word for it that she did. And a couple of weeks later when Giles accosts her in the stacks because *he's* found out about the thefts—" She made the sound of a blade ripping through skin.

Rachel thought about it. She really did. But, "Old string she left in her bag?"

Magda made a face. "Is that really more improbable than a hitherto-nonviolent academic suddenly killing two people?"

Rachel tried again. But again, "Frankly, yes. Not least because that academic is male. And so is another, who also owes a huge amount of money. If we're looking for good suspects, either of them would be much more able to commit a murder *in a men's room.*"

"I don't know about that. Boussicault said the restaurant was so busy that no one remembered seeing Laurent, right? And he was a *regular*! Who's going to remember seeing an anonymous woman disappear into the hallway that leads to the bathrooms? And if it was crowded, she could easily have managed to slip into the men's room unnoticed, too. Especially because she's so tall. People could just have dismissed her as a man with long hair."

"All right, but then why not Professor Dale? Who is also tall, and who has actual heavy debt and actual suspicious financial activity rather than imaginary thefts and love rage."

Silence. Rachel had to admit that Magda had made good points in the end, and judging from the look on Magda's face, she guessed Magda was thinking the same about her. They were at an impasse.

Except that with Magda around, you were never at an impasse. "Now," she said, "what I take from all that is that everybody's plausible. There's only hard evidence against Cavill, right?"

"Right."

"And you said the page Boussicault found was from the *Supplementum*, right?"

"Yes."

"Well, wouldn't the murderer have the other page, too? Wouldn't they have both illustrations?"

Rachel thought. "Yes, I guess so. But so what?"

"So the easiest way to find out if Cavill's really the best suspect is to find out if he also has the page from the psalter."

"That's true." Rachel was still confused. "But it's irrelevant, since we don't have any way to find out."

"Yes, we do."

"No, we don't. Not without getting inside his hotel room."

"Exactly." Magda crossed her arms.

"Exactly?"

"Yes."

"By which you mean, 'Exactly, leaving aside the fact that we don't know his hotel or his room number.'"

"We do know his hotel and room number. He told you in the interview, and you wrote it down. You said so."

Rachel didn't relish the idea of showing up at Cavill's hotel and trying to talk their way into his room. Experience had shown her that even regular civilians were suspicious of strangers with questions. Surely hotel employees, who had seen and experienced so much more, would be even more so. It was not a scenario that would end well.

"I threw that page away," she said hopefully.

"No, you didn't. You would never throw away something you thought might be useful later."

"It was in my skirt pocket when Alan put it through the wash."

"No, it wasn't. You check all your pockets when you get undressed."

Not for the first time, Rachel became aware of the downside of having a long-term best friend. "Anyway, it doesn't matter if I have the address, because we can't get inside his room. They're not going to let us in without seeing some sort of official identification."

"They don't have to let us into his room."

"Yes, they do."

Magda looked hard at her. "No, they don't. We can get in on our own."

"No we—" Then understanding dawned. "You want me to pick the lock."

Magda nodded.

"No. No way. I only did it that one time. I don't even remember how to do it anymore."

"Sure you do! It's like riding a bicycle: you never really forget."

"An *illegal* bicycle. An illegal bicycle that someone could easily catch you riding."

Magda waved that away. "We'll do a quick in and out, just check for the page and leave. No one will have time to catch us."

"And what if they have key card locks? Most hotels do now."

"Then we'll leave even sooner. It'll be a quick in and out of the hotel instead of the room."

Rachel wondered why she bothered to try. Magda's determination was nothing if not adaptable, and Rachel had long ago learned it was best just to do what she wanted. But breaking into a hotel room wasn't like buying a new dress, or even like picking the lock on an abandoned studio apartment, as she had the last time. A hotel was a business; a hotel would prosecute.

She weighed the options again. If she didn't do what Magda wanted, Cavill would remain the prime suspect, which meant LouLou wouldn't be. On the other hand, there *was* something odd about Cavill's having the woodcut in his jacket like that, which meant that if she didn't do what Magda wanted, an innocent man might go to prison. And Magda had a point about the simplicity of the test. If they could get into the hotel unnoticed, if she could still pick a lock, and if they were quick, they might just be able to search Cavill's room and see what was or wasn't there. That was a lot of ifs, but the result would allay her doubts, and that was nearly worth it. Plus, she couldn't help thinking, the whole operation would put them ahead of the police. She would have something to bring to Boussicault to show that she knew how to be a detective, that she had a use beyond spying and occasional note-taking.

"All right. But give me a couple of hours to refresh my memory."

Chapter Twenty-Eight

The Hotel Etoiles was firmly a two-star hotel. It expressed its rating not in its furniture—the lobby had a very comfortable-looking faux-leather sofa—nor in its amenities—a sign behind the reception desk confirmed that every room had a private bathroom and that the continental breakfast offered yogurt, fruit, and cheese as well as croissants and rolls and butter—but in its general air. The hotel gave off the sense of having once aimed for three stars, perhaps even four, but then found all the effort too wearying. Now the carpeting at reception was just a little too worn, the framed reproductions on the walls just a little too ordinary. Without being in any way inadequate, the hotel nonetheless breathed its two-star-ness.

Fortunately, its two-star status also meant that Rachel needn't have worried: the receptionist wasn't particularly curious about the two women who appeared at his counter. When she and Magda explained that they were going to visit a friend who was staying there, he just smiled and turned back to his computer screen.

A brief elevator ride and they were on the second floor. Room 209 was the first door on the right. "Oh, no," Magda said.

Rachel followed her gaze: the door had a key card lock. Her throat tightened. "Shit," Magda said. "I was really hoping—"

Rachel tried to sound nonchalant. "Don't worry." "I checked this out while I was on YouTube. Apparently there's nothing to it." She looked left, then right; a housekeeping cart stood midway down the hallway, but its housekeeper was nowhere in sight. She dug into her bag and brought out her wallet. Opening it, she slipped her Monoprix supermarket loyalty card from its slot.

She saw that her hands were trembling. She'd prepared, but that didn't mean she had any confidence. She gave herself a silent pep talk.

Focus. Pay attention to the lock. Respect the lock, and the lock will respect you.

She had no idea what that meant, but it calmed her.

She slid the card between the door and the frame, next to the key plate. She wiggled it. She couldn't feel anything. She tried again, higher, still with no success. She remembered all the things the man in the video had said: *This only works with a slanted latch. If you shove too hard, the card will just bend.* It had worked for him after forty-seven seconds, but he had said he was a former thief.

"How many seconds has it been?" she whispered to Magda. Then her card knocked against something solid. The bolt! She wiggled the card, felt it angle against the side of the metal—it *was* a slanted latch!—then felt it slide between the bolt and the frame. She pushed it farther in, then farther, then turned the handle. The door swung open.

"Holy crap." Magda's eyes were wide.

Rachel said, "The police should really shut down YouTube." But there was no time for bravado, or even for relief. Dropping the battered card back into her bag, she stepped over the threshold.

The room was a square box with off-white walls. A writing surface had been suspended from the wall that faced them, jutting out about a foot and a half, with two small drawers attached to its underside and a chair in front of it. There was a double bed, unmade, in the middle of the right-hand wall, a sconce on each side of it to act as bedside lamps. The bedsheets were white; the carpet and the bedspread were a shade that Rachel thought decorators might call "Juiced Tangerine" or "Bold Persimmon" but that she suspected was just orange. Sleeping in that bed must be like sleeping inside a Creamsicle.

"Close the door." Magda's voice broke into her thoughts. "I'll take the desk."

This left the bed and, Rachel saw once she'd closed the door, a wardrobe. She checked the bed first, running her hands under the disarranged sheets to see if anything was hidden there, then shoving her arms as far in as she could under each side of the mattress until they touched the center. Nothing.

"Anything?" she asked. Magda shook her head. "Let's try the wardrobe."

They opened the right-hand door to a row of five hanging shirts and a single jacket, mauve linen. Magda quickly slipped the jacket off its hanger and began to examine its lining, while

Rachel riffled through the shirts. They all had monogrammed cuffs, she noticed. She finished with them and reached up to the shelf where the trousers lay: three pairs of folded chinos that she unfolded and searched, then refolded and put back. She turned to Magda, who was placing the jacket back on its hanger. They looked at each other and shook their heads.

"You do the bathroom." Magda put the jacket back in the wardrobe. "I'll finish here." She opened the left-hand door and started searching the shelves that held Cavill's socks and underwear.

The bathroom was as minimalist as the bedroom, if not as colorful. The tiled counter next to the sink held Cavill's toothbrush and toothpaste, an electric razor, aerosol deodorant, a bottle of aftershave, and a jar of face cream. Unable to resist, she opened the aftershave. A wave of sandalwood and spices rushed out, and she inhaled deeply before recapping it; she loved the smell of men's colognes. She checked behind the toilet tank and then, in what she considered an inspired move, knocked on the bathtub panel to see if it was loose. But it wasn't, and since there was no cabinet under the sink, there was nowhere else to search.

She came out to find Magda hopping down off the chair after having checked the top of the wardrobe. "Anything?" Her friend made a face. "Me neither. Which I guess just leaves under the bed."

Each of them took a side of the rickety bed frame and flattened herself onto the carpet to look under it. There was dust, there was an old Band-Aid wrapper, but there was no page from an illuminated psalter. They stood. Just as Rachel raised her hands to brush herself down, there was a knock on the door and a slightly muffled voice said, "*Femme de chambre.*"

Housekeeping. "Get under," she said to Magda, grabbing her bag.

"What?"

"Get under the bed."

Magda was horrified. "I'm not getting under there. You saw it. It's filthy."

"Then get in the wardrobe."

"The wardrobe is eighteen inches deep!" Magda looked down at her breasts. "I'll never fit."

The housekeeper's key card hissed in the lock. "Listen, Raquel Welch," Rachel snapped, "if you don't want to get caught in here, it's either the bed or the wardrobe, and you better make up your mind fast." She dropped to her knees and wriggled under the bed. After a second, Magda joined her.

A foot propped open the door with a rolled towel; then it and its mate walked toward the bathroom. The carpet under the bed was stiff, and the mattress above gave off the oily smell of countless sleeping bodies. As the sound of a spray bottle followed by faucets turned on full blast reached Rachel's ears, she focused minutely on the shag before her eyes. Maybe Cavill had left some tiny clue after all. But there was nothing.

The feet left the bathroom and a vacuum cleaner started up. She saw its wand and brush pass over the carpet, followed by the feet. They all moved around the bed and back. Then the wand was repositioned and the brush came under the bed. It prodded Rachel's side. It retreated, then prodded it again.

There was no escape; she couldn't move with Magda on the other side of her. The brush prodded her a third time, harder—not so much a prod as a jab, really, she reflected. The vacuum cleaner shut off, and Magda and Rachel just had time to exchange a dismayed glance before first some knees and then a face appeared next to them.

"*Bonjour*," Rachel said, with all the dignity that a woman lying prone under a cheap hotel bed could muster.

The face opened its mouth and let out a yelp, then disappeared. Not a scream, but a yelp, Rachel noted. Somehow that seemed more hopeful. She wriggled out from under the bed. When she clambered to her feet, she found the woman who owned the face across from her, brandishing the wand and brush like a sword.

"*Non, non*." Rachel held out a hand. "*Ça va*." On the opposite side of the bed, Magda had emerged. "It's okay. We are—we are hotel inspectors." When the woman looked understandably dubious, she added, "Secret hotel inspectors. Checking up on hotel cleaners secretly. You did very well." When the woman still didn't lower the brush, she once more groped in her bag for her wallet, where her Bibliothèque ID card rested in the plastic compartment on the front. She flashed it at the woman fast, so she might only notice that it was official and not where it was officially from. "See?"

The brush wavered, but the woman didn't put it down. Despite seeming more unsure, she still looked determined. Rachel opened the wallet's bill compartment and took out all the cash. She had no idea how much was there, but she glimpsed a couple of twenties amid the other bills. She held it all out. The woman hesitated, then lowered the wand and took it.

"Thank you for your understanding." Rachel backed toward the door. "I know the situation is unusual, but we like to be thorough." She reached the doorway, Magda next to her. "And we might be back for further inspections, so we appreciate your silence."

* * *

Once they were halfway down the block, she took a huge breath. It was only three in the afternoon, yet she felt as if she were at the end of a week of hard labor. How did detectives deal with the tension? You never saw Sam Spade take a spa day. "Let's not do that again. Ever."

"But it worked," Magda pointed out.

Rachel wasn't so sure. She doubted that forty-odd euros was enough to buy anyone's silence for long. Nonetheless, they were walking freely down the street, they hadn't found the page from the psalter, and she wasn't going to argue with that. "Let's go through the Jardin du Luxembourg on the way to my place," she said as they stepped into their Mètro car. "I could use it."

"You've earned it."

She really had, Rachel reflected. In the space of the last hour she'd successfully hacked a key card lock, completed an exonerating search, and talked and paid her way out of a tough situation. Her best friend might have flash, and her husband might have logic, but at least at this moment she wasn't doing too badly, either.

Chapter Twenty-Nine

They had come up the escalator at the Luxembourg stop and were waiting to cross the Boulevard Saint-Michel when Rachel clutched Magda's arm. "Look!"

"What?"

"It's Aurora Dale!"

"Where? Which one?"

Rachel remembered that Magda had never seen Professor Dale. "Over there. By the entrance to the Jardin. The tall one with the gray hair. Wearing linen." She stretched her neck and gestured forward with her chin, trying to point without using her finger. "Red cross-body bag."

"Got her."

As the two of them watched, Dale walked around the perimeter of the Jardin du Luxembourg and crossed at the corner of the Rue de Médicis. She walked past Café Le Rostand on the corner and the café next to that, then stopped to peer in the window of the café next to that.

"What is she doing here?" Magda muttered.

"She lives at the Auberge des Jeunesses, remember? This is her neighborhood."

"No." Magda charged across the Boulevard as the light finally changed. "I meant right now. As in, what is she doing, in this moment?"

Rachel had no time to guess, because Dale had peeled away from the café window and continued on. She stopped at the blue front of the Libraries des Editeurs for a moment, then moved next door to the gray-green front of Editions du Boccard before walking briskly past the residential doors that followed.

"She's looking for a store," Rachel said. "She's trying to find a particular store." It was like playing charades with real life, she thought. Dale paused for a second in front of the shuttered Librairie Fata Libelli, then hurried past the garden store next to it. "She's looking for a bookstore!"

They continued to follow from the opposite side of the street. Rachel consulted her mental map of the Rue de Médicis. It took her only a few seconds to make the connection: "She's going to Bonnefoi!" She had been in Bonnefoi Librairie many times, yearning after the beautiful antiquarian books and drawings they sold.

Sure enough, at that moment Professor Dale paused in front of the storefront that said LIVRES ANCIENS: BONNEFOI. She stood for a moment, then pulled open the door and went in. They could just see her walk slowly around the interior, looking at the shelves, before disappearing into the store's shuttered second room where, Rachel knew, they kept the rarest volumes protected from the sun. Both women groaned as they lost sight of her.

Rachel poked Magda with her elbow. "You'll have to go in."

"Me?" Magda stared at her. "You're the one that knows about old books."

"Yes, but she knows who I am. She's never seen you."

This was inarguable. Anyway, Rachel thought, Magda didn't really want to argue; that was clear from the way she darted across the street. Just like Professor Dale, she paused in front of Bonnefoi's door for a moment—gathering her strength, Rachel guessed—then went in. Again just like Dale, she browsed for a few moments before turning and crossing into the other room.

Sixty seconds later she came out. She ran across the street and started walking, gesturing at Rachel to follow.

"What's going on?" Rachel speed-walked behind her. "What happened?"

Magda didn't pause, but she half turned her head and spoke over her shoulder. "When I went into the room with the shutters, the man behind the counter was telling her that the buyer had stepped out, but she would be back in five minutes. And she said, 'I'll wait. I have some items I think she'd find very interesting.'"

Rachel gave a squeak.

"I know!" Magda gulped a breath. "And then he asked about the condition of the bindings—I didn't really understand that—and she said well, some were just individual engravings . . ."

Rachel squeaked again.

"Wait, wait. Because then I heard something unzipping and she said, 'I've brought a list'!" Magda ended the sentence on an excited yelp.

But Rachel had stopped walking. "And so you *left*?"

"Well, I couldn't read the list, could I? Also—" She pulled Rachel to the crossing at the Boulevard Saint-Michel, then stood there, gasping, while they waited for the light to change. "It came to me that if she was in a bookstore discussing a list, she wasn't going to be in her room at the Auberge des Jeunesses, which is *right up the street*." The light changed, and she and her wave of enthusiasm carried Rachel across the boulevard. "While she's talking to the book buyer, we could be scoping out where she lives."

"We can't get into the Auberge des Jeunesses," Rachel said.

"We got into Robert Cavill's hotel."

"Because it was a two-star hotel with a lazy receptionist! But the Auberge is a hostel for large groups of college students. They're going to be a lot more careful about allowing random people to wander their halls."

Magda put a finger to her lips. "I have a plan."

Behind the reception desk at the Auberge des Jeunesses was a young woman resplendent in a kente cloth head wrap tied in a huge bow. She looked up from her book as they entered the foyer, then put it down as they came to stand in front of her. Rachel caught a glimpse of its cover, on which a man with a broad naked chest gripped a young woman whose blonde hair streamed down her back.

"*Bonjour*." Although Magda was speaking French, Rachel noticed she had broadened her American accent. "I apologize for interrupting you. But I'm visiting Paris for the first time in years, and I stayed here when I came last time. I was on a summer program, and I was only twenty, but this is where I met my husband. If you can believe it!" She gave a little laugh, as if marveling at this extraordinary occurrence. The young woman looked interested. "Now we've been married for twenty-three years, and there's never a day that we don't talk about how we first met in the City of Love."

Rachel realized that Magda had seen the book cover, too.

"This is our first trip back," Magda continued, "and I've spent twenty years telling my friend here about this place, and about how Jack and I met. I'd love to show her the hall I lived on. Would that be all right?"

The young woman said, "We're not allowed—"

"Oh, no, I understand! But we'll be quick, I promise. Only five minutes. Just to show her my hallway and the terrace where Jack first told me he loved me."

"We've been told not to let strangers—" The woman looked down at her book and back up. She was clearly torn. "Your husband really told you he loved you on our terrace?"

"Oh, yes. I remember because there was a full moon, and we could just see the Eiffel Tower." Rachel worried that Magda might be laying it on a bit too thick, and as if she'd come to the same conclusion, Magda's hand went to her bag. "I could leave you my wallet. It has ID in it. Would that help?"

The woman started to reach out her hand, then changed her mind and touched the edge of her headdress, frowning again. Finally she said, "Five minutes. Any more and I could get in trouble." She picked up a pen. "And what is your name?"

"Bernard." Magda took her hand out of her bag. "Jeannie Bernard. Thank you so much. You have no idea what this means to me!" She pressed the elevator call button.

When the doors had shut completely, she turned to Rachel. "What floor?"

"Five. Room five-twelve."

They stood in silence as the elevator rose. After a few seconds Rachel said, "You have no shame." Magda opened her mouth, but she held up a hand. "Don't worry. I'm not condemning you. Far from it. I thought I did well with the hotel housekeeper, but you . . ." She shook her head in wonder. "You're at a whole different level."

"I am shameless in the service of detection," Magda said loftily.

"That would be a great slogan for an agency. 'Levis and Stevens: shameless in the service of detection.'"

"Stevens and Levis, I think you'll find." Magda kept staring straight ahead, but the corners of her lips twitched.

They stepped out onto a grand landing, all carved wood and high windows, but with a linoleum floor to deal with the heavy foot traffic. To the left a corridor stretched into the distance, occupied only by small trash cans that stood in front of most rooms waiting to be emptied. Room 512 was in almost the exact middle, its can neatly placed to the right of its door. Magda leaned against the wall just as she had in the hotel. "Go ahead." She nodded at the door. "Do your thing."

"My thing?" They had been moving so fast to get to the Auberge, and then to manage to get into it, that Rachel hadn't stopped to wonder what Magda had planned for when they actually reached Professor Dale's room. "This is where she lives. You said we were going to scope out where she lives."

"We are. But we can't scope it out if we can't get into it. Go 'head.'" She nodded toward the door.

Rachel marveled at her friend's ability to let her memory burnish the past. It had taken her three tries to manage the key card door and she'd picked a key lock once, eighteen months before, but from the way Magda lounged against the wall, anyone would think Rachel was an experienced picklock with an extensive set of tools in her bag and a string of successful larcenies behind her. "No," she said, feeling a sense of déjà vu. "Absolutely not."

"Why not?"

"Because—because one lock a day is enough. One lock a *life* is enough."

And because, she couldn't bring herself to admit to Magda, she liked Professor Dale. She hadn't particularly cared about breaking into Robert Cavill's room, because even if he wasn't a murderer, he was loud and had an irritating laugh. But even though Aurora Dale was a suspect, she was also a sensible widow who contributed to her grandchildren's school fees, valued fiscal discretion, and had never annoyed Rachel. Rachel couldn't pop the lock of such a person and rifle through her belongings. But she knew that if she said any of that aloud, Magda would try to argue her out of it, making remarks about the detective's objectivity and the need to check out every possibility, when all Rachel really wanted was to get out of the hallway before they were caught crouching in front of Professor Dale's door.

So instead she said, "Because this isn't *To Catch a Thief.* I'm not going to go around breaking into any place we feel like exploring, like some sort of female Cary Grant."

"I should be so lucky," Magda snorted. "And you're remembering the movie wrong." She rocked back to a sitting position, accidentally knocking over the trash can, and massaged her thigh muscles. "Cary Grant isn't the thief. Grace Kelly and her mother think he's the thief, and so do the police." She righted the trash can and started putting its spilled contents back inside it. "But it's actually his buddy's daughter—"

"Hush," Rachel said.

"Right, sorry." Magda looked up. "You don't want to know the ending. Do you want to watch it again? We could—"

"Be quiet." Rachel's voice was urgent. "Be quiet and look."

She pointed at the trash that still lay on the floor: several balled-up tissues smeared with blotted lipstick; a few strands of dental floss; some crumbs of used eraser. And amid it all, nearly hidden by one of the tissues, lay the crumpled innermost portion of a ball of string.

Rachel took her key ring out of her bag and handed Magda the tweezers from the Swiss army knife. "Here. Pick it up. And then we need to leave."

Chapter Thirty

The length of string lay in a plastic baggie on Rachel's kitchen table, where she, Alan, and Magda sat and stared at it. It was about four inches long, slightly unraveled at one end, cleanly cut at the other. It wasn't wet; it wasn't stretched. Rachel imagined a full ball of string with the piece that had been used to strangle Guy Laurent somewhere in its midst and this one, like a tangential witness to a crime, attached but far enough away to be innocent. She put out a finger and touched the plastic bag.

"It's a problem," Alan said. "I don't know how the police would deal with a breaking and entering that didn't involve taking anything, but I'm sure they wouldn't be pleased to find out that in a non–breaking and entering you'd still removed and held on to something that might be important evidence. Especially since, given that you obtained it by entering a building under false pretenses, and from her private trash, it might not be admissible now."

"We couldn't just leave it there for housekeeping to dump out." Rachel fought to keep her voice level.

"That's why I said it was a problem."

"Exigent circumstances!" Magda's tone was triumphant. "And it was in a trash can outside her door, so I don't think there was a reasonable expectation of privacy."

"I don't think that comes into it, since you're not police officers," Alan pointed out.

Magda looked personally wounded. "Well, no, we're not."

"And I think if you're just a private citizen, taking something from somebody's trash can counts as stealing. I really don't know, since I'm also not a policeman. Or a lawyer. In fact, I'm not even sure about reasonable expectation of privacy and so on—things may be different under French law. Why don't you ask Benoît?"

Benoît! Rachel hadn't thought of Magda's boyfriend since the dreadful moment when she'd worried that he and Alan might be secret sadists. Now that his name came up, though, she saw how perfect a resource he would be. He was a lawyer at one of the top legal firms in Paris. His advice would be sound.

Alan and Rachel waited, staring at the string, while Magda called Benoît from their bedroom. When she returned, her face was sober.

"So it is considered stealing," Alan said.

"It's a problematic legal area."

Alan took a breath. "I know neither of you is going to like hearing this, but I think your best choice is to take it to Bouscicault. Since both the string and your hotel adventure complicate the idea that Cavill's guilty, he might be glad, even if it's only because you make him aware of evidence he needs to refute."

Normally Rachel would have objected to the phrase *your hotel adventure*, but she had larger worries at that moment.

"He won't be glad," she said. Boussicault had originally seemed to her to be a vaguely avuncular figure, but the exchange in his office the week before had somehow transformed him in her mind into a permanently grouchy father. When she imagined presenting him with the string and the story of their search of Cavill's room, he moved from grouchy to enraged.

"Okay, he'll probably be angry," Alan began, but her phone pinged a text, and he waited.

She looked at the screen. "Speak of the devil. It's Boussicault." She read silently, then looked at Magda. "He wants us to come to the commissariat."

Chapter Thirty-One

Two tiny black-and-white figures emerged from a black-and-white elevator into a black-and-white corridor. They briefly stood still in front of a door. Then one of them looked left and right, took something out of her shoulder bag, and appeared to bend over the doorknob. After some seconds—fewer than forty-seven, Rachel saw with pleasure—the door opened and they entered a room. The door shut behind them.

Capitaine Boussicault tapped his mouse, and the video stopped. He turned the monitor back to face him, carefully aligning its base precisely with a dust-free square on his desktop before he spoke.

"So you broke into Docteur Cavill's room." He looked at Rachel and Magda meditatively.

Neither woman said anything. *What is there to say?* Rachel wondered. They *had* broken into Robert Cavill's room. Besides, Boussicault's remark didn't sound like a question.

"Did you think the police wouldn't search the room? Did you think we wouldn't ask to see the security readings?"

Again there seemed to Rachel to be no good answer. She was hardly going to admit that yes, frankly, she hadn't thought the police would go to Cavill's hotel, since the engraving seemed like more than enough evidence on its own, or that she had forgotten all about the possibility of security cameras. And even now that Boussicault was asking questions, it still didn't sound like he expected answers. She felt a sinking feeling in her stomach that she remembered from her one and only visit to the principal's office.

"But we didn't find anything," Magda said. "And not only is that significant to your investigation, but I don't see how it affects your case if we went in but didn't take or find anything."

The *capitaine* took a deep breath. "Did you wear gloves when you searched the room?"

Magda shook her head.

"So it is now covered in your fingerprints, which cannot be explained away because you had no reason to be there, and which raise the possibility that you planted anything there that we might want to use as evidence. And although you were right to deduce that the murderer presumably would still have the second illustration . . ."

Magda straightened.

". . . you forgot that Docteur Cavill could easily have hidden it in the safe at his hotel, or in a bag left in a bus station locker, or in any number of places known to him and not to you. Which would render your search irrelevant."

Magda slumped down.

Rachel felt that Boussicault was being overly harsh. All right, they'd been foolish, but that was no reason to be mean to her best friend. Plus, hadn't they brought some actual evidence with them to this very meeting? And hadn't they handled that evidence carefully, and fingerprintlessly? And, unlike evidence that by its absence apparently proved nothing, their evidence by its presence at least *suggested* something important. What would Boussicault say to that?

She put the baggy with the string inside it on his desk. "Well, what about that? Is that irrelevant?"

Boussicault peered at it. "What is that?"

Rachel explained, and explained how they'd found it, ending triumphantly with, "And we held it with tweezers until we wrapped it in a tissue."

"And then put it in that baggy as soon as we got home," Magda finished.

The *capitaine* sat still for a long time, his eyes on the string. Then he picked up the baggy, held it to the light, then put it down again.

"Well?" Rachel pointed at the string. "Doesn't that open the possibility that someone besides Cavill is the killer? Isn't that important? String was the weapon in Laurent's murder!"

"And we didn't break, or enter, to get it," Magda added. "We found it in Dr. Dale's trash can."

"You found this string," Boussicault clarified. Magda nodded eagerly. He looked back down at it, steepling his fingers in front of him. His voice didn't rise as he spoke, but it grew progressively tighter and tighter. "This string, which you brought home—thus breaking the chain of evidence—and held in both a tissue and a bag from your home, thus opening it up to contamination? This string that a defense counsel could argue you *stole*, since you acquired it after entering a private residence under false pretenses, then rummaging around in someone's rubbish without permission."

"We didn't rummage!" cried Magda. "It fell into my lap."

The *capitaine* looked at Rachel and took a deep breath. "Madame Levis," he said calmly, "I am angry. I told you that the police no longer needed your help, but it does not seem that you understood me. I fear that your success in the case of Edgar Bowen may have given you false ideas about what it means to be a detective. And I may also be at fault. By involving you in the earlier part of this investigation—although your work was very helpful—I think I made you feel a competency which you don't possess. At least"—he seemed to try to soften the blow—"not yet.

"Now, however, I must be plain. Your help is no longer helpful. In fact, now your help is interfering with an investigation and compromising evidence, both of which can be chargeable offenses."

He inhaled deeply once more, and his face softened. "I understand how frustrating it is not to know the end of a story. I promise I will contact you when I have closed this case. Meanwhile, relieve yourself of unnecessary exertion and go sit in some air-conditioned café where you can enjoy an *apéro*. I wish I could join you." He half rose from his chair. "*Merci*."

He couldn't have indicated the end of the meeting more clearly if he had ushered them to the door and shut it behind them.

* * *

On the street the heat hit like a cement wave, fueling Rachel's fury. "We were patronized!" Her face blazed. "He patronized us!" It didn't sound any better in the active voice.

"And he kept our string!" added Magda.

They stood, linked in frustration, until Rachel said, "Fine, let's take his advice. Let's go somewhere air-conditioned and have a drink."

They went to the same café they'd visited the last time they'd been dismissed from Boussicault's office. Rachel asked for two glasses of red wine, still so angry that she inadvertently spoke in English, only realizing when she saw the blank look on the waiter's face. "*Deux verres de vin rouge*," she self-corrected, and when they arrived, she took a long swallow from her glass.

"Whoa there, Nelly." Magda held out a hand.

"I know, I know. But—" Rachel took another, smaller, swallow, then put down the glass. "First of all, I hate to say it, but he's right: I do want to know how the story ends, and I don't want someone to tell me. I want to see it for myself."

"Or make it happen," Magda pointed out.

"Or make it happen." Rachel took another sip. "But more importantly, we did a lot work for him. I found that sheet of Laurent's, and that's what linked the murder to the thefts!"

"And you noticed the paper in Cavill's jacket."

"*And* I noticed the paper in Cavill's jacket." She took a larger sip. "And what about LouLou? She must still be a suspect, especially if they don't find that Cavill hid the illustration somewhere. She's the next obvious suspect." She finished her glass and gestured for another. "Who's going to help her?"

"I don't know."

The waiter put a fresh glass in front of Rachel. She took a mouthful from it, ruminating for a minute before she swallowed. "You know what?" she said.

"What?"

"We have to keep going."

"You're kidding." Magda put her own glass down in surprise. She was normally the one who said such things.

"No, I'm not." Rachel took another sip, then pointed at her friend with the glass. She had begun to feel that she was not quite herself, but at the same time she felt filled with powerful conviction. "We have to do it. We have to show him by succeeding. We have to do it for women everywhere!"

If Magda felt this was extreme, she didn't give any sign. Instead she said, "Okay."

It seemed to Rachel that her head contained a whirlwind of half-formed yet extremely good ideas. She tried to focus. One separated from the rest and burst to the front of her brain. She swatted Magda's arm. "I know!"

"What?"

"You're right; everyone in the reading room knows me now. But they don't know you." She swatted her again. "You could do it! You could go to the reading room and observe! You could be the detective."

Magda looked thoughtful, so she kept going.

"Think about it: Cavill won't be there, but the other two will. And now that Cavill's been arrested, they're bound to notice his absence, and if one of them's the killer, then they might relax. They might give themselves away. You could go for a couple of days and keep an eye on them to see what they do. And in the meantime I could . . ." She found she couldn't think of what she could do. She had suddenly run out of steam.

"I'll do it." Magda spoke so quickly that she actually exhaled a little wine onto her lower lip. "I'll absolutely do it. Can I start on Monday?"

Rachel waved a hand. "You can start whenever you want."

"I want to start on Monday."

"Then you can start on Monday." Rachel nodded, one firm jerk of decision. Then she stood up and walked, a little unsteadily but with a great sense of purpose, to the bar to pay the bill.

Chapter Thirty-Two

Long before her forty-third year, Rachel had come to understand that although each person is the star of her own life, she is at most a secondary character in other people's. She knew that for someone out there she had at some point just been Girl at the Bus Stop or Woman Behind Me in Line. What she had never thought about, though, was what it would be like to *know* that you were a secondary character, to be left to while away the time as someone else took the starring role. She and Magda had agreed to meet after the Bibliothèque closed, and now she had eight hours of time to fill while life was happening to Magda instead of to her.

Nonsense, snapped a voice in her head. What had happened to all her meditations on order, on the value of life? Magda might have her feet under the table at the Bibliothèque, but if she, Rachel, still felt there was something odd about the idea of Cavill as the murderer, and something worrying about Lou-Lou's interview, she didn't have eight hours of free time. She had eight hours in which to join Magda in doing something about it.

Like what? she asked.

Like not wait around to see what suspicious things the others in the reading room might get up to, but investigate what they've already done.

Fine, she thought. She would start by finding the answer to her easiest question, the one that had been bothering her for days now. *How much does a man who monograms his cuffs pay for his jackets, and is it so little that he'd be willing to slash their linings?* She opened her computer.

Ede and Ravenscroft's cheapest jacket cost 250 pounds, their cheapest suit cost 350 pounds, and in both cases those were sale prices. Without much effort she managed to find the exact mauve jacket that had been hanging in Robert Cavill's wardrobe: it cost 450 pounds. At a bare minimum, allowing for sale shopping—although Cavill didn't strike her as the sort of man who waited for a sale—the tweed Ede and Ravenscroft jacket he had worn in the interview cost 300 pounds; if he hadn't bought it on sale, it had cost nearly twice that. Cavill was a spendthrift, but Rachel didn't think even a spendthrift would willingly slash open the lining of his 500-pound sport coat. Her doubts about Cavill's guilt grew.

Her next move was to do a Google search for Peter Harrington Rare Books, London. She checked her watch; it was two PM in England.

"Peter Harrington Books," said a young female voice with an English accent.

"Uh, yes, hello." Rachel straightened in her seat. "I'm calling regarding one of your customers. Professor Aurora Dale."

"Who is calling? It's not our policy to give out information about our customers."

Who *was* calling? Rachel asked herself. She should really prepare better for these phone calls. Who would the most useful choice be?

"This is Professor Dale's accountant. I'm calling from her accounting firm . . . Bernard and Twombley."

Where did that come from?

Wherever it came from, it seemed to mollify the girl a little. "I see. And what is this regarding?"

Stop asking such hard questions! Rachel silently snapped at her. She'd been equally badly prepared the last time she'd done this, she remembered. She'd have to start planning more thoroughly.

"Well, uh, Professor Dale is a new client and, uh, we're in the process of going through her past taxes. There are some payments she's tentatively identified as coming from Peter Harrington, and we just want to check if that attribution is correct." Remembering the result of Magda's offer at the Auberge, she added, "Would you like our tax ID for verification?"

There was a long pause. *Please let that work*, Rachel thought. And please let the girl not stop to wonder why the English Professor Dale had an American accountant.

At last the girl said, "No, that's all right."

Computer keys clicked; Rachel hurriedly made a rough plan of action.

"Aurora Dale. I found her."

"Very good. Now"—she braced herself—"we have a payment of five thousand pounds. Is that right?"

"Mmm . . ." From the way the sound was elongated, she could tell the girl was scrolling down the page. "No."

"Ah." All right, Rachel asked herself, should she go lower or higher? The goal was to try to get a sense of the kind of prices Dale was paid, and thus get an idea of the kind of thing she might have been selling. "How about this payment of seven hundred and fifty pounds?"

The girl gave a little laugh. "Oh, that wouldn't be us. We aren't interested in items that go for that little, I'm afraid."

"And how about this one for twenty-one thousand, eight hundred and forty-two pounds?"

Rachel had no idea why she'd selected this bizarrely precise sum, but it seemed to do some trick with the girl, because she laughed again and said, "That's more like it. But no, I don't see that amount. I do see a payment for twenty thousand, and one for seventeen . . ." She laughed once more, then said, "Mrs. Dale does bring us some rare items. Very unusual. Very *interesting*."

Rachel swallowed. "Like what?"

"Oh, I couldn't say. That information is private." The girl sounded faintly amused. "Any other amounts?"

"No, no, that's all. Thank you." Rachel hung up. She sat for a while, biting her thumbnail. Rare and unusual. One payment of seventeen thousand pounds and one of twenty thousand. She found a currency conversion site and did a quick calculation. Twenty-three thousand euros! She thought of the number on Laurent's sheet. Some had been around that amount. Her feelings about Aurora Dale began to darken.

She glanced at her watch again. In forty-five minutes it would be nine AM in Tanisqua, Tennessee. Stibb had said he'd promised his mother's retirement home a "large payment," but he hadn't been clear about precisely what that meant. Was it a thousand dollars sort of large or a ten thousand dollars sort of large? It would make a difference to his suspect viability, she pointed out to herself. She was pleased by the sound of the phrase.

Another Google search revealed that although Tanisqua was small, it had fifteen retirement homes. Were retirees flocking to Tennessee? She made a note of the main phone number of each place, then checked her watch again: four PM. She picked up the phone.

Ten communities told Mrs. Stibb's daughter that she was mistaken—her mother wasn't a resident there. The eleventh wouldn't tell her anything unless she could provide Mrs. Stibb's social security number. At the twelfth, no one picked up the phone. But the thirteenth time was the charm: Indian Star Senior Village was happy to put her through to the finance office to discuss a billing matter.

The woman who answered had a voice like syrup. "I didn't even know Mrs. Stibb had a daughter! We usually deal with your *bruhthuh*."

Rachel tried to give the impression that she was ten years older than her actual age and used to the habits of a wayward sibling. "It's probably because I live abroad. I sometimes think Homer forgets about me!" She gave a laugh that she thought might be transcribed "tee-hee." "You know what academics are like."

The woman agreed emphatically. "A lot of professors place their parents here—because of the university in town, you know—and I'm always tickled by the way they forget things, or neglect to mention things that don't seem important to 'em. Sometimes I wonder how they make it through a day!" She tee-heed, too. "Now, where abroad do you live?"

"France." That would cover any problems if the woman had caller ID. "In fact, Homer's here now, too, visiting me."

"France! Oh, gosh, that just makes me think of *wahn* and the Eiffel Tower and those little hats—whaddyoucall'em?—*burrays*!"

"Well"—Rachel made her voice warm—"that's pretty accurate, actually. Of course, when I moved here for work, I was upset at being so far away from my mother—"

"Oh, honey, now you can't let that stop you. We all have l*ah*vs."

She came down so hard on the vowel sound that Rachel briefly thought she'd said *we all have lies*—which, she reflected, in this case was completely true.

"I'm sure your momma was proud when you went off. What kind of work do you do?"

Her accent made it a little like being questioned by Dolly Parton. "Oh, I'm an international systems administrator." She'd come up with this in the forty-five minutes since she'd called London. It sounded both complex and boring, she thought, two attributes likely to put people off further inquiry.

Apparently she was right, because the woman said only, "Well, that sounds challenging! But I don't want to keep you answerin' my questions all day. What can *ah* do for *you*?"

Rachel took a deep breath; this time she had prepared. "Homer and I have been talking about paying Mother's bills there and the most effective way to keep up-to-date with the payments." What finance administrator could fail to be seduced by the idea of someone who wanted to pay their bills promptly? "He told me he'd promised you a large amount in September, and I'm just calling to find exactly how much it is. Could you tell me?"

"I sure can. Just give me a minute." Rachel heard the usual clicking and imagined the tips of glossy Dolly Parton nails hitting computer keys. "Now, is this payment going to be from a foreign bank? Because I'm not sure how we'd process that."

"No, no." Rachel made her voice soothing. "I still have an American bank account. I haven't given up on coming home!"

They tee-heed together, and then the woman said, "Here it is. Mr. Stibb promised us payment to cover the last three months and next month, so that's a total of twenty-four thousand and eighty-eight dollars."

Rachel almost choked. She heard Stibb's voice saying, "I say big, but I pay little." But if you owed over twenty thousand dollars, could you really get away with paying off just a little and promising more the next month? And in the face of twenty-four thousand dollars, what constituted a little, anyway?

"Miss Stibb? Miss Stibb?" The woman's voice echoed in her ear.

"Yes, I'm still here. I was just, uh, writing the amount down." Recovering her wits, Rachel realized she hadn't planned how to get off the phone. She groped for an excuse. "Now, uh . . . I just need to confer with Homer, and we'll get back to you about—" About what? What had she told this woman she was calling about?

"About your payment plan. Sure, that'll be great. I'll look forward to another call from France!"

"Yes. From France. That's right. *Au revoir!*" She clattered the receiver back into its cradle. Although she hadn't much cared for Homer Stibb's financial shell game, she felt a little more sympathy for him now that she knew the amount he was up against. What academic—what regular person—could afford to pay that?

The whole conversation had taken less than fifteen minutes, which left plenty of time for her to make a final call before meeting Magda. She straightened her spine, swallowed hard, and picked up the phone again. She had decided to take the bull by the horns and talk to LouLou, but she was going to need some help contacting her.

Docteure Dwamena sounded harried but pleased to hear from her. "I was just thinking of you, Rachel! *Ressources Humaines* have given me three new members of staff, and they are all like little newborn calves. I was thinking of how easy it was when you and LouLou and—when you all were here. What a pity you are police; you would have made a fine librarian!"

Well, now I'm neither, Rachel thought, but she wasn't going to tell Docteure Dwamena that. "Thank you. It's LouLou I wanted to talk to you about, in fact."

"Ah!" The doctor sighed. "*Pauvre* LouLou! I suggested she come back to work to take her mind off things, but she refused."

"You've spoken to her recently?" Good, she did know how to reach her.

"Yes, I called her a few days ago." After the interview, then. "I wanted to check on her."

"I'm glad to hear that, because I was hoping . . . Do you think she would speak to me?"

The doctor sounded confused. "I thought she'd spoken to the police already."

"Yes, she has." Rachel nodded as if Docteure Dwamena could see her. "But I meant to me personally. As a friend who wants to check on her. If she would consider me a friend, after I—"

"I'm sure she still considers you a friend." The doctor's voice was warm. "And I'm sure she would have been glad to talk to you, but I think she's already left."

"Left? You mean left the job? Yes, you said that."

"No, left for Spain. Her mother lives in Madrid, and she's going to live with her."

"In *Madrid*?" All thoughts of what she wanted to ask LouLou fled from Rachel's mind. LouLou was leaving France—and leaving French justice. She pulled her lips between her teeth. Was LouLou escaping justice that was harassing her, or fleeing justice that was hunting her?

"I was surprised myself," the doctor admitted. "But she said she couldn't take Paris anymore. She said she was leaving as soon as she could. She said she wanted to move somewhere where she felt safe."

"'Felt safe?'" Another ambiguous phrase. Rachel felt her heart thump.

"Yes." The doctor gave a little sigh. "It's a pity, because I was so hoping she would come back. She's a real find for a library—degrees in both information science and book conservation, hands-on experience with ancient books . . . I was going to ask her to fill Laurent's post. But hopefully she'll be an asset to some library in Spain. In any case, I can telephone to see if she's still in Paris and tell her you would like to speak to her. I'm happy to pass on your number, if I may."

"Sure." Rachel wasn't really listening. Madrid! As soon as she could pack! Of course France and Spain had an extradition treaty, but it would certainly take the police a lot longer to bring LouLou in if she weren't in Paris, and who knew where she might go from Madrid? And then, Stibb's twenty-four-thousand-dollar retirement home debt! Dale's big-money sales to antiquarian booksellers! Even Cavill's preposterously priced jackets were cause for thought. Maybe she wasn't going to be a secondary character after all.

Chapter Thirty-Three

". . . to Spain as soon as she can. *As soon as she can.*"

"Uh-huh." Magda took a sip of her spritzer.

"And Homer Stibb! Twenty-four thousand? That's a lot of money. I thought we might be talking ten thousand, but twenty-four? He's not going to be able to manage that without something extra coming in. Unless he was telling the truth about his little bait-and-switch plan. But what business would wait four months for twenty-four thou and then be satisfied with only a bit of it?"

"Mmm." Magda folded her lips together.

"*And* Professor Dale pulling in those big prices. She has to be selling something special for that. Even the girl said so. 'Rare and very unusual.' And she's exactly the sort of person who wouldn't attract attention in a library: an older woman with gray hair, sensibly dressed, quiet . . . You'd never think to check what she was doing."

"Mmm."

Rachel took a breath. She suddenly realized she'd been talking almost from the minute they'd sat down. Looking across the table, she noticed for the first time that Magda was almost bursting with excitement of her own. So much for being a secondary character in someone else's life! "I'm sorry. I didn't mean to—My mistake. Tell me about your day. Did you find anything out?"

Magda let out a gasp as if she'd been holding her breath for hours. "Aurora Dale uses long pieces of string to mark pages!"

"*What?* You're kidding."

"I certainly am not. And that's not even the best thing. I—No, hold on." She inhaled deeply, then started again. "I need to explain the setup. There are ten people using the reading room now. Plus me, that's eleven. The way it worked out, I was able to grab a table to myself, over by the computers. That area gets the least light, so I figured I'd draw the least attention there. Stibb and Dale sat at the table farthest from me. The other people sat between us, but because I sat close to the outer edge of my table, I could still watch them." She looked at Rachel. "Okay?"

"Okay."

"So that's what I did: I watched them. Well, I pretended I was researching medieval clothing, and I watched them while I looked through books I ordered up. And I saw Professor Dale use the string."

Rachel felt her heart give a thump. "How long were the pieces?"

"About, uh . . ." She held her hands up, roughly eighteen inches apart. "Like that."

Was that long enough to strangle someone? It seemed long enough, but what was the circumference of a neck? Especially a male neck? Frustrated, she realized she would have to wait until she could go home and run a test on Alan.

Magda cleared her throat. "Wait. There's more."

"More?" *What more could there be?*

Magda put her hand in her bag. Rachel leaned forward. Had she managed to steal a piece of the string? Had someone wiped their mouth and Magda stolen the napkin for a saliva sample? But when her hand came out, it held a plastic baggie containing what appeared to be a stub of shiny eraser.

"What the hell?"

"Look at it!" Magda's voice echoed with barely suppressed excitement. She thrust the baggy toward Rachel. "Go on, look closely."

Rachel reached out.

"Don't open it!"

Rachel let the baggy flop over her hand so that the object inside lay on her palm and held it to the window. What she had thought was a shiny eraser was in fact a small eraser stub, in one edge of which someone had cut a slit. Into the slit they had inserted, so deeply that only about a quarter inch of its sharp tip appeared, the blade of an X-acto knife.

"What is it?"

"What is it? What is it?" Magda was outraged. "It's a shank! A shiv! An Arkansas toothpick!"

"What?" Rachel looked more closely, bending her hand back so the baggy flattened against the eraser. The tip of the blade winked where the light hit it.

"It's a knife!" Madge sat back with satisfaction. "I found it in the reading room."

"In the reading room!"

"Under my table, right next to the leg. I dropped a pencil, and when I bent over, something glinted. Then I saw what it was, so I picked it up and put it in the baggy."

"You had a baggy with you?"

"Yes." She nodded vigorously. "Before I left this morning, I remembered what the *capitaine* said about the chain of evidence, so I took a baggy and wiped the inside down with *alcool isopropylique* and took it with me."

"Wow. Good prep work."

"Thanks." Magda smirked a little at her own cleverness. "Boussicault won't be able to catch us out this time. The implement is coming to him clean, sterile, and untouched by human hands."

She seemed so pleased that Rachel hated to pull her back with a question. "The implement?"

"Of the crimes! This is what was used to take the pages from the books!"

Rachel felt even worse. "No, it's not."

"How do you know?"

"The page stubs had frayed edges, remember? I told you after the first book was found. And this would make clean cuts. No fraying."

Magda looked so disappointed that Rachel picked up the baggy and peered at the blade once more, wanting to give her something to cheer her up. There was a long silence before she spoke.

"I'll tell you what this could be, though. This could be what was used to cut Robert Cavill's jacket lining."

Magda lifted her head. "You think so?"

"Yes, absolutely. That was a clean cut."

"Cavill brought it with him to use when he needed it, then threw it away when he was finished!"

This was not an easy conversation. "Not exactly." But before Magda could deflate once more, she said, "While you were working, I did some research on Cavill's jacket." She explained about the prices. "I don't think he would slash the lining of his own four hundred–pound sport coat."

"I don't know . . ." Magda frowned. "The prices on Laurent's list were pretty high. And Cavill wasn't exactly careful about money. He doesn't seem like he'd balk at cutting up a four hundred–pound jacket if he was stealing something he could sell for twenty thousand euros."

"No." Rachel shook her head. "Cavill spent money to look a certain way to other people, and to provide a certain kind of life for his family. That might seem foolish to us, but it wasn't wasting money as far as he was concerned. But ruining a four hundred–pound coat by slashing the lining is a waste."

"Not if you're going to be able to buy fifty more as a result."

Magda looked mulish. Rachel decided to try using logic rather than psychology. "Okay, I can see your point. But why would he cut open his coat lining in the reading room? He could have cut it in his hotel room, or even in the men's room at the Bibliothèque, if he wanted to dispose of the knife blade somewhere where it couldn't be traced back to him. Why would he wait until he was in the place where it was most important that he not be caught? Or let's say he did slit it somewhere else. Why would he keep carrying the blade after that, so he could lose it in the reading room?"

This seemed to work. Magda didn't concede, but she did say, "Do you have a better scenario?"

Her voice was sulky. Rachel understood: first her big moment had fallen flat, and now it was being undermined. Still, she knew she had to go on. "I think so."

"Fine. Let's hear it."

"I think someone else slashed Cavill's lining. And I think that someone also planted the woodcut on him."

She waited. Magda's arms were crossed, but she didn't say anything dismissive, so Rachel continued. "I think they must have done that, then either deliberately dropped this thing next to the table leg, where they thought it wouldn't be noticed, or just lost track of it because it wasn't important anymore."

Magda considered. "Okay, it's a hypothesis. But in that scenario both Cavill and the slasher are in the reading room. How could the slasher cut the coat without Cavill seeing him?"

Rachel had been puzzling over this very question for the half hour before their meeting, with no luck. "I don't know."

"They'd have to be quick about it."

"They would."

"And they'd have to be unobtrusive. You'd need to bring out the blade, get access to the jacket, then to the lining, then make the cut, then slide the folded page in, all without anybody noticing. Who could do that?"

"I don't know. That's the part I haven't been able to figure out yet."

"It's a pretty big part."

"It is."

They sat in mutual silence until Magda said, "I have an idea, but you won't like it."

"I can take it. Tell me."

"It's LouLou."

Rachel didn't like it. She made a face.

"No, think about it. Who could linger by an empty reading room table for any length of time without creating suspicion? A member of the staff. She pretends to drop off some materials while Cavill's at the computer or in the bathroom, knocks his jacket off a chair, and while she's picking it up she makes the slash and slips the page in. No one would pay much attention. Who would know where to dispose of the blade quickly and with the least notice? A member of the staff. She drops a book in the right place, kneels down, shoots the blade under the table, stands up with the book in her hand. Perfectly normal."

Rachel still didn't like it, but she had to acknowledge that it wasn't completely out of the realm of possibility. She turned the scenarios over in her mind. "But we didn't find the woodcut in Cavill's jacket until a week and a half after Giles's death, and LouLou hadn't been in the reading room since the day before Giles died. Would Cavill have wandered around for eleven days with a cut in his lining and a piece of paper inside it and not noticed? And, anyway, why would LouLou have put the woodcut in his jacket before she killed Giles? She had nothing to worry about then."

"Those are very good questions, Watson." Magda raised an index finger. "But I can answer them. First, Cavill apparently didn't notice his lining was cut until you pointed it out. Maybe he's not much of a noticer. Or even if he is, maybe he wore the jacket on the relevant day, hung it up in his tiny hotel wardrobe, and then didn't wear it again until the day of his interview. It *is* tweed, and the other one was linen—a much better hot-weather fabric." Her voice became thoughtful. "If you think about it, time and timing have always been a problem in this case." Rachel could tell she loved saying *case* in a casual way. Which was fine, because she loved hearing it.

"We don't know when the page was taken out of the *Supplementum*," Magda went on. "We have no idea when Laurent did his blackmailing, or when the page was removed from the book of psalms."

"Psalter."

"Psalter. Thank you. And you yourself pointed out that Giles's reaction to the missing page suggested he'd known about some earlier theft from a book. It's perfectly possible that LouLou is an advance planner. Lots of murderers are." Magda said this as if she'd interviewed thousands of murderers on just that topic. "What if we got the timing wrong? What if Giles already knew that she'd stolen a page from the psalter before he found out about the *Supplementum*? What if he'd already started to blackmail her, and she'd already planned to kill him over it? She put the page in the jacket *in advance* because she figured it was worth it to sacrifice one illustration to get rid of suspicion and be free to sell the other, more valuable one."

Magda stopped, waiting for a response. Rachel felt that perhaps she did deserve to be a secondary character that day after all. Maybe Woman Who Found Out Some Mildly Interesting Stuff, but Nothing as Good as This. Magda's suggestions were plausible, and in their plausibility they made it impossible to dismiss LouLou as a suspect.

"Okay, those aren't *entirely* unlikely hypotheses. But neither is the hypothesis that someone else was able to slash the lining and throw away the blade, too. So we have a number of hypotheses that are equally likely to be wrong."

Magda cleared her throat. "Or equally likely to be right."

Rachel sighed, looked at the baggy, then sighed again. "I'll tell you what else we have. We have what could be a major piece of evidence, which we found as a result of investigating. And we have to hand it over to a police captain who explicitly told us to stop investigating."

They mulled the grim prospect. At last Magda said, "Do we, though?"

"Do we what?"

"Do we have to give it to him? Couldn't we just . . . not?"

"I'm pretty sure your lawyer boyfriend would tell you that withholding evidence is even worse than compromising the chain of evidence—probably even worse than breaking and entering and finding nothing but leaving your fingerprints everywhere. Ask him if you don't believe me. We have to give it back."

"I will ask him." Magda gave a determined bob of her head. "In fact, I'll ask him tonight."

Chapter Thirty-Four

Later that evening Benoît and Alan sat with them around a table at Fauchon on the Place de la Madeleine. In front of them was one of the patisserie's most decadent pastries, a cake in the shape of a pillowy mouth airbrushed bright raspberry red. Magda sighed mournfully as she cut off a bite.

"I *am* sorry"—Benoît shook his head—"but the law is very clear. Impeding an investigation is a serious offense. You must hand it over."

Magda swallowed. "But we're not impeding an investigation. The police have Cavill, but we also gave them the piece of string that suggests someone else could be the murderer. So they have all the evidence they need to continue to investigate from both angles. The knife is just extra."

Benoît turned to face Magda, a lock of his hair falling over his forehead and the light glinting off his glasses. He gave her a sad smile. "*Amour*, the police will not share your reasoning. You may be correct in your thinking—certainly you are scrupulously logical—but the police will argue that any piece of evidence, at any stage, is important. And"—he tilted his head to one side—"we must admit that a piece of string found in a rubbish bin and a homemade weapon found near the scene of a crime are very different sorts of evidence."

"Also," Alan pointed out, "not handing in the eraser keeps Robert Cavill in police custody when he might not deserve it. And of course"—he flashed a smile of his own in Rachel's direction—"it keeps Boussicault from knowing about the excellent detective work you did all on your own."

Benoît frowned. "I think Docteure Cavill may have been released in any case." He added hastily, "Although you should still hand in the evidence."

"How do you mean, he may have been released?"

"Well, criminal law is not my area, but I do know that the police can only detain a suspect for forty-eight hours before they must bring him before a magistrate to request an extension. And no magistrate would agree to an extension based on the evidence you have described. Nothing shows clearly that Monsieur Cavill murdered anyone, and the theft of the page with the woodcut is a *délit*—what you would call a misdemeanor." He said the last two words in English with an impeccable American accent. "He would probably be required to remain in the country and to check in at a police station regularly, but he wouldn't be detained in custody." He frowned again. "Excuse me a moment."

After he left, Alan leaned in. "I know I sound like a broken record, but I think you have to turn this in, too. Even if Cavill has been released, that thing raises all sorts of questions. Who could smuggle it into the reading room? How could it have stayed where it was without being noticed and for how long? And you don't have the ability to test it for fingerprints, which the police do." He put his hand over Rachel's. "I know Boussicault treated you badly, but he is the law, and he really will know how to use this most effectively."

Rachel though of how angry Boussicault would be—how angry he would be *again*. She winced. But then she thought of Giles, whom she'd grown to like despite herself, and who had probably loved LouLou, and who had had hopes and dreams that were ended prematurely by a knife in the chest. And then, because she prided herself on not falling for sentimental clichés, she thought of her belief that solving a crime was a way of ordering the world. And then, because she couldn't help it, she thought of Giles again.

Benoît reappeared. "Monsieur Cavill has indeed been released." He sat down.

"How did you find out?" Alan asked.

Benoît gave another, smaller shrug. "I called the commissariat and explained that I was a lawyer recently retained by the British embassy to represent Monsieur Cavill. I asked when I might come to see him. The *gardien* told me that he had been released and could be reached at his hotel. He even very kindly gave me the address."

Alan exhaled a sharp cry. "Am I the only law-abiding citizen at this table?"

Benoît waved his hand. "I did nothing illegal." He turned to look at the women. "And neither will you, I believe. Please promise me that tomorrow morning you will go to the commissariat and hand over this knife to the police. Without this evidence the police may devote themselves to building a case that unintentionally convicts an innocent man—and one that allows the real murderer to walk around free."

Rachel looked at Magda across the sponge-cake lips. Magda had found the blade, so the decision about what to do with it belonged to her. Rachel tried very hard not to let her face show that she wanted her to take it to Boussicault. Instead, she let it show another fact: that she would stand by her whatever she decided.

Magda chewed thoughtfully for a moment. She put her fork down, swallowed her bite of cake, then wiped her lips. She looked at Alan and Benoît. "How about a compromise?"

Chapter Thirty-Five

Early afternoon the next day found Rachel sitting with Magda by the side of the boccie court in the Jardin du Luxembourg. Elderly Frenchmen as short and broad as fireplugs measured their shots, cackled at their friends' misses, and gossiped about each other as they waited their turns at the game. The sun still blazed out overhead, but Rachel spotted a few brown leaves on the path in front of them. Autumn was coming, even it if it seemed as if it never could.

"How long did you say you were going to wait?" she asked.

"Until two this afternoon. I just wanted a bit more time to think." Magda sighed. "I *am* going to turn it in. I promised Benoît, so I will. But it feels so significant . . . if only we could figure out what it signifies! And I don't see why we have to rush to help Boussicault. You said yourself that he patronized us."

She had said that.

"And we're good. We're *good* detectives. We're doing well. I don't see the police successfully planting an observer in the reading room."

Well, if he were a successful plant, you wouldn't see him, Rachel pointed out silently. But she was too wise to say it aloud. Besides, they *were* good detectives. Instead she said, "So we have two hours."

"Two hours is more than enough time to have a revelation."

Normally Rachel would have rolled her eyes at Magda's optimism, but just this once she almost agreed with her. Three hours was a valuable commodity when it came to detection. She closed her eyes and moved her mind backward, pulling at the clues and possible clues. She thought about Aurora Dale, always keeping her handbag close. Was it because there was a stolen page in it, a page she meant to sell at Bonnefoi? She was the least likely suspect, and by the law of mystery novels that meant she was the killer. But what about Homer Stibb? He was American, which in the eyes of any European mystery novel made him guilty of *something*. And LouLou? She could have killed out of rage and fear, or out of economic ruthlessness. In a fiendishly plotted noir novel, it would be out of both.

The trouble, she thought, was that she didn't know what kind of mystery novel this real-life mystery was *in*. If she were Hercule Poirot (had she remembered to bleach her upper lip?), Cavill would be guilty, having engineered the situation with Mrs. Cavill to free them from all debt and suspicion simultaneously. If she were one of Wilkie Collins's characters, Dale would be guilty, conniving behind an exterior of charming eccentricity. If she were in a Raymond Chandler book, the doer would be Stibb, playing fast and loose with his money and his promises. But then again, if she were in a Raymond Chandler book, she would be the moll or the faithful secretary and never get anywhere near investigating. This was the problem with real life: you got to do more, but there was less clarity. At least, that was *one* of the problems with real life.

"Madame Levis?"

Rachel opened her eyes and looked up. Aurora Dale stood in front of her.

"It is Madame Levis, isn't it?"

"Professor Dale!"

"Oh, please do call me Aurora." She gestured at the bench on which they sat. "I thought I recognized you from the interviews! May I join you?"

Rachel nodded. "And please call me Rachel."

Aurora settled herself so that she was facing them, her knees pressed against the front edge of the bench. She held her bag firmly on her lap, Rachel noticed. "How fortuitous for me! I was just debating whether to contact the police. I don't know if you're someone I could talk to . . ."

Magda leaned out from behind Rachel. "Hello, I'm Magda Stevens." She held out her hand. Aurora looked somewhat confused, but she shook it. "Rachel's friend and colleague. Yes, we're the right people. You can absolutely talk to us."

"Oh, how do you do. I'm so sorry to break into your afternoon. I wouldn't do it under normal circumstances, but I've been thinking about those interviews." She took a deep breath, then sighed it back out. "I think I've behaved poorly."

"I can't imagine how." Rachel tried to think back.

"Well, foolishly, then. Certainly foolishly." She paused, seeming to gather herself together for some sort of launch. "You see, when I was growing up, and even now really, in Britain anyway, money just . . . wasn't talked about. Money is a private matter. And I fear I rather took this attitude when talking to the police captain."

She looked away for a moment. "If it hadn't been for certain, well, inhibitions, I could have explained those payments into my current account quite easily. I put the personal above the common good, which is always a mistake."

She snapped back to attention. "You see, as it happens, over the years I've managed to pile up a collection of relatively unusual books."

Rachel's ears pricked. *Unusual* was the word the girl from Peter Harrington had used.

"A number of which have since become very valuable. They are, ah, items of"—she looked slightly bashful—"well . . . erotica. Nineteenth-century erotica."

Realization came to Rachel in a rush. "Very unusual"; "very *interesting*"; the amusement in the girl's voice. Professor Dale had been selling dirty books. And, judging by the prices the girl had quoted, she'd been making some tidy sums from it.

Aurora must have seen Rachel's startled expression, because she said quickly, "It's a very profitable area these days. The bookseller tells me it's terribly trendy to own rare pornography. It's a, well, a seller's market. And, well, once the savings ran out and the overdraft started growing, I became, well, a seller. I just couldn't bear having debt like that, and so over the past year I've been, well, selling my rarest items. To Peter Harrington." She smiled bashfully. "I've been managing some, ah, good prices, actually. But I didn't want to mention it in the interviews because, well, money is awkward. And a woman with a sexual appetite, or even an interest in sex, is . . . you know."

Magda and Rachel nodded: they did know.

"But now I've come to feel that if I'd told the captain about this in our interview, he could have written me off as a suspect. And he might have been able to put more energy into finding the real culprit."

"I don't think you need to worry about that." Rachel put a hand on her arm. "They've arrested Dr. Cavill, you know. There was material evidence against him." She felt a twinge of conscience, but at that moment it was more important to her to allay Aurora's fears than to voice her doubts about Cavill's guilt.

"Yes, I heard that. And also that he had to be released. They're terrible gossipy in the reading room—just like an English faculty." But instead of looking amused or even relieved, she seemed even more troubled. "And I've been thinking about his arrest and release as well. I presume if they've released him, they must be looking for someone else." She sighed, then pursed her lips. "Do you remember that I said in my first interview that detective work is like literary criticism? That in both cases you look a text over repeatedly to see what you might've missed during the previous examinations?"

Rachel nodded.

"Well, I've been reexamining my text. I've been running over and over in my mind what I saw before the library opened that morning, trying to see if I could remember anything more. Only the opposite happened. I remembered less. Oh, I'm sorry. I'm so unclear!" She shook her head once, hard, as if trying to dislodge something inside it. "What I'm trying to say is, I think I made a mistake. I think what I told you in my interview was wrong. I remembered something wrong."

What should a person do in this situation? Rachel asked herself. She knew that Benoît and Alan would say that she should tell Aurora to take any concerns or reconsiderations to the police. But would that really be the right thing? After all, she had appeared in front of them just as they were trying to come up with possible leads, and she might be handing them a lead. Was this a sign? Rachel didn't believe in signs, but was this a sign?

"This is fate," Magda muttered.

"Pardon?"

"Nothing." Magda smiled at Aurora. "Doesn't matter. You think you made a mistake about what?"

"About what I saw. Or rather, about what I didn't see." Another sigh. "Rachel, when you and the captain asked if I'd seen anything that seemed strange, I told you that I thought I remembered seeing someone go round the corner into the back of the library. I did see them in my memory, a tall person going round the corner. But I've been running the morning through my mind over and over these past few days, and it's come to me that I didn't remember seeing that person until after we'd all been talking in the waiting room together—Dr. Cavill, Professor Stibb, and I. That is, I only remember remembering the person once we started talking about what we remembered."

Rachel checked to be certain she'd understood this rather confusing explanation. "You mean all the witnesses waited together in the same room?" Aurora nodded. "And you talked about what you'd seen?"

"Of course they did," Magda said. "Wouldn't you?"

"Well, we didn't at first. At first we wondered about what was going on. Then I said I thought it must be a murder because—as I said to you—there were all those police. And after I said that, everyone started trying to remember what they remembered that might be significant. I mean, we really were cudgeling our brains."

Rachel smiled at this old-fashioned expression.

"And when I ran all that through my mind over the past week, it began to seem to me that I couldn't remember remembering I'd seen this person, if you see what I mean, until after we'd all talked about what we remembered. And this morning when I was thinking about it again, I realized that in fact I must have remembered wrong.

"You see, I was having my usual cigarette, and this morning I suddenly remembered that when I had my cigarette *that* morning, I stood right over by the entrance to the Bibliothèque, in the corner farthest from the courtyard gates. And from there you can't see if anyone is going round the back of the library." She said confidentially, "I checked again before I left just now, to be sure. And I'm quite sure I was standing there at the time I said I'd seen the tall person, because I remember I had time to walk over to the bin by the gate and back to throw the butt out—you know, before they unlocked the library doors." Her revelation over, she rushed to finish the story. "Then I made a beeline for the ladies' to wash my hands, as I always do. And I bumped into that terribly gloomy girl from the reading room on the way in, so you can check my story with her."

She sighed luxuriously, relieved, and smiled at Rachel and Magda. "This kind of false memory isn't unheard of, apparently. I looked it up on the Internet. Studies have shown that it's fairly common for people to manufacture memories, especially if they're eager to help someone, and especially if a crowd of people are all trying to remember together."

"But someone must have started it," Magda said reasonably. "Do you think you could try to remember who?"

"I can try." She sat to attention, gripping her bag even more tightly. "We were all in the room together, and I said I thought it must be a murder. Professor Stibb was on my right, and Dr. Cavill on my left. The Frenchwoman was standing up, looking out the window. And we all started talking about whether we'd seen any actual evidence that would suggest it was a murder, and then . . . well, you know how it is when you all speak the same language. You just speak that language naturally. And the Frenchwoman didn't seem terribly interested anyway—standoffish, you know. So the two men and I were chatting in English, and then when I was called in for the interview, I remembered I'd seen this tall person." She continued to stare into the distance for a few moments, frowning. "Sorry, that's all I can remember. But as I said, I felt I ought to tell someone, so I left the library and was just on my way home to think about whom to contact."

She gave a pleased smile, and Rachel remembered her comment that she was interested in mysteries. She smiled back. "I wouldn't beat yourself up over what you did or didn't do. But I do think you should tell all this to Capitaine Boussicault."

"Yes." Magda leaned forward once again. "And the commissariat is on the Rue de Vaugirard, just over there." She pointed over her shoulder.

"Yes, that's all wise advice. I probably should have already gone. But I didn't feel terribly confident in my own memory until now. You know how it is. I wonder if Dr. Cavill or Professor Stibb . . ." She trailed off—cudgeling her brains once again, Rachel thought—before giving a little shake and standing up. "In any case, yes, I shall go to the police. And I'm sorry to have bothered you while you were chatting. Makes the day a bit of a busman's holiday for you. Sorry." She said good-bye and strode off, heading for the Auberge des Jeunesses.

Magda waited until she was out of earshot before she spoke. "So there was no tall person!"

"Well, maybe."

"What do you mean?"

"She only said she wasn't sure. And we have to remember that she could have just made it up. We only have her word for it that the idea didn't originate with her. What better way to put us off her scent? And didn't you notice that she just walked off in the opposite direction to the commissariat?"

"Toward her home!"

"But you told her the commissariat was close by. Why not set off right away, if she was really so eager to unburden herself to Boussicault?"

Magda made a face. "I think you're overly suspicious."

"We're investigating two murders! Is it possible to be over suspicious?"

"It is if it makes you second-guess somebody who hands you vital evidence on a platter."

"Putting it that way makes it sound even *more* suspect." It wasn't that she was untrusting, Rachel thought; it was that she didn't know whom to trust. Another real-life problem.

After a while she said, "How long do we have left?"

"About an hour." They sat silent for a bit longer. Then Magda said, "How about a gelato?"

"If we can eat it on the way there."

So they ate gelato and walked slowly toward the commissariat, their tension keeping them quiet. Rachel thought about Aurora's recovered memory. Only after she replayed the professor's monologue in her head did she spot that she had mentioned seeing LouLou. There was an alibi for LouLou! Her spirits soared. She must let Boussicault know. Surely he couldn't object to information she'd acquired via an accidental meeting?

Then her spirits fell again. Who knew what Boussicault would object to when faced with evidence that they'd furthered disregarded his orders? He'd probably have them locked up, not sit down with her and listen to some story about memory gone bad.

Chapter Thirty-Six

When they arrived at the commissariat, however, the young *gardien* behind the reception desk informed them that Capitaine Boussicault had been called away to help with an organized-crime shooting in Sentier. They sat, both disconsolate and relieved, in the strange scoop-shaped chairs of the lobby, whispering to each other.

"What do we do? Do we just go home?" Magda's voice was hopeful.

Rachel shook her head. "We said we'd hand it in, so we'll hand it in. We'll give it to the *gardien*, and we'll put a note on it that says Boussicault should call us as soon as he gets it."

"Be sure to tell him about Aurora, too." Magda sat back in her chair. Rachel gave her a look. "What? You're the writer."

Rachel might have been less reluctant than Magda to hand over the eraser-knife, but she wasn't any more eager to explain herself to Boussicault. Taking out her pad and pen, she just wrote, FOUND ON FLOOR OF READING ROOM. EXPECT A CALL FROM AURORA DALE ON ANOTHER MATTER, signed it neatly, asked for a stapler, then handed the baggy, note stapled to its neck, to the *gardien*. "For Capitaine Boussicault." He nodded; they left.

When they were back on the street, Magda suddenly said, "What's a busman's holiday?"

"I don't know. I've been wondering that myself."

"And why did she keep apologizing?"

Rachel shook her head. "The English do that. A lot."

"The English are weird."

Rachel just shrugged and hugged her good-bye. Who wasn't weird today? She herself had just left a carefully elliptical note to avoid a policeman's wrath, listened to an elderly woman tell her about the advantages of collecting and selling pornography, and delayed turning in significant evidence in a murder case by eating a gelato. *We're not in Kansas anymore.*

Her *portable* rang with a number she didn't recognize. "*'Allo?*"

"Rachel? It's LouLou."

Thus proving my point, she thought. She felt that she'd lost the ability to be surprised by anything. "LouLou, how are you? You're still in Paris!"

"Yes, just barely. And I'd like to see you. Would it be possible? I want to tell you something before I leave."

I want to tell you something, too, Rachel thought. *Something that might actually make you happy.* "Name the time and the place."

* * *

The time turned out to be half an hour later and the place the Goguette café inside the Louvre. Since the Louvre air-conditioned itself to freezing to combat the heat of the summer sun that sizzled through its glass pyramid, Rachel stopped at the Starbucks next to Goguette and bought a tea. Sipping decent hot tea in Paris in August fit right in with the oddness of the day.

Dressed in her usual head-to-foot black, LouLou was easy to pick out amid the bright tourists. She smiled a little when she saw Rachel, but she didn't get up, so Rachel sat down, putting her cup on the tabletop.

"Thank you for coming," LouLou said. Then, with no further preamble, "I spoke to Alphonsine to say good-bye, and she said you'd telephoned and asked after me. I had wanted to say good-bye to you, too, but I didn't know how to reach you. So when she gave me your number . . ."

"I'm glad you called." Rachel smiled across the table. "I have something to tell you."

But LouLou put out a hand. "No, I have something to tell you." She peered at Rachel from under her bangs. "I felt so good after our drink that evening. I know from Docteure Dwamena that you were there for the police, but still, I felt like we really connected. You—you *listened* to me, and I felt like you really wanted to understand." She took a breath, and in that tiny pause Rachel wondered if it was a detective's fate always to feel torn, gathering information while pretending friendship. It seemed to be her fate, at any rate.

But LouLou had started again. "So I want to share this with you. Don't worry, I'll be fast, because I'm not very brave." She folded her hands on the table in front of her. "About two years ago, on the way home from work, I was . . . attacked. I wasn't raped, but it was . . . bad. Very bad. And afterward was just as bad. I went to the hospital to report it, I made myself go, and the doctor who saw me asked me if I really thought it was a good idea to walk home alone in hot weather, especially past Les Halles. Then the policeman who came to take my statement looked at my bruises and said he was sure that I *felt* I'd been assaulted, but could it be that my boyfriend had just been a little rougher than I was used to?"

Rachel closed her eyes. She wished she could be shocked, but she'd heard similar stories from other assault victims.

LouLou continued. "After that, I started carrying a kitchen knife in my bag." She swallowed. "It made me feel better. For a long time it was the only thing that made me feel better. But then my mother persuaded me to go see a counselor, and that helped. It helped a lot. I started to feel safe again. But I took chances I shouldn't have. With Guy Laurent. He . . ." She shook her head. "I don't want to talk about it again. All that matters is . . . My counselor once told me that fear is like a hibernating animal that feeds on trauma. She said that if an old fear smells new trauma, it will wake up again. Only it will be worse, because it wakes up hungry. After Laurent, it was worse. He made me worse, and I hated him so much. He took pleasure in doing cruel things; what kind of person does that? If anyone ever deserved to die, he did. After him I hated men, any man. Giles and I, we were friends once, if you can believe that. But after Laurent, just having Giles near me made me tense. Having *any* man near me."

She met Rachel's eyes. "I'm telling you this because I want you to understand. I was traumatized by my attack. I was traumatized again by Laurent. And I know that the police arrested someone else for what happened, but Docteure Dwamena tells me that he has been released. And the police interviewer told me that the witnesses said they saw someone tall entering the back of the Bibliothèque before Giles died, so I have no doubt the police will want to question me again. And I just want to get away from this whole thing, away from Paris and its police."

Rachel looked into LouLou's burning eyes and was glad to be able to bring her some relief. "Well, that's actually what I wanted to talk to you about. You don't have to worry so much anymore. Aurora Dale—you know, from the reading room—doesn't think she really did see a tall person. Apparently she's been going over that morning in her mind, and she's come to the conclusion that the supposed person was an implanted memory, or a shared delusion, something like that. Oh, and"—she moved forward in her seat—"you have even less to worry about, because part of what makes her think she got it wrong is that she remembers what time it was when she came into the library, and she brushed by you on her way into the bathroom."

"What?"

"Yes, so you have your alibi. Someone saw you!"

"Is that true?" LouLou's eyes were wide, Rachel saw, and her face white with relief.

"Yes."

"And Docteure Dale is still in France? Is she still using the reading room?"

"Yes. And she's going to the police"—Rachel remembered

that Aurora Dale had set off in the opposite direction to the commissariat—"at some point soon to set the record straight."

"But this is . . ." LouLou cleared her throat. "This is wonderful news! I must go call my mother. She will be so relieved!" She stood up and slung her bag strap across her body. She gave Rachel a final smile. "Sisterhood is powerful."

Chapter Thirty-Seven

"Pick up your phone," Alan's voice said. "Pick up your phone!"

Rachel swam up from sleep. Alan's tie was dangling over her face and his hand was on her arm, but now he was speaking into her *portable*. Outside the sky was gray, and the room was cool enough for her to know that it was early morning.

"*Oui, oui,*" Alan said. "*Un moment.*" He handed her the *portable*. "It's Boussicault. Don't let him grind you down. See you tonight." He waved as he left the room.

"*C'est* Boussicault," the *capitaine*'s voice said in response to her greeting. Rachel steeled herself for his reaction to the eraser, but instead he said, "Please come to Salpêtrière immediately."

It is never a good thing to be woken from a sound sleep by a policeman, but it is an even worse thing to be woken by a policeman demanding you hurry to Paris's best teaching hospital.

"Why? Has something happened?" Ridiculous question, Rachel thought as she reached for her bra; of course something had happened. "Is it Magda?"

"Why doesn't matter." She remembered that brusqueness was the *capitaine*'s business mode, so she was grateful that he had the empathy to add, "But Madame Stevens is fine. It has to do with our murders. *Urgences générales, immédiatement, s'il vous plait.*"

* * *

Rachel had always thought the screech of tires as a car stopped abruptly was an affectation of the movies, but when her taxi pulled up to the *urgences* entrance at the hospital, she realized it existed in reality, too. Through the plate glass windows of the lobby she could see Magda waiting, holding a cardboard cup in each hand. She paid the driver and hurried through the hospital's doors.

Magda handed her one of the cups. "It's Aurora Dale."

"Aurora Dale? Is she—" She stopped; if they were in Emergency, Aurora Dale couldn't be dead. "What's happened?"

"I don't know. I just got here myself."

They set off down the hall, only to find Aurora sitting up in bed, lively but bruised around the neck, with the *capitaine* leaning on the window ledge across from her. When they entered, he stood up. "Ah! Professeure Dale asked me to telephone you. I only arrived myself a half hour ago; SAMU contacted me at a crime scene in Sentier."

So he hadn't yet been to the commissariat, Rachel thought, carefully not catching Magda's eye. As for Aurora Dale, Rachel was sorry she had ever thought she might be the murderer, or even questioned her veracity. The red marks around her throat were proof of the foolishness of those ideas.

"What happened?" Rachel asked.

She had gone to the Bibliothèque, Aurora explained. "I

was still bothered by the question of what I did or didn't remember from that morning in the courtyard—the one I talked to you about. Mr. Stibb gave me his email address when we first met, so I emailed him, and he emailed Mr. Cavill, who emailed me. I'm sorry"—she held up a hand to forestall impatience no one had expressed—"I know this must seem like unnecessary detail, but it does all matter. I arranged to meet both of them at the Bibliothèque late yesterday afternoon, separately, because I wanted to find out if they'd actually seen the person or if they only remembered remembering the sighting, like me." She touched the livid bruises on her neck and smiled ruefully. "I don't know what I was thinking. I've been reading too much Lord Peter Wimsey, I suppose. In any case, I went to the ladies' before the first meeting. And as I was washing my hands . . ." She touched her neck again.

"Holy God." Now Rachel did exchange a glance with Magda. "But what did you do? I mean, how did you . . . ?"

Capitaine Boussicault took over. "Professeure Dale tells us she used something called the 'sing method.'"

"You *sang*?" Rachel sat back in her plastic chair. Was Aurora that bad a singer? Had her voice stopped a murderer in his tracks?

"No." The older woman gave a hoarse cough. "I'm sorry, let me explain. S.I.N.G. stands for *solar plexus, instep, nose, groin*. I saw it in a film."

"*Miss Congeniality*," Magda interjected.

"Yes, that's right. When he threw the, well, the garrote, I suppose, over my head, I grabbed it with my hand, just instinctively—so it wasn't fully pressing on my throat. Then I put my other elbow in his stomach, stamped on his instep, and smacked him in the face with my knuckles. I didn't do very well on *groin*, I'm afraid." She looked abashed. "When I tried to hit him there, he jumped back. Although that did make him break his grip. Only then he ran before I could grab him."

"Did you get a look at him?" Magda asked.

Boussicault said, "Professeure Dale has told me that she is unable to identify her attacker."

The older woman shook her head sorrowfully. "He stood behind me, you see. And when he was running away, I was trying to get my breath back."

"You keep saying *he* and *him*. You're sure it was a man? It was in the women's room, after all." A terrible realization had begun to make its way to the front of Rachel's mind.

Aurora looked taken aback, then abashed. "I'm sorry. That must be because I was expecting Mr. Cavill or Mr. Stibb. I suppose it could have been a woman, although she'd have needed to be a tall woman, given my size. But why *would* it be a woman?"

"No reason. I just wanted to be sure it was a man." Under the guise of folding her hands in her lap, Rachel pressed her fingertips into her knuckles. Hadn't she told a tall woman the previous afternoon that Aurora was going to the police? That she was still working at the Bibliothèque? She thought of Lou-Lou's face, white with what she had read as relief. Calming herself, she asked, "What happened next?"

"Well, once I'd got my breath back, I asked to use a phone. Then I rang emergency services and they sent an ambulance."

"*You asked to use a phone?*"

"Yes." Aurora seemed surprised at Rachel's surprise. "I didn't bring my mobile to France with me."

"And the ambulance brought you here? Surely there's a hospital in the second arrondissement that they could have taken you to."

"Oh, I asked them to bring me here."

"You asked them?" Rachel glanced at Boussicault. He raised his eyebrows and nodded.

Aurora shrugged. "It's the most famous hospital in Paris. I wanted to see it."

Rachel looked at her smiling face underlined by the bruises around her neck. *Doughty*, she thought. That was exactly the right word to describe Aurora Dale: doughty.

Chapter Thirty-Eight

They sat on a bench outside the hospital, watching some of the nurses smoke together, chatting and waving their cigarettes for emphasis as they talked.

"Jesus, what a woman!" Magda said.

"I know. Let's hope that's what we're like in twenty years."

They kept looking at the nurses. One of them laughed and waved her hand at another in a shooing motion. The shooed one mock-dodged away.

"I have to tell you something," Rachel explained about her meeting with LouLou, about Rachel's revelation that Aurora was going to change her story. "It didn't occur to me until just now in her room that Aurora's description of what actually happened contradicted LouLou's own story to the police. She said she was in the record room until she went through the stacks and found Giles, but Aurora said she ran into her coming out of the bathroom!"

"Well, that's not so bad." Magda switched from LouLou's prosecutor to her defender. "I mean, it's not unreasonable that you might forget to mention you'd washed your hands."

"It's a lot less reasonable when you've been found next to a stabbed man, holding a bloody knife with perfectly clean hands!" Rachel grabbed her own hair in frustration. "And when she said, 'I'm telling you this because I want you to understand!' I thought she meant understand why she was so bitter all the time!"

"Maybe she did. You have her number in your phone. Call her up and ask."

That's right, she did have LouLou's number! She poked at her screen and waited. No reply. No voice mail. Just endless ringing.

"Nothing. She's not picking up. And the way she smiled when she said, 'Sisterhood is powerful.' I thought she was thanking me, but what if she was reminding me to stay quiet?"

"Calm down." Rachel had just enough sense left to appreciate the irony of Magda saying that to her. "You're acting like she's our only suspect. There's still Cavill, for one. We could go question him."

"I'm guessing that by this time Cavill's been told not to talk to anyone. And Stibb"—she headed off another suggestion—"wasn't exactly obliging in his interviews with Boussicault, so when it's just us . . ." She shrugged.

One of the nurses flicked her cigarette into the standing ashtray and went back into the hospital. She waved her fingers at her companions over her shoulder, like algae drifting underwater.

At last Magda said slowly, "All right, so either we can't talk to our suspects or it's not a good idea. Then what if we tried some victimology? We could try to learn about the victims instead."

Rachel frowned. She couldn't see how they'd even start investigating Laurent and Morel. Both men had been killed near work, so there were no neighbors to draw on, even if they could get the addresses. But still, presumably they'd made friends and contacts through work . . . well, she knew they had. "I guess we could start at Chez Poule."

"What?"

"Chez Poule. We could try a different waiter, maybe."

Magda laughed. "I don't mean those victims. I mean the *other* victims." At Rachel's blank look, she said, "The books. Why don't we see if we can find out anything from the books?"

"The books?"

"Yes. Remember that time when you were thinking about becoming a bookbinder?"

Rachel nodded. It had been during a period when the poetry was going particularly badly.

"You told me that when books were damaged, you could take them to conservators, who could look at the damage and tell you the best way to fix it. They knew all about bindings, and about how different things interacted with different papers to cause damage, and they could use that information to fix them. What if we took the books to someone like that? Someone who could tell us what happened to them and what it means? A . . . a . . . forensic conservator."

"I don't think it works like that. I think they can tell you what happened to a book, and how it could be fixed, but they can't tell you who might have done it."

Magda huffed. "Yes, but they could tell us *some*thing.

Which might lead us somewhere. And at the moment we don't really have any other options."

Rachel tried to think of other options, with no luck. "But who would we even get? We don't know any conservators."

"You do." Magda was triumphant. "Dr. Dwamena. She's Head of Rare Books for heaven's sake. Presumably she knows all about them. She could look at the books and tell us what she sees."

* * *

Docteure Dwamena had not let the police take the *Supplementum Chronicarum* and the psalter to the commissariat; they might have been potential material evidence in a homicide, but they were also rare works of art and literature that were under her care. And since the Bibliothèque Nationale was technically an arm of the Ministry of Culture, and the police were technically an arm of the Ministry of the Interior, neither outranked the other; the police couldn't order her to hand over evidence. The books, she told Rachel over the phone, were sitting safely under lock and key in a controlled environment. As she and Magda sat on the Mètro to the Bibliothèque, Rachel wondered if the doctor would be any more receptive to the two of them than she had been to the police.

In the end, the question turned out to be irrelevant. Docteure Dwamena heard them out, then said simply, "But I am not a book conservator."

"You're not?" Magda looked bemused.

"No, I am a book historian. That's quite a different thing. I can tell you the circumstances surrounding a book's production and history, what kind of materials it's made of and so on, but I cannot tell you anything about the means of its destruction. And unfortunately our conservation team is away for the August vacation. So I don't think I can help." She looked genuinely disappointed.

For a moment they all stood quiet. Then Rachel remembered, "We know another conservator."

Magda looked confused again. "We do?"

"Yes. She helped us with Edgar's Bible." Then, realizing those sentences would make no sense to Docteure Dwamena, she turned to her. "We know a woman named Camille Murat. She works for Librairie Pierre Brunet, a shop for antiquarian religious books. She's a bookseller there, but she trained as a conservator. She's helped us in the past."

"I know of Brunet. In the Rue des Carmes, yes? It has a good reputation." The doctor nodded. "And this woman, is she someone who can be trusted in dealing with a priceless book?"

"Yes." Rachel thought of the way Madame Murat had assisted with the identification and preservation of a rare facsimile of the Gutenberg Bible. "She's the one who originally told us that antiquarian books can hold on to evidence for centuries."

"You can meet her yourself if you come with us," Magda put in.

"Come with you?"

"In the cab. When we take the books to her."

"The cab?" Docteure Dwamena's voice didn't rise, but her face told a whole story. "You want to take a rare sixteenth-century Latin chronicle and a medieval psalter across Paris in a taxi cab?"

"An *air-conditioned* taxi cab," Magda replied, as if this canceled out all objections. She added, "Air-conditioned there *and* back."

"No." Docteure Dwamena said flatly—and definitively. "The books remain here. You may arrange for your conservator to visit us. I will research her background while we wait, and I will evaluate her in person when she arrives. What happens afterward will depend on what I learn."

Chapter Thirty-Nine

Camille Murat sounded surprised to hear Rachel at the other end of a telephone line after a year of silence, but once she heard the name Alphonsine Dwamena, she didn't hesitate. She would be right over.

Rachel, Magda, and Docteure Dwamena stood in the foyer waiting for her. "A promising CV," the doctor had said as she locked her office door. "North Bennet Street School in your country, followed by an MA at West Dean College in England. Two of the best programs outside France."

Now, standing next to Rachel, she suddenly said, "Why did you need Madame Murat's help?"

"I'm sorry?"

"You said Madame Murat had helped you in the past, and that made me wonder under what circumstances you had met her. I wasn't aware that you'd had any experience with rare books before coming here. How did you come to know a book conservator?"

Rachel and Magda exchanged a glance. How did you explain to someone that although you were not really interested in rare books, you knew this particular rare book expert because someone else had sold her a rare book—well, a facsimile of a rare book, but one that was rare in its own right—that was evidence in a murder case you had been investigating before anyone else thought it was a murder; a book that, once the case was resolved and after you made sure she got her money back, you claimed for yourself in accordance with a promise in the will of the murder victim whose unsuspected murder you'd been investigating?

"We met professionally," Rachel said. "When I was responsible for cataloging a friend's library."

* * *

Madame Murat looked precisely as she had a year earlier, even down to her white blouse and straight black skirt. Her low heels clicked across the granite floor, and as she approached she switched an old-fashioned doctor's satchel from her right hand to her left so she could shake hands.

"Madame Levis, what a delightful surprise to hear from you! And Madame Stevens, it's good to see you again as well."

Rachel took her outstretched hand, then indicated Docteure Dwamena. "And this is Docteure Alphonsine Dwamena, head of Rare Books and Manuscripts here."

"Docteure Dwamena!" Madame Murat was obviously delighted. "I have read your recent work on ascribing pamphlet authorship by clustering false publication information. Most exciting, most suggestive. *Vraiment, un honneur*."

Docteure Dwamena gave her a skeptical look. "Suggestive in what way?"

"It made me wonder what might happen if one paired the

clustering with paper type and watermark information. This might help to narrow the date quite tightly."

Docteure Dwamena thawed. "Yes, this is an interesting idea. I have been thinking about it myself. There are some risks involved if one doesn't know how long the paper was held before use." She gestured down the hallway toward the reading room. "Let me tell you about my ideas as we go."

The doctor had cleared her desk of everything but two lamps, wiped the surface clean, and placed two boxes tied with tape on its right-hand side. Madame Murat turned the lamps on; their light was dazzlingly strong. From her bag she took a pair of white cotton gloves like those Docteure Dwamena had worn when examining the *Supplementum*, tweezers, and a pair of black-framed glasses with the thickest lenses Rachel had ever seen. All of these she laid on the desktop before pulling toward her the nearest of the two boxes. She opened it carefully, untying the ribbon and folding out four flaps so that the container became a flat surface. Then she pulled on the gloves and put the glasses on her nose—she looked like Mr. Magoo, Rachel thought, trying not to laugh—and opened the cover of the psalter.

There in front of them was a page of stark black calligraphy, relieved by an initial B that stood out like an elaborate jewel. Outlined in red, it held in its upper loop a tiny representation of a Madonna and Child, in its lower loop a small crucifix. Even from where she stood Rachel could see the love that softened the Virgin's face and the lines of pain on the Christ's, each bellying chamber surrounded by twining vines tipped here and there with gilded leaves.

"Ah!" Madame Murat looked at Alphonsine. "Beautiful, beautiful."

It was beautiful, Rachel could see; although the ink had cracked in places, the colors still sprang out vividly fresh.

Madame Murat turned the pages reverently until she arrived at the stub of the missing sheet. She bent over, flicking her enormously enlarged eyes up and down. Rachel could hear the breath of every person in the room as Madame Murat moved her head, carefully taking a survey of the damage. Then she began to talk.

"Books are unique objects because they speak to us twice. They have words and pictures on their pages, but they also speak to us with their *form*, with the matter that makes their existence. Every book—" She tugged gently with the tweezers at the stub's fringe of fibers; She tugged gently with the tweezers at the stub's fringe of fibers, peered at their feathery tips and at the pages that flanked them, inhaled deeply, smelling. Then she continued. "Every book is a history. It contains the story of the world that made it."

She moved the psalter carefully to one side and unpacked the *Supplementum*. Rachel held her breath, and she could feel Magda doing the same.

"Now"—Madame Murat opened its cover with her gloved hands—"here you had a *Supplementum Chronicarum*, printed in Venice in 1490, its particular pages printed in a particular typeface on sheets folded and stitched in a particular way and with illustrations interleaved at particular places and for particular reasons—perhaps because that was the hallmark of the printer, perhaps because it was expected that such books would be created in such a format, or perhaps because it wasn't expected." She looked up at Rachel and Magda for a moment with her magnified eyes. "This book contained numberless answers, some to questions we don't even know we should ask yet, all waiting to be discovered to help us trace the evolution of books, of printing practices, and to help us understand the expectations and desires of people in fifteenth-century Venice. This book might have told us a little bit about how different the current world is from that of Venice, or how similar it is to it. It might have illuminated for us something about human nature.

"And now—" She lowered her head over the *Supplementum*, peered at the pages flanking the stub, and inhaled as deeply as she had with the psalter, then lifted her head again. "Now you have a book with a page missing. Now it has a new story, perhaps a story that will still ask and answer questions—certainly a story that illuminates something about human nature. But your thief has destroyed a history. On the other hand, of course, he has also created a new one."

She pulled off her gloves and glasses, and as she did so it seemed she shed her philosophical skin and resumed a practical one. "*Alors*. Here is what I can tell you: the lines in your psalter have been drawn with lead, and at least one of the monks who worked on it was blond—a hair was preserved in the binding. Your *Supplementum* was preserved, but it wasn't opened very often. The pages show scarcely any wear, and the binding is still very tight. And your thief is clever and careful, as well as very, very discreet, because the pages in both books have been removed with liquid."

"Liquid!" Rachel didn't know what she'd been expecting, but certainly not that.

"Yes. It's not unheard of, although I myself have never seen it before. The page is softened with liquid so that it can be pulled away easily and quietly. Hence the little hairs sticking out from the stub. You would need to be familiar with ancient papers and parchments to manage it—one second too short and the page would rip; one second too long and the string might dry to the page. But if done right, no ripping, no slicing, just a soft wiggle, and—" She clicked her tongue. "One shouldn't admire destruction, but . . . such ingenuity! I recently read an article in which someone even did it using string. A map seller, I think. He would go to a library with a length of string tucked in his cheek. He would keep it wet with saliva—you know." She moved her jaw to demonstrate. "And when no one was looking he would take it out, straighten it into the book margin, and rest it there until the saliva softened the page."

Rachel went cold. "Say that again."

Madame Murat looked confused. "Which part?"

"The end. Just the end. No, wait, never mind. Saliva!" Rachel held out an arm as if stopping an advancing horde. "I've got it. I mean, I get it. I've got it. I know who did it."

"Who?" Magda sounded breathless. "Was it LouLou? It was the familiarity with papers that made you realize, wasn't it?"

"No, it wasn't LouLou." *Thank God*, she added silently.

"It was Cavill?" Magda shook her head. "Man, all along! We should stop discounting the most obvious—"

"Hush! It wasn't Cavill." She turned and looked at Magda. "It was Homer Stibb!"

Chapter Forty

Of course there wasn't a taxi, Rachel thought. There was never a taxi when she needed one. She bounced up and down on her toes, looking in both directions with no success. Then Magda, always a taxi-whisperer, stepped to the curb, and a sleek white Peugeot with a lit sign appeared. They tumbled in.

"Hotel Palais!" Rachel said to the driver.

"But Madame"—the man turned around—"that hotel is a ten-minute walk from here."

"I can't run and dial a phone."

The driver stared, mystified by this explanation.

"Drive, please!"

He shrugged and pulled into traffic. Rachel dug into her bag and found her *portable*. "Boussicault?" she said after a few seconds. "It's Rachel. I know who did it. Please come to the Hotel Palais. Yes, right away. Yes, I'll explain. In person."

She broke the connection and turned to Magda. "It was the jaw, the thing Madame Murat did with her jaw." She imitated the conservator's back-and-forth motion, her lips rolling in and out. "Homer Stibb did that in his interviews. I thought it was a nervous tic, and I suppose it is, but I see now that it's a tic acquired from moistening the string. He was nervous that his string wouldn't be wet enough when he used it on the books, so now whenever he's nervous he automatically tries to produce saliva!"

"And *that's* why there was saliva on Laurent's neck."

"Yes. No one was licking people while they murdered them." The cab gave a jerk, and Rachel saw the driver's eyes in the rearview mirror. "Stibb used string he kept in his cheek to strangle Laurent, so his saliva was on it, and that transferred. I bet if that police lab ever gets around to testing the string from the bathroom floor, they'll discover that it's got saliva all over it." She sat back in satisfaction just as the cab drew up outside the hotel.

"Perfect," she said to the driver, handing him ten euros.

Like the Hotel Etoiles, the Hotel Palais was clearly a two-star establishment, but this time Rachel didn't try to figure out how or why. She crossed to the check-in counter and rapped on the marble-look Formica to draw the receptionist's attention.

"What room is Homer Stibb in, please?"

The young man behind the desk jumped slightly. "Homer Stibb?"

Rachel stifled her impatience. "Yes. I need the room number for Homer Stibb."

"But, Madame, Monsieur Stibb is no longer a guest here. In fact, you just missed him. He checked out ten minutes ago. I called a cab to take him to Charles de Gaulle airport myself."

"Where was he going?"

The receptionist stared at her, confused. "To the airport. As I said."

"No." Magda craned her neck over Rachel's shoulder as she spoke. "Where was he *going*? Did he say he was going back to America, or somewhere else?"

"Oh!" The young man gave a little laugh at himself. "No, back to America. Tennessee, I think he said it was?" He pronounced it *Tenn-ay-say*.

They recrossed the lobby in a few long steps, Rachel calling "*Merci!*" as they went.

Outside, the taxi was standing where they had left it. No wonder she could never find one, if they were all idling by the curbs of their last drop-offs. They climbed in again.

"Charles de Gaulle! Hurry!"

The driver looked up from texting. He seemed surprised to see them, although he recovered quickly. "But Madame, you can get to Charles de Gaulle via the TGV. It's much cheaper than a taxi."

"Please just drive." As the car began to move, she turned to Magda. "The train stops; a cab doesn't. If we want to have any real hope of catching Stibb, a cab's best. How much cash do you have?"

"I don't take cards," the cabby called back warningly.

Magda opened her wallet and counted, held up five fingers, then used two to make a zero. Rachel had twenty. Well, seventy euros was more than enough to get them to the airport. "Don't you worry," she said to the driver.

For a few seconds there was silence. Magda scrolled down

her phone's screen while Rachel unearthed her own phone from the depths of her bag. She dialed Boussicault once again, but this time when he answered, she said only, "He's already left the hotel. Come to Charles de Gaulle."

"What terminal?"

She had no idea what terminal. Why hadn't she thought to ask the receptionist what terminal Stibb had asked for? What airlines even flew to Tennessee from Paris?

Magda's pad appeared before her eyes. TERMINAL 2, it said, 3:40 FLIGHT. "Terminal two. The flight leaves at three forty." When she hung up, she turned to face Magda. "Thank you. Thank you, thank you."

"No problem."

"How do you know the flight time?"

Magda shrugged. "The only flights still left to fly from de Gaulle to Tennessee today are at three forty and six thirty. I assumed it was the three forty. If it's the six thirty, we'll have plenty of time to catch him."

They sat in tense silence, each staring out her window.

"A friend has left his passport behind?" the cabby asked at last.

"What? No." Rachel shook her head.

"One of you is trying to reunite with her boyfriend?" He grinned into the rearview mirror.

"No."

Magda leaned forward. "We're detectives. Trying to catch our man."

His reflected eyes took them in, trying to decide if they were joking. When both their faces remained serious, the car suddenly bucked, then leapt forward. He grinned into the mirror again. "This is every taximan's dream!"

Once they regained their composure, Magda turned to face Rachel. "What about the saliva on *Morel*'s neck? He was stabbed."

"I don't know. I'm guessing it takes a lot of effort to stab someone to death, so maybe the saliva came from exhaling at the exertion." The cab took a sharp right, then a left, then merged onto the highway at top speed. Rachel began to feel slightly nauseated, and she noticed Magda turning pale. The rest of the trip passed silently.

They jerked to a halt outside the terminal, and Rachel shoved their money at the driver as they clambered out. "*Bonne chance*!" she heard him yell as the automatic doors slid open.

Terminal two was packed. Snaking lines full of disconsolate college students traveling home from summer programs and tourists exhausted by foreign exposure crowded the floor. Exasperated parents tried to corral the small children who ran shrieking across the polished granite, while airport soldiers wandered the edges of the crowds clutching the assault rifles that always seemed like too much to Rachel. Today, though, she hardly noticed the soldiers or their guns. She was too busy wondering how they were ever going to find Stibb in this mess.

Magda stared at her phone. "He's checking in at either Delta or Air France. Given these lines, even if he was twenty minutes ahead, he probably hasn't finished bag drop yet. We should go right to their check-in areas."

They looked around desperately, trying to spot a sign that would help. And then suddenly, "There he is!" Magda grabbed Rachel's arm.

"Where?"

"Over there at Air France! See? The bag drop desk all the way over there."

Rachel saw. Homer Stibb was standing in front of an Air France economy counter, smiling at the agent while a large suitcase slid down the conveyor belt away from him. As Rachel watched, he tucked his passport and boarding pass in the front pocket of his khaki traveler's jacket, settled the strap of his satchel more comfortably on his shoulder, and strolled off toward passport control as if he didn't have a care in the world.

"Come on!" She grabbed Magda's hand. "We can't follow him into security. We need to reach him before he goes through passport control."

They tried to move through the crowd as swiftly as they could without drawing attention. They speed-walked by couples standing next to giant suitcases and through clumps of extended families bidding tearful farewells; they overtook a flock of flight attendants whose clicking heels and shiny roller suitcases moved briskly toward the barrier. They were going to reach him, Rachel thought. Her heart soared with triumph just as a tiny girl wobbled into a clear space a few meters ahead of her, stumbled for a moment, then fell flat on the floor.

The girl's outraged screams echoed through the terminal. Homer Stibb turned toward the noise. His eyes darted around, looking for its source, and instead fell on Rachel. She had a fleeting glimpse of them widening before Stibb began to run toward security. He zigzagged between people, as fleet as a man could be while a satchel slapped against his hip. She and Magda chased behind him.

Stibb reached the retractable barriers that marked off the passport control area. Heading for the opening, he turned swiftly to his left, but his satchel, pulled away from his body by the abruptness of the turn, caught on one of the poles. It jerked off his shoulder and fell, its snaps popping and papers flying out. Some scattered, but most stayed in a stack as they hit the floor, where they fanned out. There, in almost their precise center, Rachel saw a yellowed sheet with thick black writing, its entire left-hand side taken up by a square once colored bright red, now softened to a hazy rose.

It was the missing psalter page.

Stibb fell to his knees, scrabbling to collect the sheets. He stuffed them in the satchel and scrambled back up, turning to run into passport control. But Rachel stretched out her arm as far as she could—and she just managed to grab the strap of his satchel. Bracing herself, she gave it a jerk. Stibb's feet slipped on the granite and he stumbled, but he recovered. Grabbing the satchel, he jerked back. Rachel felt Magda grip the back of her shirt to offer added ballast, and she yanked again. Stibb slid a few centimeters across the floor, still gripping his bag.

Really? Rachel thought. She was playing tug-of-war with a grown man in the middle of an airport and no one was going to intervene? *Where are those idiots with the rifles when you need them?*

No sooner had this question formed in her mind than Stibb gave a vicious pull and the strap slid burning out of her hands. He reeled, recovered once more, clutched the satchel to his chest, and began to run the few meters left before the entrance to passport control. Reaching out a hand to steady himself on the first pole, he turned sharply to enter.

Rachel stooped over. She was prepared to chase him all the way to the border control counter if she had to. She began to slide under a strap, but a figure ran out of the crowd ahead of her, crashed into Stibb, and brought him sprawling to the floor.

It was Boussicault.

"Homer Stibb." He panted slightly. "I am detaining you on suspicion of the crime of murder against Giles Morel on thirtieth July, suspicion of the crime of murder against Guy Laurent on sixth July, and suspicion of thefts from the Bibliothèque Nationale of Paris, number unknown. You have the right to answer questions, to make statements, or to remain silent. You have the right to an interpreter, if you need one. You have the right to an attorney and the right to notify your embassy, or to have us notify them for you." He took a breath and snapped the handcuffs closed.

Chapter Forty-One

In the holding room of Charles de Gaulle airport, Rachel found all her interrogation-venue dreams come true. Here the furniture was welded aluminum and the floor cement. Here the windowless walls were painted a dull institutional cream and the door had a buzzer that went off each time it unlocked. A small ceiling-mounted camera trained its monocle eye on the table and four chairs that crowded against one wall.

Homer Stibb sat on one side of the table; she, Magda, and Boussicault had arranged themselves around the other. Between them lay the psalter page, now encased in a plastic protector.

Stibb stared at it silently for a long moment. Then he said, “Would you believe me if I said I had no idea how it got in my satchel?”

“Well”—Rachel’s tone was practical—“not now that you’ve asked that.”

His eyes moved to it again, as if dragged by magnets. After a minute or so he said, “Will I go to prison for stealing it?”

What a weird opening question, Rachel thought. But when Boussicault nodded, it was as if all the air went out of Stibb.

He gave a deep sigh and slumped back in his seat. Tears came into his eyes. "For how long?"

"Certainly not less than three years."

"Three years! Three years without—" Stibb stopped as if overwhelmed. He put his left hand on the table, palm down and fingers slightly spread, like a spider at rest. It was far enough away from the page that there was no fear of his coming into contact with it. He seemed just to want to feel something under his touch.

"It's beautiful, isn't it?" he said. "It's so beautiful." He raised his head and gazed at them across the table as if they were students and he wanted to teach them something very important. "They're all beautiful. You can look at hundreds of them, over and over again, and they never become ordinary. They always take your breath away."

"Do you have hundreds of them?" Boussicault's voice was mild, but it was determined. If Stibb looked like a teacher, the *capitaine* sounded like one.

Stibb smiled. "I have—" A sly look came into his eyes. "I have more than one. If I give you the ones in my suitcase, will I get time off for co-operating?"

Boussicault's features revealed nothing. "The French government takes theft of its national treasures very seriously, Docteur Stibb. I wouldn't count on the effectiveness of any bargaining."

Stibb's face fell.

"You got them using string, right?" Rachel couldn't help breaking in. She needed to know if she'd guessed correctly.

Stibb stared at her for a moment, then nodded. "I read

about it in a magazine. You put the string in your cheek and keep it wet with saliva until you can use it. I had to practice a few times before I got it right; it's hard to work up the saliva you need."

"That's why you do this." Rachel mimed Stibb's convulsive lip and jaw gesture. "To produce the spit. And after a while it just got to be a tic. Maybe to soothe yourself when things got stressful?"

He nodded again.

"And then you'd detach the pages by putting the wet string in the margin until the saliva softened the paper enough to remove it easily, right?"

"Parchment," Stibb corrected. "Paper is made from vegetable matter. Medieval book pages are usually made of animal skin stretched very thin." He gave a little smirk at his superior knowledge.

Boussicault took over once more. "Is that why you used the string to strangle Guy Laurent? Because you had it with you?"

Stibb turned a blank face in his direction. "Who is Guy Laurent? Is that the man in the stacks? I thought Cavill killed him."

Boussicault grew impatient. "Docteur Stibb, you know full well who Guy Laurent is."

Stibb grew polite. "I assure you I don't." He raised curious eyebrows. "Could you remind me?"

The *capitaine* leaned forward. "Docteur, we have saliva in the ligature in Monsieur Laurent's neck, and we have tested that saliva for DNA. We have a piece of string from the scene of Monsieur Laurent's murder with saliva on it, and its DNA matches that in the ligature. We have that same DNA in saliva on the neck of Giles Morel. When I apprehended you earlier, the force of our collision caused you to exhale sharply as you hit the terminal floor. An officer I had standing by specifically for this purpose collected the saliva you exhaled, and it's on its way to our lab. I have no doubt it will match what we found on the string and the victims."

Rachel felt Magda tense up. She reached out under the table and put a gentle hand on her arm. She, too, remembered Boussicualt's assertion that the saliva on Laurent's neck was too degraded to yield DNA, and she was betting the rest of his statement was equally untrue. But Stibb didn't necessarily know that.

In the silence Stibb looked down into his lap, then back up again. His eyes moved rapidly back and forth. "Well," he said finally. "DNA. Well." He thought for a few seconds more, then swallowed. "Can I get some water? When I've had some water, I'll tell you what happened."

* * *

When he put down his plastic cup a few minutes later, he closed his eyes, then opened them and looked at Rachel. "Yes, I remove the pages with the string. I get it out of my mouth by coughing, or by pretending to clear my throat." He mimed bringing a hand up to cover his mouth politely, then switched his focus to Boussicault. "That's how it began with the first librarian. I coughed, but I was too loud. It caught his attention, and he saw me spit the string into my hand. He kept watching, and eventually he also saw me roll up the page and put it inside my shirt." He shook his head. "You should really thank me for getting rid of that man. He was loathsome. He watched me do it twice, just to be sure he had enough on me. He didn't care about the books at all."

"And he blackmailed you," Rachel prompted.

"Yes. He called and told me to meet him at that restaurant. When I got there, he told me what he'd seen and demanded a thousand euros not to say anything." He shrugged. "I don't have a thousand euros. Well, you know that. I suppose I could have pleaded with him, but he made it clear he wasn't going to negotiate. He started telling me about other people he'd blackmailed in the past, and how he'd turned them in if they'd refused. It was so *unfair*!" They jumped at this sudden shout. "He didn't care about the illustrations one bit, but he expected *me* to pay *him* for them? He said he was going to go to the men's room to give me some time to think. That's when I realized I still had the string, and it came to me how easy it would be to solve the problem." He made a little *hmm!* noise. "And it really was. I just held the string tight around his neck for a few minutes, then paid the bill and left."

Just like that, Rachel thought. She hadn't been too far off when she'd imagined the murderer all those weeks ago. "And Giles Morel?" She was genuinely puzzled. What had poor Giles ever done to Stibb?

"Oh, that one! When I handed the psalter back in, he noticed the page was missing. He said he happened to flick through it because he had a spare second. He asked me to come in early the next morning because he wanted to find out the 'concatenation of circumstances'—that was his phrase—that could bring a man like me to destroy books. But I knew his goal was to get money too. He let me in around back, but then he said he thought we'd be more comfortable in the reading room while we 'talked.'" Stibb made quotation marks in the air on the last word. "And while he was leading me through the stacks, I just—Well, I'd bought a knife the previous evening, thinking I'd slit his throat, but I realized in the moment that if I did that, his blood would get all over the books. So I stabbed him in the chest." For a moment he looked pleased at his ability to adapt to circumstances, but then he frowned. "Stabbing is a lot more difficult than it looks in the movies. It really takes the breath out of you. I had my mouth open, and my string dropped onto his neck. But I collected it again when I finished, before I wiped the knife handle with my sleeve. I didn't want the two crimes connected, obviously." He looked at Boussicault. "So much for that, huh?"

Oh, Giles, Rachel thought. Killed by his own lack of common sense. How could he have thought a thief would stop by for a chat about his theft? Still, death was a harsh punishment for ignorance of human nature. She sighed.

Magda leaned forward. "And then you made up Jean Bernard to confuse things?"

"Yes."

"But how did you do it?" Rachel broke in. The question had been puzzling her ever since Alan's explanation that Jean Bernard didn't exist. "You need an ID number to place book requests."

"Not exactly." Stibb looked pleased with himself again. "You need *an* ID number, and you need *a* name, but there's some kind of glitch in the system that means they don't connect. I found that out one day when I accidentally typed an author's name into the patron's name space. So I just typed in the most generic French name I could think of and a number I found when someone forgot to log out." Rachel raised her eyebrows. She could see how this fault could go unnoticed by the Bibliothèque and its honest patrons, but the library was still going to have some explaining to do.

"Of course, there's always a risk that the person whose number you've stolen might figure it out," Stibb continued. *Shades of Charlotte Loftus*, Rachel thought. "So I was irritated when Cavill told me about his debt. I could've saved myself the risk. He was scared at that point, and wanted someone to confide in, I think, but obviously the debt made him a great suspect. So I figured, better safe than sorry . . ."

"And you put the woodcut in his jacket."

"Mm-hmm. Although that was harder than I thought. I was able to bring the blade in by putting it in my pants cuff, and I avoided the risk of cutting myself by shoving most of it into an eraser I could use as a handle, but I had to move very quickly to pull the whole thing off while he was over at a computer ordering books. I really thought I might not make it. And I did feel bad about it. I loved that woodcut. But I needed to take this illumination home with me." He gestured toward the plastic envelope. "You can see why."

Try as she might, Rachel couldn't see. The page was beautiful, yes, but not as beautiful as the one Madame Murat had shown them. And according to Laurent's calculations it wasn't worth much outside its book—certainly not two murders and an innocent man in jail. But she could see from the look in Stibb's eyes that it enchanted him.

Boussicault must have agreed with Rachel's assessment of the page, because he said uncomprehendingly, "You did all of this over two pieces of paper. Two illustrations you could have asked to have photographed, or could have found reproductions of in a book."

Stibb looked at him. His face said plainly that other people were very strange. He gestured at the illumination once again. "Look at this. This was made to bring readers closer to God, to entice them to holiness by means of beauty. Libraries keep things like this shut up in the dark. They make complex rules about who can access them, and where, and for how long." He barked a laugh. "What kind of lover never looks at his beloved? I look at my illustrations every day—I'd look at them every hour if I could. I feel ecstasy in their presence. I feel what they were made to make men feel. And my love is pure. Someone else might be interested in profit, but I'm not. I want them for themselves. I'll be struggling financially until the day I die, and I don't care because my eyes will be filled with beauty." He took a breath and looked at Boussicault. "Now you tell me: who deserves this beauty if not the man who loves it most?"

All three sat stunned by his sudden eloquence, and in their silence Stibb's left hand suddenly came to life. He pressed its fingertips down hard on the surface to brace himself, then shot forward. The other three instinctively reeled back for a moment, long enough for him to grab the psalter page. In a blur of movement he shook off its plastic protector.

Boussicault jumped up and stretched his arm across the table, but Stibb simply leaned away. Just out of the *capitaine*'s reach, he looked at the page for a split second, his face a vision of tender joy. Then he tore a strip from the side with the illumination and stuffed it in his mouth. Raising some saliva with the familiar jerk of his jaw, he swallowed it.

Chapter Forty-Two

"He ate it?" Alan's voice was disbelieving. "Why?" He, Magda, and Rachel were at a table in Bistrot Vivienne with a bottle of the restaurant's best rosé in front of them. The women were celebrating; Alan was trying to understand.

"He didn't say." Rachel lifted her shoulders. "In fact, he didn't say anything. He literally did not speak again, and Boussicault told me this morning that he still hasn't offered a word of explanation. But my thought is that he wanted to—to make it part of him. He knew he was going to prison for the rest of his life, and that was the only way he could keep what he loved with him."

"I don't think it was love," Magda put in. "I think it was more like addiction. Didn't you see the way he couldn't keep his eyes off the page while we were questioning him?"

"But doesn't an addict love the thing they're addicted to? They end up needing it, but it all starts with love."

They considered for a moment. Then Magda turned to Alan. "Actually, eating's the least of it. After his arrest Stibb gave Boussicault permission to let the Tennessee police go in his house, and they found *stacks* of illustrations. Hundreds, they said."

"So he'd been stealing for years?"

"Yes," Rachel cut in, "but even that's not the bizarre part. The bizarre part is, they were all in a safe in an empty room."

"He didn't even have them on display?" Alan's tone said, *Then what's the point?*

"Not just that. He didn't have *anything* on display. Anywhere in the house. All he had were the pages in the safe. And the Tennessee police told Boussicault there was nothing else in the room except a chair. I guess Stibb would just shut the door, open the safe, and sit there looking at them."

"And he didn't feel guilty at all about stealing them," Magda added. "Or about the murders. He really seemed to think the pictures were better off stuffed in a safe in Tennessee with him." She shook her head in disbelief.

"Well, you got your psychopath," Alan said to her. "No guilt, convictions of superiority . . ."

"I guess." Magda looked disappointed. "But I thought a psychopath would be more unusual. You know, a ruthless murderer, not some skinny guy with dusty aviator glasses."

"Although he was a murderer in the end," Rachel pointed out. "His glasses were dusty, but he saw through them well enough to kill two people."

"I thought it was LouLou." It was Alan's turn to shake his head. "You told me that Aurora Dale said she saw LouLou coming out of the bathroom when LouLou said she was in the records room."

"Yes. But, well, LouLou lied. Boussicault told me he called her to let her know they'd caught the murderer, and she was so relieved that she came clean. She was really scared, because everyone knew she hated Laurent and was jumpy around Giles. She'd gone to wash her hands before going back to the stacks, and she knew how that would look. So she lied and said she was in the record room the whole time until she went into the stacks. She didn't remember passing Aurora, so she didn't know Aurora had seen her."

"People, eh?" said Alan. "They never do the sensible thing. She should've just told the truth at the start."

Magda, disappointed by her psychopath, nodded agreement. "I will never understand the human mind."

"Ah, the human mind," Rachel said philosophically. "It is indeed a mystery." She paused. "For example, sometimes someone seems set. Their path seems secure. You might even say that you know them. But then they change course completely. Well," she qualified, "not completely. But a lot. Or they begin to. They make a decision to begin changing course."

Magda stared at her. "I have no idea what you're talking about."

"Yeah, sorry, I got a bit lost at the end. Hang on . . ." Trying to regain the drama, she reached into her bag and took out what looked like a miniature day planner. She put it down in front of Magda.

Magda looked at it. "What's that?"

"You're supposed to open it." She pushed it toward her. "Open it."

Magda unsnapped it. It opened like a day planner, too,

but each of its four pages was made of fabric, and each had a series of slots holding small rods of different shapes and sizes.

Magda was still confused. "You're going to start training as a dental hygienist?"

Rachel rolled her eyes. "It's a lock-picking kit! The picks all fit different locks! And wait, that's not all." She reached into the bag again, this time pulling out a business card that she laid next to the kit.

Alan recited the card aloud. "'Levis and Stevens, Investigatrices.'"

"'We are shameless in the service of detection,'" Rachel added.

Magda met Rachel's eyes with her own across the table. Her face was grave. "Stevens and Levis, I think you'll find." But the corners of her lips twitched.

Rachel grinned at her. "We can talk about that later."

A Glossary of Relevant French Words and Phrases

alcool isopropylique—Rubbing alcohol.

apéro—Short for *apéritif*, a before-dinner drink.

Arsène Lupin—The gentleman thief and amateur detective hero of a series of French early-twentieth-century novels by Maurice Leblanc; Lupin persistently outwits the police inspector chasing him, Ganimard.

Aux armes, citoyens—To arms, citizens. A line from the French national anthem.

bloc-notes—Writing pad.

bonne chance—Good luck.

ça va—Okay.

carte d'identité—Identity card.

chef—Chief, boss.

choucroute—Cabbage with sausages, often also served with other vegetables and potatoes.

Coca Light—The European version of Diet Coke. Although it has the same label and appears identical to the U.S. version, this version has different sweeteners and so tastes noticeably different.

d'acc—A shortened form of *d'accord*, which means "okay."

de rien—It's nothing.
délit—Offense (see "French Law and Police" section on page XXX for an explanation of how this differs from a crime in France).
un escroc—A swindler.
ecoutez-moi—Listen to me.
eh, bien—Oh, well.
enculé—Motherfucker.
excusez-moi—Excuse me.
fils de putain—Son of a whore.
flic—Policeman.
hein—Huh.
un honneur—An honor.
immédiatement—Immediately.
la bonne—The good. It can also be used for men ("le bon") and is the equivalent of saying, for example, "The good Dr Kildare has cured her wounds." It is used to express exaggerated politeness for charming effect, which is very French.
les vacances—Vacation.
mais bien sûr—Of course (literally, "but of course").
mais oui—Of course (literally, "but yes").
maître des conferences—The equivalent of an American assistant professor.
mec—Guy.
médecin légiste—Medical examiner.
métier—Area of expertise.
par exemple—For example.

pardonnez-moi—Pardon me.

patron—Owner, boss.

plage—Beach. Every summer Paris turns a stretch of the banks of the Seine into an urban beach by covering them in sand.

portable—Cell phone.

portefeuille—Wallet.

Ressources Humaines—Human Resources.

resto—Short for restaurant.

rillettes—A coarse terrine.

salaud—Bastard.

SAMU—The emergency medical services (Service d'Aide Médicale Urgente).

séjour—Living room.

s'il vous plait—Please.

souche—Counterfoil, one of two identical halves of a receipt or slip of paper.

tabac—A shop or café that sells cigarettes and other tobacco products.

tarte flambée—a French tart with a very thin crust that is piled with cheese, onion, and bacon, then baked in an oven.

tapis roulant—Conveyor belt.

tiens—Wait.

urgences générales—The emergency room.

*V*élib'—One of Paris's rentable public bicycles.

vraiment—Truly.

French Law and Police

French law recognizes three kinds of illegal offenses: *crime*, *délit*, and *contravention*. A *crime* would be a felony (such as murder) in the United States; a *délit* would be a misdemeanor. Murder is a *crime*; stealing a page from an antique book is a *délit* and would only earn a relatively short sentence (up to five years) and/or a fine. A *contravention*, which doesn't come up in this book, is a minor infraction—although it still results in a hefty fine.

Below are police ranks with rough American equivalents:

gardien—roughly equivalent to a police officer
brigadier—roughly equivalent to a sergeant
capitaine—roughly equivalent to a detective

A Word About First-Name Usage

The French remain refreshingly formal when it comes to names. In professional relationships such as the one between Capitaine Boussicault and Rachel, neither party would dream of calling the other by his or her first name without receiving permission. Younger people would not call older people by their first names unless invited to do so, and employees would not call their superiors by their first names unless invited to do so. People of the same age working at the same level may use first names, but it helps if—as when LouLou first meets Rachel—someone clarifies that the familiarity is acceptable.

Author's Note and Acknowledgments

Before I do anything else, I want to apologize to the Bibliothèque Nationale. Although I've been in its courtyard, its foyer, and its lounge, I've been no further. The interior that I describe (and map) in this book is entirely the product of my imagination. I also entirely made up the Hotel Etoile and the Hotel Palais. I have no doubt that both exist in Paris, but I'm also sure they are much, much, much better than the ones I describe.

As with my first book, I must begin my acknowledgments by thanking my agent and my editor. Laura Macdougall, receiver of worried emails and sender of reassurance, made my writing career, and I can't thank her enough. Chelsey Emmelhainz is a living demonstration of the importance of editors, and I'm both proud and fortunate to have her as mine.

I couldn't have written this book without the help and support of Janice Duffin, Jemmelia Jameson, Frances Kee, Stephen Markman, and Xandy Wells. A writer's life, which consists mostly of sitting in one place for large amounts of time, could look very much like a con job to unsympathetic viewers, but all of the above never questioned my right to disappear for hours every day, emerging only to make tea and gloomy prognostications. Thank you. I am also thankful for the support and diversion provided by Isabel and Jeoffry Jackson.

Richard Fox gave me much-needed help in an area about which I knew nothing, as did Ash Bowen. Lydia Burton graciously allowed me to take inspiration from her. Sakeenah Feghir and Aurora Murgo Aroca pinch-hit in ways that solved a central problem. And once again, I thank the AirBnB hosts who put me up in their Paris homes—as well as all the unknowing tenants in their buildings whose surnames I copied off the mailboxes when I realized I didn't know any "real" French names.

This book wouldn't have been produced without the love and certainty of Jennifer Piddington and Ashley Bruce.

Moving from the human to the digital, I must once again, and even more profusely, thank Google, Google Satellite, Wikipedia, and countless other websites, without which I couldn't have walked the streets of Paris, found out how much it costs to go from central Paris to Charles de Gaulle airport, or learned about the holdings at the various sites of the Bibliothèque Nationale.

I also used the following books to help me get law and pathology details right: Pekka Saukko and Bernard Knight, *Knight's Forensic Pathology* (Hodder Education Publishers, 3rd edition, 2004); Walter Cairns and Robert McKeon, *Introduction to French Law* (Routledge-Cavendish, 1995). Homer Stibb's method of detaching pages came from an article in *The New Yorker*: William Finnigan's "A Theft in the Library: The Case of the Missing Maps" (October 17, 2005, pages 64–78). The quotation from Mallarme is from "So Dear" by Stephen

Mallarme, in *Un Coup de Dès and Other Poems*, translated by A.S. Kline (Poetry in Translation, 2004–09).

Both my parents died while I was finishing this book. My mother, Gabriele Bernhard Jackson, would have got all the jokes and been appropriately surprised by all the bits I wanted to be surprising. She also told me from a very early age that I was a wonderful writer, and always insisted that her belief in this had nothing to do with the fact that she was my mother. In other words, she was as motherly a mother as could possibly mother, and I owe her almost everything.

What I don't owe to her I owe to my father, Thomas Jackson. Daddy loved France, and he loved me, so I think he would have enjoyed what I produced here—and without years of his wise writing instruction I would never have produced it.

I am unmoored without them.